Accolades for America's greatest hero Mack Bolan

"Very, very action-oriented.... Highly successful, today's hottest books for men."
—*The New York Times*

"Anyone who stands against the civilized forces of truth and justice will sooner or later have to face the piercing blue eyes and cold Beretta steel of Mack Bolan, the lean, mean nightstalker, civilization's avenging angel."
—*San Francisco Examiner*

"Mack Bolan is a star. The Executioner is a beacon of hope for people with a sense of American justice."
—*Las Vegas Review Journal*

"In the beginning there was the Executioner—a publishing phenomenon. Mack Bolan remains a spiritual godfather to those who have followed."
—*San Jose Mercury News*

ONE MAN'S WAR

So many weapons and so much ammo in one secret place is an unarguable sign that something evil is going on and growing. Mack Bolan confronts the menace of international terrorism wherever he finds it, with whatever means he considers best. It isn't his job to wonder when this global war of evil will end. His mission is to fight evil wherever he sees it, to do what governments and international organizations are too timid—or to corrupt—to do.

He hits back.

Hard.

DON PENDLETON's
MACK BOLAN®

BLOOD FEVER

A GOLD EAGLE BOOK FROM
WORLDWIDE®

TORONTO · NEW YORK · LONDON · PARIS
AMSTERDAM · STOCKHOLM · HAMBURG
ATHENS · MILAN · TOKYO · SYDNEY

First edition November 1989

ISBN 0-373-61417-9

Special thanks and acknowledgment to
Gayle Stone and Mark Sadler for their contribution to this work.

Go into emptiness, strike voids, bypass what he defends, hit him where he does not expect you.

—Ts'ao Ts'ao, A.D. 155–220

I believe that much of the success I have achieved in this crusade can be directly linked to the advantage of surprise.

—Mack Bolan

PROLOGUE

On an unimposing side street, behind the simple black door of 10 Downing Street, the prime minister folded her small hands on the big desktop. "Well?"

"Yes, ma'am," the general said. He stood opposite her, starched and pressed. There was no reason to wait for her polite invitation to sit. He brought bad news. He knew she would send him away immediately. "The material is weapons-grade. It's not dangerous now, but if it's enriched properly..."

The general let the consequences hang in the cool air between them. The PM's thin mouth grew momentarily thinner. Then the face returned to normal, betraying none of the worried turmoil the general knew she must feel. From bombs to missile heads, the possible uses of the enriched ore were something neither of them wanted to dwell on.

"Get the uranium back," she said brusquely. "Use whatever means you must."

The general nodded and left the room. He returned to his office, sat in his big soft chair and picked up his telephone. He took a deep breath, then turned on the scrambler and dialed. After two rings, the phone was picked up on the other end. There was no greeting, no sound of any kind.

The general counted to five, then said, "Wolf's Head." He hung up.

Fifteen minutes later he entered the alley behind the Wolf's Head Pub in Chelsea. Eyes straight ahead, he strolled through the alley and continued over the winding tree-lined streets to the Thames River and the Chelsea Embankment.

Steve Barr would be following.

The general paused on the Embankment and lit a cigarette. He waited. The summer sun was bright and warm. The sky was Wedgwood blue. He seemed to be admiring the Thames as it flowed slowly to the sea. The river glistened like mercury in the golden English sunshine.

"Nice day," a voice said at his elbow. "Good for cricket, cottage pie and burners. Mind if I have one?"

It was the correct code. The general handed Steve Barr, his agent, a Player's cigarette and lit it for him. Barr was in his late thirties but looked a decade younger. He was slender, of medium height and had sandy hair and freckles. He was blessed with an innocent air that he wore like a mask. He was among the general's best.

Without looking at Barr, the general talked in a quick, quiet voice, describing the uranium theft. "A slick job all round," he concluded. "So slick there had to be inside help."

"You want me to find the ore and the thief?"

"Precisely." The general puffed on his cigarette. "Bring the bloody stuff back, will you? Before it becomes dangerous."

HIDDEN IN THE HEART of a vast triangular wedge of sand and hot desolation on the Gulf of Aqaba stood

Israel's nuclear research center, a top-secret cluster of squat, temperature-controlled buildings located in the Negev Desert where the heat and loneliness attracted no tourists.

Irascible, Dr. Claudius Lev watched carefully as his technicians pulled rods, the first step in restarting the plutonium-producing N reactor. He stood high above in a room with a wall of glass, from which he had monitored the overhauling of the hazardous machine. Israel's 150-megawatt reactor was large enough to produce plutonium for ten nuclear bombs, and more than large enough to create a Chernobyl-size radiation catastrophe.

Completely involved in the technicians' progress, Dr. Lev didn't notice the swift opening of the control room's door or the masked figures in flowing white robes who swept into the room. Suddenly uneasy, he turned and looked into black, glittering eyes swathed in a cloud of white muslin. The eyes were the last thing he remembered.

"What the devil are you...?" the peppery old man said.

The man in white lifted his Uzi and swung the butt down on the scientist's head. Hard. The scientist collapsed. Around him, the other scientists and technicians stood stunned, their hands held high above their heads, fear on their faces.

One of the robed figures picked up the Israeli scientist while the leader continued on to a file drawer and pulled out a stack of papers. He knew what he was looking for and where to find it. Surrounded by his men, with the unconscious scientist carried safely like a sleeping baby, the leader strode toward the door.

After the others were out, the last man turned in the doorway. His Uzi barked again and again. Blood appeared as if by magic, splattering the room's white walls and shining equipment. The remaining scientists and technicians spun, slammed back against their consoles, crashed into one another and toppled over dead.

The white-robed figures escaped through the building, all sentries in their path already eliminated. They piled into three waiting Jeeps. At last the compound's security system screamed. But it was too late. Dust and sand billowing behind, the Jeeps roared away across the desert.

A week later in the ancient city of Jerusalem, the director of the Israeli intelligence service, Mossad, met with his underchiefs to inform them of the situation.

"They got old Claudius Lev," he told them. "Whoever *they* are. Brutal, quick and efficient. Professionals. And one of our top atomic scientists has disappeared without a trace."

"What about a ransom?" a small, angular agent asked.

"The government's received no demand," the director said. "If there was going to be a demand, there'd be one by now."

The men and women around the table looked at their longtime director. A ransom meant a simple kidnapping. It was a fact no one needed to state.

"No terrorists have claimed responsibility?" asked another in the group.

The director shook his head.

"Wasn't Lev working on that top-secret bomb project?" asked a woman across the table.

"That's right," the Mossad chief said grimly.

"Then who . . . ?" she wondered.

"Perhaps another nation," suggested the man at her elbow. "One greedy for power. Or afraid of its neighbor. Or worried about the superpowers. Most likely a Third World country."

The group was silent. It was a good possibility.

"The Brits report that an important load of weapons-grade ore has disappeared," the director continued. "My sources tell me high-placed scientists in other countries have vanished recently, probably kidnapped. And several months ago in France someone stole blueprints for a uranium-enrichment facility."

Again the group was silent. The most difficult part of building a nuclear bomb was creating, or acquiring, uranium ore enriched above the normal grade necessary for peaceful purposes. But once that technology was achieved, a country, or an individual, could do whatever it or he liked.

"We must find whoever is behind these technological thefts," the Mossad director said. A taciturn, unexcitable man, he now did something that shocked his staff: he leaned forward, and his voice rose with urgency. "We must *stop* them. *Fast!*"

THE ARMY PFC DROVE the lieutenant through the sagebrush and across the flatlands toward the tubular gates of the Nevada weapons installation. Cars, trucks and motorcycles were backed up a quarter mile on the other side of the road, exiting the installation. It was Friday afternoon, the beginning of a three-day summer weekend, and the excited soldiers were headed toward all the Las Vegas alcohol, glitz and hot women their paychecks could buy.

At the kiosk the busy guard looked at the lieutenant's badge and waved the truck onto the base. The PFC knew the right turns to make on the asphalt roads. He'd had an excellent map to memorize. At last he backed the truck up to the loading dock of a concrete building. The lieutenant got out, rang the bell and waited for visual inspection.

Sweating more from tension than the desert heat, the lieutenant held up his papers. The bay doors rose. He stepped inside and signed in while the sergeant checked the papers and filled out the proper documents.

Two privates loaded a crate onto the truck bed. The lieutenant watched, then got back into the truck cab and sat next to his driver. "Let's go."

The PFC drove the lieutenant and the crate back toward the guard kiosk.

"Pull over," the lieutenant told him. "We'll wait here. No one will suspect the last truck out."

The lieutenant and PFC parked between two corrugated prefabs and watched the long line of vehicles snake toward the kiosk and the weekend's freedom. Finally the lieutenant nodded.

The PFC started the engine and pulled out. He followed the last car toward the busy sentries. The line crept along. When it was their turn, a weary guard flipped through their papers, looked at the labeling on the crate—Rations, Field, Tropical FTR-C-12-X9—and waved them through.

Once out on the open plain, where sagebrush was the only sign of earthly life, the PFC hit the accelerator. The truck leaped ahead like a jackrabbit with its tail on fire. The two men leaned back and laughed.

A few miles down the road they pulled off behind a deserted Shell service station, where they changed into polyester pants and open-necked shirts. Then they moved the heavy crate onto a beat-up old pickup, tied a tarp over it, got in and drove off again.

This time they followed a dirt side road that led straight into the desert. Mirages shimmered on the heat-drenched surface. Sweat poured down the private's face. The lieutenant reached up and peeled off a complete latex facial mask. Beneath was a handsome red-haired man with a thick mustache and sideburns. A long scar made a ragged purple mark on his left cheek from eye to jaw. He was slender and of medium height. Wiping a hand across his sweat-drenched features, he laughed in triumph.

A few hours later a government car stopped beside the Army truck. The civilian got out and smelled the sickly stench. Soon he found the two bodies in the brush, bloated from the heat, at least two days old. In his car he radioed the information to his superior, then drove off onto the dirt road.

Five miles later he found the second truck. It was empty. Nearby, helicopter runners had made a faint imprint in the sandy soil. The rotors had probably washed out most of the track. Now he searched the area. He found nothing obvious, but well-developed instinct told him to dig up a small, too-perfect mound of sand and dirt. In it he found two polyester shirts, trousers and some papers.

"Damn!" Again he radioed. "Cecil Olds here. I found a second truck but missed the bastard. Yeah. It's Haggarty all right. What now?"

He listened, nodded, then got back into his car and returned to the weapons installation. In the commander's air-conditioned office he sat in a canvas chair and listened to what his news had started. The older man was on the phone to Washington.

"Two men murdered," the commander growled. "Looks like a renegade British soldier named Miles Haggarty. The bastard swiped that special alloy for making weapons-grade uranium. If they've got it, they're sitting on top of the real thing. Somebody better get his ass in gear and find out what the hell's going on!"

CHAPTER ONE

On long cross-country skis Mack Bolan slid across the
November snow and through the dark forest of ponderosa pines. Skillful and silent, he was a shadow
among the multitude of night shadows that wavered
over the white ground beneath the tall branches.

He kept up a constant, sweaty pace. His skis ate up
the icy miles as wind whispered through the trees and
over the dark mountainside. Mounds of snow fell with
soft plops from the pine needles. The air was arctic
fresh. Diamond-bright stars sparkled in the sky's
black dome.

At last he saw it. In the distance two faint pin-
points of yellow electric light twinkled. There was his
destination: a small cabin set alone in this isolated
chunk of Colorado's Rocky Mountains.

He herringboned up a slope, then paused to survey
the swaying forest ahead. The trees were stark and
black against the cold white mountain. The moon was
low, just above a ridge. When it rose high in the sky,
the snow would reflect a silver light that, when added
to the moonlight, would illuminate the area and make
his job more difficult.

As always, he was prepared. He wore a skintight
combat whitesuit that covered his muscular frame. A
white ski mask hid his dark hair and protected his
craggy, determined features from the frigid air. He

carried his 9 mm Beretta 93-R automatic holstered in a shoulder rig beneath his left arm, while a G-11 caseless assault rifle was slung across his back and tied down so that his hands and arms would be free to pole. A half-dozen Misar MU 50-G hand grenades hung from his belt.

Pressing his ski poles into the snow, he pushed off. Speed was critical if he wanted to beat the moonlight. He moved across a flat area, sweat coating every inch of his body. He'd already skied fifteen miles, a long distance when you had only the moon, a memorized map and the rugged, endless mountain terrain. Now he had another mile to go, mostly uphill.

His long skis slapped the snow, plowing fresh tracks through the virgin powder. His cool blue eyes studied the forest as he passed massive granite boulders and young pines bent double with heavy snow.

He skied downhill, herringboned uphill and sped across vast expanses of white that would turn into lush green meadows when spring came. Finally, he slowed as he neared the log cabin.

Smoke curled up through a chimney and disappeared against the stars. Breathing deeply, he angled north around the cabin. The lights inside glowed brightly—a big mistake.

The building was in such a remote region that those inside had no fear of discovery. Bolan nodded grimly. They were foolish to think they had covered their trail so completely.

At last he reached the far side of the cabin. Here a narrow road ended. Parked inside a carport next to the cabin was a Land Rover with chains on its wheels. The snow on the road was chewed up from other vehicles that had come and gone since the last snowstorm.

One branch of the road angled uphill and seemed to disappear right into the mountain slope. This part of the road had wide, black ruts where heavy vehicles had dug in to climb the grade. Bolan studied it. There was something important about this offshoot of the road—someone had deliberately built it so that it vanished into nothingness. When he finished with those inside the cabin, he would check it out.

He skied on across the road and then dipped back down toward the forest on the other side of the log cabin. Pine needles brushed his cheek as he slid through the thick trees.

And then he heard a soft click.

He squatted over his skis, coasted and waited. A brief, bright flame appeared and disappeared ahead— a cigarette lighter. Soon he saw the tip of the cigarette. The ember burned orange, then grew faint. The acrid aroma of tobacco smoke floated toward him.

Patiently he continued to coast. Then he saw the figure. The guy was wading through the snow back toward the cabin. He'd been taking a break. Now he was batting his arms across his chest and smoking furiously.

Bolan stood up, stabbed his poles deep into the snow and pushed hard. Skis whining, he hurtled down the white slope toward the figure. The man looked up, startled. He pulled a gun from beneath his coat and opened his mouth to shout.

The smoker was Japanese, a member of a Red Army unit sent to make a terrorist raid on a top-secret

U.S. missile command base nearby. Bolan had received the information from private, absolutely reliable intel.

As the Executioner flew past, he slammed an arm into the terrorist's chest. The guy flew back, winded, and fell into the snow.

Bolan skid to an abrupt stop. Immediately he herringboned back up the slope, pitched off his skis and jumped onto the terrorist. The man tried to suck in air as Bolan pulled out his long commando knife and slid it across the gasping terrorist's throat. The dying man's dark blood poured onto the white snow.

The Executioner rolled off and snapped his feet back into his skis. And then, suddenly, gunfire erupted from the cabin.

Bullets bit into the snow and trees around Bolan. Snow, bark and pine needles sprayed the air. The debris cut like razors into the flesh around his eyes.

The warrior unsnapped his skis and shoulder-rolled down onto the snow. There was no way he could get to cover. The snow was deep. The only way to cross it with any speed was on skis or snowshoes. And his skis were now ten feet away.

But that was why he came prepared. His whitesuit was virtually invisible against the snow. Bullets rained down around him, looking for a target his attackers couldn't see.

With a minimum of movement he grabbed three of his grenades. Expertly he hurled one grenade onto the cabin's front porch, a second beneath the cabin and a third through the window opening where a rifle protruded, shooting at him. Then he ducked and covered his head.

The first explosion shattered the front porch and blew out the windows. A voice screamed with pain, while others bellowed in anger. The second explosion blasted the substructure, making the cabin list to one side. The rifle fire stopped, and someone pulled open a side door. The third explosion ripped a hole the size of a car in the side of the cabin. The man who'd tried to escape through the door flew out as if shot from a cannon. He crashed into the snow and didn't move.

Bolan waited and listened. Quiet settled over the snowy cabin. Wood creaked. A radio gave off sporadic static.

At last the warrior got up onto his knees. He studied the destruction. Curtains fluttered in the wind. Smoke curled up from the chimney. Steam from the cabin's heating system misted in the air.

He got his skis, snapped them on and skied toward the cabin. When he reached the man who'd been thrown through the door, he stopped to roll him over. The dead man was Japanese, too. There were U.S. dollars in his pockets but no identification.

In the cabin he found two more Japanese terrorists. Dead. Each had American money as well as bogus driver's licenses and credit cards.

He'd found the number of guys he'd been told to expect, but searching the cabin he uncovered a surprise. Inside a closet was an unconscious woman who was gagged and tied to a wooden kitchen chair. She had a smell of chemicals around her, which probably meant she'd been drugged. The lady was damn lucky;

she was on the side of the house that had sustained the least damage.

Bolan untied her and carried her to a sofa in the living room. She lay motionless, but her breathing was regular. About thirty years old, she was slender and tall, a Caucasian with short dark hair that framed her soft face. She wore white ski pants and a pink sweater. Her forehead was high and intelligent. Even without makeup she was lovely. He looked at her left hand and saw a wedding band. Angry red welts encircled her wrists and ankles where she'd been tied to the chair.

He found no handbag. Carefully he searched her pockets. Nothing. Again he walked through the cabin. This time in the kitchen he spotted a white ski jacket that matched the woman's ski trousers. The pockets were pulled out and the lining cut. The terrorists had wanted to know who she was, too.

He covered her with the coat and again went through the cabin, this time looking through drawers, a desk and the closets. Everything he found could have belonged to anyone—a deck of airline playing cards, a calendar with nothing written on it, the last two issues of the *Denver Post*, a couple of paperback novels.

The warrior checked on the woman again. Her eyes were still closed, but her color was good. She seemed to be resting comfortably and would eventually wake on her own.

Bolan picked up a flashlight and went back outdoors. He slogged over to his skis and snapped his feet into them. Pushing off, he skied back up the hill, past the freezing corpse of the first terrorist. On the road that ended at the back of the log cabin, he paused, then skied up the narrow road that branched off and seemed to disappear into the mountainside.

Sweat saturated his ski mask. The road was steep and the ruts were black and deep in the snow. High above the mountain the moon shone, the snow glistening silver in its light. The whole mountainside seemed to glow with a translucent pearl-gray haze.

At last he reached the top of the road. Ponderosa pines surrounded the area and overhung the road's end. It was very dark here, almost black beneath the thick branches.

Bolan let his eyes adjust, then turned on the flashlight. He moved the beam around and found the concrete face of what looked like a small building embedded in the mountainside. It had a rough exterior, shaped to resemble natural granite, which meant that someone had gone to a lot of trouble to camouflage whatever lay beyond.

The outlines of a garage-size door showed faintly, while off to the side was another door, this one regular in size. It was padlocked. Bolan's Beretta barked once, and the padlock flew off.

The warrior melted back into the trees and waited, but there was no sign or sound of danger. He opened the door and flashed his light inside. Finding a switch, he turned on overhead fluorescents.

The room was four times the width of the garage door and seemed to extend back endlessly into the mountain. Huge wooden crates were stacked from floor to ceiling in neat rows as far back as the eye could see. The boxes had various labels—Rations, Engine Parts, Mining Equipment, Medicine.

Bolan stared. There were literally thousands of crates—enough assorted matériel to supply a brigade. But why here? It didn't make sense.

He pulled a box labeled Mining Equipment off the stack next to him. Packed inside were brand-new Uzi submachine guns. He opened the next box, labeled Cookware. More Uzis.

Next he strode down the row of floor-to-ceiling crates, then stopped. Randomly he pulled out another wooden container. This one was identified as Blankets. The soldier opened it and found tightly packed boxes of M-16 ammo.

Bolan continued down the warehouse row and opened another half-dozen crates. Inside he discovered grenade launchers, night vision goggles, rifles, pistols and even rocket launchers. And, of course, ammo. Hell, there was enough firepower in this mountain arsenal to blow Denver sky-high!

CHAPTER TWO

Mack Bolan strode up and down the aisle of weapons and ammo crates, looking for the source of the munitions—and their destination.

Many boxes showed the official black stamp of import inspection. These were labeled Mining Equipment. As usual someone—or a group of people—had been paid off. The crates were addressed to the Houston Mining Supply Company, Highway 45, Houston, Texas.

There was no way to know for sure what function the warehouse played. It was obviously a storage dump, and probably a secret stop. Where would the weapons go? He answered his own question: remote jungles, mountains, deserts or rural communities. Any or all of them.

Bolan returned to the front of the building and looked for a telephone. He found one hanging on the inside wall next to the garage door.

But outside in the distance a door slammed.

The warrior ran through the arsenal's front doorway, clicked on his skis and sped down the rutted road toward the cabin. The icy air whistled in his ears, as his skis whined over the powder.

Ahead was the slender figure of the woman. The ivory light of the moon and snow illuminated her and her short dark hair, white ski pants and white ski jacket. She was leaning over next to the lopsided cabin porch, busily fastening on her own set of cross-country skis.

Bolan crouched over his skis to increase his speed as he rushed toward her. She looked up and froze, then burst into motion. Her skis secure, she slipped her hands through the leather pole thongs and pushed off into the trees, with Bolan right behind her.

She was a good skier, nimbly circling around trees and boulders and racing across flat open places, but the warrior stayed on her tail, pumping his legs to gain on her. Glancing over her shoulder, she saw how close he was. Fury and determination played across her face. Now that she was awake Bolan saw more than the smooth, pretty features. There was strength there, too, and exhaustion. The youthful face was lined and worn.

Suddenly the woman angled off, pumping her legs and heading for a thicket of tall snowy brush that glowed eerily in the pearl-gray light. Bolan angled after her, but she disappeared from sight.

The Executioner followed her into the sudden silence of the brush. Thick with snow, the vegetation formed an almost soundproof maze. The warrior slowed to avoid collision with the high white walls.

Although he couldn't see her, she wouldn't get away. All he had to do was follow the trail her skis left. He weaved through the quiet brush, listening, watching.

And then he heard it—the faint *slap-slap* of cross-country skis. But there was something strange about the sound. Then he knew—it was coming from both directions, not only in front of him, but *behind*. Someone was stalking him!

He sped ahead, rounded corners and stopped. Hurriedly he unfastened his skis and rolled away, landing in the brush within reach of his skis. Without making a sound, he picked up the skis and shoved them under the thicket where they couldn't be seen from the trail. Then he scurried deeper into the brush, out of sight, wiping his trail smooth behind him as he went.

Soon the *slap-slap* of skis grew more distinct. Bolan grasped his poles tightly.

A figure in dark ski clothes rounded the bend, swaying rhythmically with each stride—another Japanese, one guy more than Bolan had been told to expect. He had to be the cover man, the sentry Bolan had been searching for when the guys in the cabin had opened fire. Where in hell had he been? Out for a midnight run?

As the terrorist swept down on him, Bolan slammed his ski poles out onto the trail. The guy seemed to come unglued all at once. The poles jammed between his ankles midstride, and he grunted with surprise and pain, cracking one pole as he struggled to keep going. Off balance, he catapulted head over heels into the soft powder.

Bolan was out of his hiding place instantly. The terrorist tried to get his Uzi unstrapped from his back. His black eyes glittered with fear and malice—and leftover sleep. The stupid fool had crawled into some shelter and fallen asleep while he was supposed to be on guard.

The guy's right foot was still locked in its ski and propped high in the air. The guy rolled to the side, trying to stand. In one practiced motion Bolan pulled out his commando knife and knocked the terrorist back down.

But the guy was strong and quick. He kept rolling, and Bolan lunged after him. As he rolled, the terrorist unsnapped his ski. Free of it, he jumped to his feet and lunged back through the snow, throwing himself onto Bolan.

The warrior directed a fist toward the guy's jaw, but he ducked, his eyes half-crazed now. He'd gotten his three comrades killed—and it had been his own damn fault!

The man grabbed Bolan's throat in a steel grip, clamped his hands and squeezed. Red bolts of pain flashed behind the Executioner's eyes. Gasping, he couldn't get past the terrorist's arms to get his knife up to his assailant's throat. And the guy's hands were squeezing hard and fast. Bolan felt the first faintness and knew he needed oxygen immediately.

Grabbing his knife in both hands behind the terrorist's back, he raised and angled it. With all his strength he plunged the knife deep into the base of the throat where the neck meets the shoulder.

Blood spurted. The terrorist's hands loosened on Bolan's neck. Surprised, the killer's black eyes widened with shock, then pain.

Knocking the guy's hands away, Bolan cut the knife quick and clean across the front of the terrorist's throat, finishing the job. The guy gurgled, collapsed and gave a hollow death rattle.

The Executioner got to his feet and slogged through the snow to his skis. He snapped them on and raced away, following the trail of the mysterious woman.

Weaving on and on through the brush, he pushed as fast as he dared. Then suddenly he was in the open again. He herringboned uphill and turned west on a ridge, making good speed now, taking advantage of the trail she had cut for him.

Suddenly he realized he was approaching the cabin again, this time from a new direction. He should see her anytime now. Just a few more minutes and he would catch her. There was no way she could stay ahead of him on the flat....

And then he saw her—a small figure delicately pale against the black forest wall. She was signaling with a flashlight across the meadow. Three long blinks, two short ones, then she repeated the message.

Somewhere an engine started, its roar echoing over the open space. Bolan tore across the ridge and sliced down the mountainside toward the woman. A big snowmobile sped out onto the flat meadow, white powder billowing out behind it in a shimmering cloud. As soon as the woman saw the snowmobile, she leaned over and unhooked her skis.

Sweat drenching his ski mask, Bolan pumped, his stride eating up the distance. And then he knew he would never make it. And he couldn't shoot. He didn't know whether she was friend or foe.

The snowmobile roared up to her. She glanced back at Bolan, her eyes wide with fear...and something else...disgust, maybe. Something had gone wrong, and whatever she was after at the cabin was lost to her.

Shrugging off her disappointment, she gauged the distance between her and Bolan, smiling when she knew he couldn't reach her. She was safe from him and whatever danger he posed.

And suddenly she was all graceful motion. She swung her long legs up over the snowmobile's seat and sat, then pulled her skis and poles up and tied them next to her. The driver, who was wearing a ski mask, turned and said something to her and she answered. Then they sped off, their eyes focused straight ahead on the safety of the forest.

There was no way Bolan could stop them, so he skied back to the cabin. A faint cloud of mist—a combination of steam and dust—surrounded it in the gray light.

Inside the cabin, Bolan went straight to the telephone. He dialed the special numbers, spoke the right codes and waited impatiently as each connection slowly cleared access to the next.

At last Hal Brognola's voice spoke irritably—and sleepily—from his home. "Mack? Do you know what in hell time it is?"

"I've got important intel for you," Bolan brusquely told his old friend, the man from Justice. It was nearly 4:00 a.m. in Washington, D.C., but Bolan's information couldn't wait. He described the Japanese Red Army unit and their plans for the top-secret missile command base nearby.

Brognola was silent for a moment. "Glad you called," he said at last. "I'll send people to take care of the mess. The press could sniff this out in a heartbeat and we don't want it on the front pages or the six o'clock news. A panic's the last thing we need.''

''Right. Make up whatever story you think best,'' Bolan said. ''But there's more.'' He told Brognola about the arsenal hidden deep in the Colorado mountain.

Again there was silence. Brognola cleared his throat. ''You're sure?''

Bolan repeated what he'd seen.

Brognola whistled. ''Christ!''

''You know anything about it?''

''It's not ours, if that's what you mean.''

''You haven't heard rumors?''

''Not about this.''

It was Bolan's turn to be silent. ''It's a supply dump for terrorists,'' he said after a moment. ''Maybe strictly Japanese, but probably not.'' He stared out the window at the forest, already planning.

''You gonna wait for us?'' Brognola asked, although the tone of his voice indicated he already knew the answer.

''No way. Your people can analyze, put stuff under a microscope and argue to their heart's content. I'm not going to waste the time.''

''You going after the source or the destination?''

''I'll start with the destination.'' Bolan said goodbye to his old friend, then quietly hung up the phone, picked up the car keys in the kitchen and went out into the freezing night to retrieve his skis and poles. Equipment in hand, he climbed into the terrorists' Land Rover and drove down the snowy, rutted road toward the nearest town.

CHAPTER THREE

Near Houston's international airport giant jumbo jets roared low overhead. They thundered in and out just seconds apart, carrying oil barons, European princes, and New York businessmen intent on closing Texas-size deals.

Around the airport in the north section of the bustling Texas metropolis, the autumn temperature had dropped into the chilly thirties, filling the neon motels, tall hotels, dark bars and plush restaurants with residents and travelers who needed a drink or two to ward off the unusual cold.

The strains of a hot salsa melody carried on the bayou wind, along with the aromas of spicy chilies and prime beefsteak. It was cold outside, but indoors people laughed, drank and ate. It was four o'clock in the afternoon.

Inside a motel room a man and a woman sipped margaritas made with fresh California limes and fine Mexican tequila. It was the wrong drink for the weather, but the right one for Texas.

The woman spoke with a faint English accent and was tall and good-looking, with short dark hair that framed her smooth face. The man spoke with the highly educated intonations of Oxford and Cambridge and watched the woman with the hooded, hungry eyes of a man who wanted but would not get.

"He's probably with a rival terrorist group, old girl," the man speculated.

"Every damn fool has a rival these days," the woman said gloomily.

They sat next to the big window of her room overlooking the empty motel pool and veranda. The curtains were tied back, and they amused themselves with drinking and watching through the window as people scurried along the tiled motel paths toward the warmth of their rooms.

"On the other hand, Cecil," the woman continued, "he could be with the same group."

"How so?" The man drank from his tall glass.

"If they knew I'd penetrated—"

"Ah, yes," Cecil said. "They would have to take extreme measures. Eliminate the unit, find out the weak link by questioning you—"

"Torturing," the woman substituted without flinching. She knew the system all too well.

"By torturing you," he amended.

"And then backtracking." She held her glass high and admired the liquor in the yellow lamplight. "Which means discovering you." She drank.

"Really, Marsha," he protested.

He liked to watch her graceful movements, the way her fingers wrapped around the glass, the way her hips moved languidly in the overstuffed motel chair. He liked all that, and more—the dangerous way her mind worked. She'd been out of the business for five years, yet she was just as sharp and cool as ever.

"Followed by the same treatment for you," she continued wickedly, eyeing him over her glass. "They would make a very good job of torturing, I'm sure. After all, they go to school to learn how to do it well.'' Again she drank, emptying her glass.

"Don't you think you should slow down?''

"The word *torture* comes from a Latin root that means to twist. Isn't that charming?'' She stood and walked without swaying across the room to the bureau where the tequila bottle, limes and salt waited.

"Marsha.''

She ignored him and reached for the bottle. "To 'twist.' Think about it, Cecil. To twist or wrench out of shape. One's limbs, one's spine. Or just—if it's a small job and only a little piece of intel is needed—the fingers, the toes, perhaps—the genitals. Particularly a man's genitals.''

"Don't, Marsha. Put it out of your mind. You can't keep going over and over—''

"Shut up!'' She dropped a slice of lime into her glass, turned and walked back toward Cecil Olds, her face stretched with painful memories but her drink beautifully made. With great control she sat down again.

Cecil watched her, waiting patiently as she glanced around the room, then meekly lowered her head to stare at her hands. At last she looked up. "I'm sorry, Cecil, dear.''

"I know you are. But Steve wouldn't like this one damn bit.''

"You think I'm carrying on too much?''

"I think you're torturing yourself. You don't need any terrorist organization to do it for you.''

She nodded, then set her glass on the table between them. "Why wouldn't MI6 tell me where he was sent?"

He grimaced and rolled his eyes.

"Damn you!" she said.

"Look, old girl." He set his glass next to hers and clasped her hands with his own. "You've been out of MI6 for years now. Retired, remember? Wives don't have access to anything. In fact, the only reason you know Steve *is* MI6 is that you worked with him. For pity's sake, you don't even really know he's missing."

"I *know*," she said with certainty. "When he was on assignment, he always sent me notes in our secret code. The letters arrived once a week at a postal box in Chelsea. It's been a month since I've heard from him. A month!"

"Maybe he couldn't write. Maybe he could write but couldn't post it. Maybe he's being watched so closely—"

"Maybe! Maybe! Maybe! It means nothing except that he's missing. In all these years he's sent me notes every week he was in the field. He could be sick. Captured. Dead!"

Cecil Olds sighed. "Of course. Part of the hazards of the business."

Olds paused, watching Marsha Barr's anguished face. She was about thirty years old now, he guessed, and quite pretty, some would say beautiful with her high forehead and smooth, translucent skin. He decided to take a calculated risk—honesty.

"It's one of the reasons we do this kind of work," he reminded her. "The danger. We like the risk, the adventure. Man against man. Man against government. Man against nature. We have to like it, or we couldn't do it. It's too damn much of a strain. We live too close to death to tolerate it for any other reason.''

"We tolerate it because we have a job to do," she argued, thinking of her husband, MI6 top-secret agent Steve Barr. "Because if we didn't try to keep the world right, we'd be overrun by the greedy and sick, the people who think they're entitled to do whatever they please when they want to, no matter who's hurt."

"All right," Olds said slowly, "I'll accept that. It's true for some people." He finished his drink.

She stood and walked restlessly around the small room. "Let's go over what we know."

"Fine, old girl," Olds said cheerfully. "I'll begin." He paused. "We know a special alloy was taken from a U.S. nuclear installation in the Nevada desert this past summer by one Captain Miles Haggarty, a renegade British paratrooper and commando turned mercenary."

"And that the alloy is used to make weapons-grade uranium."

"Right-o," Olds continued. "When I told the Yanks who Haggarty really was and they found out what he had made off with, all bloody hell broke loose. The head chap at the base called Washington, and they had troops swarming over the desert thick as Bedouins."

"With no luck."

"That's it. Haggarty and his accomplice were long gone. Disappeared in a whirlybird. No trace."

"Haggarty could have caught Steve," she said. "He could be holding him. He could have killed him."

"Possibly. We know Haggarty and Steve are connected somehow."

"Oh, God, how I hate this!" she cried, holding her hands over her ears.

Again Cecil Olds waited. At last he said softly, "Go on, old girl. What happens next?"

She sighed and lowered her long-fingered hands to her lap. "Then I find you," she said softly, "and we stumble on the intel about the Japanese Red Army. We know they have something to do with the alloy theft, and it looks as if we're the only ones who've pinpointed them. Then we decide to go in before alerting the Yanks."

"Except that you insist on penetrating alone," Olds said. "I shouldn't have been such a gent. Rule number one: never let a lady have her way."

"I'm the one who skis, remember?" she said. For the first time that day she smiled. "You'd never have gotten close on that noisy snowmobile."

"But it came in mighty handy when you needed out," he reminded her, smiling, too.

They stared deep into each other's eyes, then looked away. She knew what he wanted from her, and that even if Steve were dead, she would never be able to give it to him. She would never feel anything but deep friendship for Cecil Olds.

"And that leaves us with two issues," she said.

"Who in bloody hell was that big fellow who eliminated the Japanese unit?" Olds murmured, asking one of the two questions they had been struggling with.

"A Yank, I think," she said. "What eyes he had! Blue and piercing. You feel when he looks at you that he can see straight into your soul."

"A warrior type," Olds added. "Strong and tough. A hell of a fighter. The Japanese were pros, yet he wiped them out. Wish we knew whose side he's on."

She nodded with the memory. "And the second issue is the big one we started with. Simply stated, the connection among Miles Haggarty, the stolen U.S. alloy, the stolen British uranium and the kidnapped Israeli scientist. You've gathered enough pieces to form a very unpleasant picture of a potential nuclear hazard. And now, at the Japanese hideout, I find a major supply dump. It looks as if the same people involved in the uranium business are supplying terrorist arms around the world, locally through this Houston 'mining' outfit next to the airport."

"And there it all stops," Olds said. He crossed the room to fix himself another margarita.

"I'd like another, too, please," she said demurely, smiling up at him.

"Sorry, old girl," he told her. "If you want another drink, you'll have to make it yourself. If you can't make it, we'll know you shouldn't have it."

"You are a bastard, Cecil!" she said.

"Thank you, my dear. I couldn't have put it better."

She stood and strode to the bureau. As she made her drink, she said, "We have the place staked out, but nothing's happened."

"Not a damn thing," he agreed.

"It feels hopeless to me right now," she said. "We'll never find Steve!"

"Sometimes," Olds said philosophically, "we don't appreciate inactivity. Sometimes it's best to close one's mouth, quit worrying and relax, because something really quite bloody dreadful is off in the wings, just waiting to happen. And there's not a damn thing a body can do to stop it."

IN A TALL HOTEL BUILDING of gleaming glass and concrete, two men looked down at the man and the woman who sat in the window of the Houston motel room. The men studied the handsome couple as they talked, drank and made more drinks. Sometimes the woman seemed almost to cry. Other times she was enraged. Her male companion watched her as if she were a precocious, beloved pet that he wanted to tame so he could own her.

"Nice-lookin' tail, huh?" one of the men high above in the hotel building said to the other.

"Naw, boss," the second man said. He glanced at the woman with no interest. He was small and dark with a wrinkled weasel face. "You got plenty better than that."

"Wouldn't mind having her," the first man continued. "Looks like the bastard has his hands full with her."

The boss inhaled deeply from a marijuana joint, held the smoke in his lungs, then exhaled in a long stream. He had a big frame that had once been full and muscular. Now, because of the coke and grass, his skin hung loose over his emaciated body. His smile was a leer. He thought about sex, talked about sex, but he and his assistant both knew real sex for him was history. Until he could give up the seductive drugs.

"Hey, boss, you forget her. She's trouble."

"A broad that fights always makes it more interesting."

"Sure, boss, then I got to get you outta trouble," his assistant reminded him. "The broads, they don't like it when you got another girlfriend. A pissed broad's the worst kind to fight."

The skeletal boss laughed, remembering the old days when he'd been the toughest on the street, then the toughest in the gang. Now he was the toughest in his secret import-export business. "Broads, booze and guns," he told his little assistant with satisfaction.

"Crazies and flakes!" the assistant said worriedly.

"Maybe, but not those two," the boss said, nodding down at the motel, where the pair sat in their window, talking. "They're straight as arrows. They may have been watching our warehouse, but they're pretty much nothin'. We can play with them all we like."

"Play with them?" A smile crossed the weasel face of the assistant.

"All we like," the boss repeated, then pulled again on his joint. He closed his eyes, held the smoke in his lungs and waited for the hit. At last he exhaled, disappointed. Grass just didn't do it anymore. He'd switched back to grass, trying to get off the coke, but nothing was as good as coke.

"Yeah!" the assistant said, rubbing his hands on the tops of his thighs. "Yeah, yeah!"

"You, too pal," the boss said, not forgetting the silent Navaho who stood behind them, arms crossed as he leaned against the hotel wall next to the door. "You get to play, too, pal."

The Indian nodded, his dark eyes cool, unexcited. The boss had a hard time figuring out the inscrutable Navaho. But when he needed him, the Indian was there with his strong, big hands and lethal weaponry. Best damn bodyguard he had ever had. He owned the Indian body and soul, had his complete loyalty. That's what a man needed when he was boss.

There was a knock on the door.

"Who's there?" the assistant called out.

"Manuel."

The boss nodded at the Navaho, and the man opened the door. The boss resumed watching the woman in the window below, thought about tearing off her clothes, wondering whether she would scream or fight first.

"Yeah?" he asked as he sensed Manuel's footsteps cross the hotel carpeting. It was a damn good hotel. The fixtures were gold plated and the carpeting was thick. If he ever needed another office....

"Bad news, *señor*."

"It's not those voodoo crazies again?" the assistant asked with trepidation.

Behind his back the boss sensed the evil look that Manuel gave the weasel.

"The Japanese, they dead, *señor*," Manuel said.

The boss turned and glared down at the small man. "What Japanese?" he asked sharply. He pinched off his joint and threw it into an ashtray.

"The ones at the cabin in Colorado. The Feds got all the guns and ammo. They hauled off the bodies before the newspapers and TV knew anything about it."

Manuel had bright, intelligent eyes and an unassuming manner that fooled most people into trusting him. He was an ideal courier and could slip in and out of most places, even banks, unnoticed. The boss had learned to trust him.

"I'm listening," the boss said. His heart pounded in his emaciated chest.

"It was those two down there," Manuel said, pointing to the window.

"What! How?" the boss said. "No way. Those Japanese were smart, tough, experienced guys. They *had* the woman. That guy down there couldn't have gotten her out alone!"

"Sorry, *señor*. I only say what I'm told."

"Get your ass back to those mountains!" the boss ranted. "I want that whole area examined, front, back and sideways. Find out what happened!"

"Examine the area?" Manuel said. "No way, boss. The Feds are everywhere."

"You heard me, asshole! Get back up there and find out what's going on!" He paused. His heart was pounding so hard his hands shook and his eyes felt as if they'd pop out. He knew getting excited wasn't good for him, and that he shouldn't talk to Manuel like that.

Manuel was a good man. Useful. He took long, deep breaths, while his assistant watched with alarm.

"I go, boss," Manuel said. "You can count on me."

The boss nodded. "Our business depends on it. We don't want to spook the clients. Just remember, we can take anyone! I don't care who rescued that broad."

For a long while the boss stared down at the couple in the window. They seemed to be having a good time. He was envious. Then his heart started to pound again. He didn't know what thought or idea had started the pounding, but the feel of it scared the hell out of him. When he was young, he'd thought he'd live forever.

"Get those people," the boss told his assistant and the Navaho. His voice was cold as ice. They knew what he had in mind. "Choose your own time and place, but make it soon. Very soon."

CHAPTER FOUR

Called the North Highway, Interstate 45 ran almost due north-south through downtown Houston, routing tourists and residents toward the pleasures of the Astrodome, exclusive shopping at Neiman-Marcus and a glittering array of nightclubs and restaurants.

Mack Bolan took the I-45 south from the airport toward the city's bustling hub. He pulled off after only a few miles, heading into an industrial area and looking for the address he'd found on the crates in the mountain arsenal.

It was twilight and unusually cold. Warmed by frequent hot winds off the Gulf of Mexico, Houston more often needed air conditioners than heaters. Bolan wore a tweed jacket and slacks over his skintight combat blacksuit. His Beretta 93-R rested snugly in its shoulder holster under his arm. Next to him on the seat, hidden under a blanket, was his Heckler and Koch G-11 caseless assault rifle.

As he drove along the frontage road toward a cluster of buildings, the moon was barely over the horizon. Darkness had fallen. It was a good night for recon and penetration.

He was going in.

He slowed the car to a stop as he approached the address. The size of a football field, the building had the company's name—Houston Mining Supply,

Inc.—painted in bold, illuminated letters on its front. No light showed in the windows. Quickly he stripped to his blacksuit.

A tall concrete wall with barbed wire rolled on top encircled the property. There were gates on both entrances to a circular driveway inside the wall, which led to the dark entrance of the building. Both were closed and locked. A service drive branched off the circular drive inside the wall and disappeared around the building.

Houston Mining Supply looked like a fortress—or a prison. A dark Ford sedan was parked in the circular drive inside the gates.

Bolan drove by twice. The second time, inside the gates, a couple ran out from around the side of the building. A man and woman. They were dressed in dark jumpsuits, and their faces were blacked. The woman kept looking over her shoulder. The man shouted at her. They hurried toward the car in the circular drive.

Bolan stared. He studied the way the woman moved, saw the short dark hair, the tall, slender figure...

It was the lady from the cabin.

He floored the accelerator and skidded to a stop at the first gate to the circular drive. Four men barreled out of the building inside the gates, running after the man and woman.

Bolan grabbed the caseless assault rifle and jumped out of his car. He didn't know who the man and woman were, but he wanted them alive so he could talk to them. To the woman especially. How had she known about the Japanese Red Army unit hidden in the cabin in the Colorado mountains? Was she with a rival terrorist group, maybe planning to steal the munitions for her own people? Or was she after the terrorists, too, working with some governmental agency trying to stop them?

Two of the men knelt in the drive and squeezed off careful rounds. The man and woman zigzagged as bullets bit into the concrete drive and sparks erupted in a fountain of red, blue and white. While the couple dodged and continued running toward the Ford, Bolan opened fire.

The rounds slammed into the two kneeling goons, who pitched back, weapons spinning into the air. They crashed bloody and unmoving onto the circular drive.

The man and woman ran to their car, firing at the last two guys behind them as they pulled open the front doors. The pursuing gunners ducked behind the low brick wall that ringed the drive, safely out of Bolan's sight.

The couple jumped inside their car, the woman looking around, trying to see who had killed two of their attackers. Bolan slung his G-11 over his shoulder, leaped up and grabbed the top of the concrete wall. He had to be careful; the barbed wire on top was probably electrified. He'd decided not to shoot open one of the gates and go through that way. With such a complete security system, the gate would most likely be hooked up to an alarm system.

The warrior pulled himself up, balancing on his toes at the top. He stepped over the barbed wire to the narrow lip on the other side.

As the man started the Ford's engine, the last two killers let loose a hail of bullets. The woman leaned out her window and returned fire. She glanced up, saw Bolan and frowned with disbelief.

For a moment Bolan teetered precariously, then he jumped down into a flower bed.

The Ford roared around the circular drive, causing the goons to leap up and fire another volley.

Bolan ran across the compound, G-11 blasting away. But the little Ford was going to beat him to it. He stopped and watched with respect. The couple in the car knew what they were doing.

The two goons stood in the middle of the drive, firing their two Uzis at the Ford as it tore around the circular drive and finally bore directly down on them. Like drugged zombies, they stood their ground, their bullets striking the Ford's hood.

A cloud of steam erupted from the car's radiator, but the vehicle continued to hurtle toward them. They looked at each other, eyes popping in horror. Almost in unison they turned to run away. But it was too late.

The car was doing at least sixty miles an hour when it smashed into the two guys. Screaming, they flew up over the hissing hood, bashed against the windshield and arced up over the car in long loops, their bloody, battered bodies crashing to the ground.

Its windshield cracked, the car sped on, trailing steam. Bolan watched as the vehicle plowed through the wire-and-iron entry gate and zoomed out of sight down the dark street.

Instantly the warehouse alarm system shrieked. Bolan turned and raced around the warehouse to where he had seen the couple, then their pursuers appear. Powerful body straining, he devoured the distance down the drive to a door left half-open. He ran inside and flipped on bright overhead lights. There was no reason to maintain secrecy. Outside, the alarm still shrieked.

The warehouse was packed with crates, many of them larger than those in the Colorado arsenal. All the boxes he could see bore the names of various mining supplies. He paused long enough to rip one open. It was filled with Colt Commandos.

Bolan ran on to a stairway that led to a row of offices overlooking the giant warehouse floor. He slammed open the doors until he came to the biggest one. An enormous desk stood gleaming off to the side, with a grouping of leather chairs and sofas on the other side of the large room.

The name on the desk was Albert Leonard. Bolan went through the desk drawers and saw shipping manifests from South America—Brazil in particular. That was a natural area for mining equipment to be shipped *to*. But *from*?

Time was running short, and sirens reverberated in the distance. Just as he was about to leave, he saw a strange address on one manifest—a Houston address, and above it the name Leonard had been penciled in. He looked at the size of the shipment. Too damn big for a residence, but that was what it appeared to be. What was Leonard sending to his own home that was disguised as mining equipment?

Bolan memorized the address, slammed the drawer shut, turned off the lights, closed the door and ran through the warehouse to the exit. Again he turned off the lights, then closed and locked the door.

Screeching sirens filled the air, and cars squealed to sudden stops in front of the warehouse. There was no way he was going to get out the front now, so he ran across the drive to the concrete wall.

"There he is!" someone bellowed from the front of the building as he tried to hoist himself over the wall.

"Stop him!" another ordered.

"Hey, you! Stop!" a voice boomed authoritatively. "Stop or we'll shoot!"

Private cops, Bolan thought. Real police would have shouted an ID.

The warrior pulled himself straight up the wall and stepped nimbly over the barbed wires as a gun barked and a bullet blazed past his ear. He leaped off the wall and onto the moist bank of a bayou, shoulder-rolling expertly until he regained his feet. Circling back, he listened to the voices of the patrol as the men discussed where he was, whether anyone else was with him and what they should do.

While they talked he moved. He was just another black shadow on the dark bank in an underlit, ignored industrial section of a big metropolis. Small animals scurried away. Probably rats.

Soon he emerged among tall cottonwoods. Part of the private security patrol had spread out over the warehouse grounds, while the rest had run around outside to the other side of the enclosed warehouse property to look for him. They were behind him now. Obviously they weren't the smartest hired guns he'd run into, but they were still dangerous.

His rented car was straight ahead, exactly where he'd parked it. Crouching, he ran for the vehicle, keys in hand.

"He's getting away!" someone yelled.

"The car!" someone else warned.

Feet pounded toward him. It was no use; they weren't going to let him leave. Bolan stood away from the car knowing full well he'd have to make a stand. He pulled the caseless assault rifle in front of him and squatted. The street was empty behind him where his attackers' bullets would do no harm.

The security cops ran at him from all directions, but he waited patiently for the right moment. Then they opened fire, their bullets screaming and whining. Instantly Bolan returned fire, pivoting once on his heel as his lethal weapon mowed a bloody path across them. They pitched over like bowling pins, a dozen guys, maybe more.

But there were more gunners behind them, and the warrior dashed toward his car, pulled open the door and slid into the driver's seat, starting the engine before the door was even closed.

As he roared out of there, the bullets of the remaining attack squad uselessly pelted the concrete, the cottonwoods and the other buildings along the deserted street. He watched the frenzied goons in his rearview mirror as they grew smaller and smaller. When he could no longer see them, he pulled out his map of Houston. Using a penlight, he figured out where the address was. He'd been right. It was in the old, beautiful section of Houston called River Oaks, which was ten minutes west of downtown. Sprawling over a thousand densely wooded acres, River Oaks was easily the city's premier residential community.

Bolan drove past the manicured terrain of the sixty-year-old suburb, still within sight of Houston's serrated skyline. Impressive Georgian, Tudor and colonial mansions stood back on large rolling lawns.

As the warrior read the numbers on the wrought-iron, carved-wood and split-rail gates that guarded the mansions, a security patrol car drove past at a steady pace. This was River Oaks security—hired by a community, not an individual.

Bolan parked beneath an overhanging willow tree. The address he wanted was on the other side of a white plaster wall. His G-11 secure on his back and his Beretta holstered under his arm, he got out of the car, trotted over to the wall and boosted himself up.

The sign on the wrought-iron gates that closed the estate off from the rest of the world warned: Beware! Attack Dogs! So Bolan dropped quietly and warily onto the turf of a man called Albert Leonard, a man who gave every indication of running a halfway house for illegal weapons. Bolan wanted to know whether Leonard was behind the whole terrorist operation.

Dogs barked in the distance as the Executioner melted into the trees. The forest was cold, damp and aromatic, full of the good odors of earth and trees. He saw the mansion about a quarter mile ahead: a grand French château with balconies and a sloping roof.

The dogs barked louder, excited. Bolan trotted toward the mansion, keeping to the shadows. He paused at a small white building, a miniature of the château that waited ahead. Edging around the side, Bolan saw a sentry sitting in front of the door, a rifle across his knees as he leaned back against the wall. The man wore earphones, and there was the faint sound of rock music.

Bolan slipped out his combat knife and crept silently toward the guy. Involved with his music, the guard didn't even turn around. The soldier yanked him to his feet, pulled him back and cut the knife straight across his throat, holding the guy as he thrashed. The job done, he dropped the lifeless body on the ground.

Suddenly the dogs erupted in a frenzy of barking. Someone had let them out of their cages. Bolan entered the little building and found a couple of dozen crates stacked along one wall—a private cache. They were labeled Mining Equipment, K-rations, Boots, everything under the sun. He didn't need to open them to know what they contained.

The warrior exited and threaded his way through the woods toward the château. The first dog appeared on his left, then there were two more, and then a dozen. Fangs dripping, the first one hurled itself at Bolan, aiming for his throat.

CHAPTER FIVE

The Executioner ducked and pulled out his Beretta 93-R. Snarling, the Doberman hurtled over his head without touching him. It landed lightly on its feet and spun mindlessly back toward Bolan.

The other Dobermans circled in a tight pack, their ferocious growls echoing eerily through the trees. Speed was crucial. No doubt the handler was nearby and soon the woods would be crawling with guards.

Two dogs sprang at Bolan. Almost instantly four more lunged. The warrior rotated, his specially modified Beretta firing again and again. The muffled shots thudded and the flash-hider masked the night glow.

The first dog flew back dead, its black lips frozen in a snarl. Then the second dog died, and another, and the rest. Their fangs dripped saliva even in death as their bloody carcasses hit the ground.

Finally the woods were silent, and Bolan faded back into the trees. Soon he heard shouts.

"Where are they?"

"I can't hear them anymore!"

"Damn dogs!"

Soon three guys ran into the little clearing where the Dobermans' carcasses lay in the cold night air. The handler had a big hunting rifle, while the other two carried Uzis. Moaning, the handler dropped to his knees beside the first pile of bodies.

"Who was it?" one of the guards asked, head snapping as he surveyed the forest.

"Where'd they go?" asked the other.

"We'd better tell the boss," said the first, and he grabbed the walkie-talkie from his belt.

Bolan raised his silenced Beretta and smoothly squeezed the trigger. Suddenly a black hole appeared in the forehead of the guy with the walkie-talkie. Blood gushed out and he fell back, landing on the Dobermans' handler.

"Hey!" the handler yelled, shocked. "What's goin' on?" He pushed the guard off.

The other guard crouched and raised his Uzi, looking for a target. But he wasn't very smart, or his eyes weren't sharp. Before the man could decide where to fire, Bolan pressed the Beretta's trigger and the guy's skull exploded.

The dog handler jumped up. He was the only one left, and his face twisted with hate and rage. But it was anger over the dogs, not the guards. "Asshole!" he screamed, aiming his hunting rifle at where he thought the bullets had come from.

Again Bolan pressed the Beretta's trigger, and the quiet bullets landed square in the handler's chest. Confusion, then renewed fury gripped the guy's leather face. But it was too late. The guy was helpless. And dead.

He fell back with the impact of the bullets, landing on a pile of his well-trained animals. Bolan holstered the Beretta and sprinted toward the château.

If he was lucky, he'd have time to get in and out before the dogs and men were discovered. So much depended on the routine of the place, how often sentries were replaced, how often they were expected to call in.

The Executioner moved through the woods, his eyes coolly scrutinizing the dark trees. He saw no one, but that wasn't surprising: the sentries, along with the dogs who'd guarded this section of the big estate, were dead.

The warrior slowed and took out his Beretta as he approached the château. The great house rose ghostly pale in the moonlight. There were lights in the big multipaned windows downstairs. A couple of the big rooms, he guessed. One had a gray-blue flickering light inside, no doubt a television set.

More light shone upstairs in a corner room where a wrought-iron balcony overlooked an outdoor pool. Carefully Bolan edged along the outskirts of the house, past the pool and spa. He didn't want some guy out for a cigarette or a midnight swim to surprise him. And there might well be a perimeter guard.

Then he smelled hamburgers cooking.

The Executioner moved flat against the château's stucco wall, Beretta in his fist. The aroma of coffee and hamburgers was strongest here. The top half of a Dutch door was open, and inside the château's kitchen a man was whistling a popular tune.

Bolan leaned around the corner. The guy was frying hamburgers in a heavy iron skillet and drinking from a bottle of beer. On the floor next to him, his Uzi leaned against the stove.

The warrior reached over and unlocked the bottom door. The guy continued to flip hamburgers and whistle loudly. Bolan turned the handle, and the door swung open.

As he stepped inside, the heavy skillet sailed across the room straight at his head. Bolan dropped into a crouch. Eyes narrowed, the cook reached inside his shirt and pulled out a knife.

The skillet went on through the open door and landed somewhere outside. A spray of hot grease burned Bolan's face, and the knife thudded into the doorframe next to his cheek. Before the guy could grab his Uzi, the Executioner opened fire. The bullets hit the guy in the belly and slammed him back against the stove.

"Who the hell...?" the man grunted as he grabbed his belly and slid to the floor.

Bolan ran past him into the downstairs hall. He heard laughter, oaths and the loud noises of a television car chase. Padding farther down the hall, he found a door ajar. Inside, guys were sitting around a poker table.

"Raise you twenty."

"You got twenty, Nate?"

"Hey, Nate's got twenty!"

"You gonna bet, asshole?" Nate said good-naturedly.

Bolan moved softly past and up the stairs. Somewhere there was an office, and in the office...

He paused at the top of the stairs. Thick carpeting extended the length of the wide, old-fashioned corridor. Heavy-framed paintings decorated the walls. The hall was dim, and light showed beneath one of the big oak doors. Bolan pressed his ear against the door.

Silence.

He tried the knob. It turned. The latch was quiet, well oiled. Swiftly Bolan swung the door open, slipped in and closed the door. A skeletal man sat behind the big mahogany desk. Behind the guy were tall French doors that framed the wrought-iron balcony he had spotted from below.

The skeleton looked at Bolan with hollow, drugged eyes. Was this half-dead guy the kingpin of the arms shipments? Bolan didn't believe it.

"Who are you?" the guy asked listlessly.

"You Albert Leonard?" Bolan countered.

"Who's asking?" the guy said automatically. "Zeke's supposed to bring my crack. Where's Zeke?" The guy hauled himself unsteadily to his feet. "Zeke?" he croaked.

"There's a change of plans on those arms in the warehouse," Bolan told the skeleton. "But my orders are to give the information to Albert Leonard and no one else."

"So give," the skeleton said. "I'm Leonard."

"Prove it. Tell me where they were shipped from first."

The skeleton was annoyed. "Zeke!" He stared at the door and shouted again. "Zeke!"

Bolan realized the guy was beyond fear or threats.

"Zeke, you fuck!"

Bolan jumped quickly for the balcony, flattening outside against the wall where he could see back inside the room through the space between the curtains and the window frame.

The door opened and a tall, thick, stern Indian filled the opening.

"Tell this guy where the shipment come from," Leonard said to the Indian. "Can't remember... Gimme the crack!" He fell back into his chair, panting slightly from the exertion, his dull eyes eager.

The Indian's dark, intelligent eyes looked around the empty room. "What guy, boss?"

"The guy from...from... Hell, I don't know. Just tell him and gimme the crack."

The Indian stared at the skeleton without expression.

"Boss, you're no good no more," he said simply and tiredly. He pulled a Colt .45 from beneath his armpit and dropped one slug between the skeleton's dull eyes. Albert Leonard didn't look surprised as the heavy slug knocked him across the room against the wall. He almost seemed to smile as he pitched forward onto his face.

The thunder of the shot reverberated through the house. Downstairs someone yelled. The Indian ran to the French doors, threw them open and leaped off the balcony and into the Grecian-style swimming pool.

Bolan could have killed him, but he wanted answers. Feet pounded up the stairs toward the office. The warrior strode across the balcony. The Indian was already out of the pool and running into the woods. Lowering himself over the edge, Bolan dropped silently to the ground and cat-footed after the Indian.

Marsha Barr and Cecil Olds sat in their rental car outside the New York dive. They were parked just off the Minnesota Strip, where derelict buildings and humans collected like scum on oily water.

This was an area where thugs robbed their own mothers and mothers killed their sons. The miserable residents were ground down to less than animals. The stink of alcohol, urine and unwashed bodies filled the brown air, and every morning behind trash cans and piles of rubbish the cops found skinny corpses who'd overdosed sometime during the long, hopeless hours of the night.

"He's bloody hard to tail," Cecil observed in his Oxbridge accent. He'd already had to get out of the car once to shoo ragged children who were sizing up the vehicle for the local chop shop. He looked now at Marsha with the old hunger, and she looked kindly back, ignoring it.

"A cautious sort," she agreed. "Wish we knew who he was."

"First that big Indian goes in."

"Then our man follows, tough and silent as ever," Marsha said. Last night she'd dreamed about their mystery man, his tall, muscular body. It had been unsettling.

"What-ho!" Cecil said in quiet triumph. "What have we here?"

The long black stretch limo parked across the street. It glistened with polish, care and expense. Two sleek young toughs got out of the back seat, buttoning the jackets to their business suits. A dapper, slightly older man leaned out after them, giving instructions.

The two toughs nodded with respect, then went into the dive. The chauffeur got out, closed the back door and returned to the driver's seat. The large bulge under his arm warned the neighborhood to stay away.

Marsha and Cecil looked at each other, surprised at the new arrivals.

"Know them?" Marsha asked.

Cecil shook his head. "What now?"

"Indeed," Marsha murmured, and was suddenly afraid for their mystery man.

BOLAN HAD TAILED the Indian to the Houston airport, where he'd bought a tourist-class ticket to New York City under the name Ezekial Chee. The warrior had taken the same flight to Kennedy, followed the guy to a fleabag hotel off Columbus Circle and then to this dive off the Minnesota Strip.

The Indian was careful. He had doubled back, always wary, constantly watching. So Bolan had let him get far ahead and out of sight sometimes. Once he'd almost lost him. Chee was worried about something, and expected to be tailed. If not by Bolan, then by whom?

Now Bolan sat across the dim, sleazy bar in a shadowy corner and watched the eye contact between the Indian and the bartender. The bartender wanted Chee to order a drink, but the Indian just sat there on a high bar stool, his broad face impassive.

Bolan leaned back in his chair, arms crossed, an amused look in his eyes. He didn't have a drink, either, but he was out of the bartender's line of fire.

"No drink, get out!" the bartender said at last, furiously polishing the dusty bar.

Chee just blinked.

"Can't have no freeloaders takin' the chairs of payin' customers!" the bartender said indignantly.

The Indian rotated his head and looked down the long bar. There was only one other customer. He shrugged.

"Listen, guy!" the bartender said, then stopped in midsentence. He looked at the door where two young toughs in expensive suits stood. He resumed polishing the bar. "Help you, sir?" he said meekly to the taller of the two.

The pair ignored him. They walked directly to Chee.

"Okay, Indian," the taller said. "Come on."

Chee's eyes blinked slowly. He didn't even bother to look at them.

The tall guy leaned over and snarled, "Move it!

Bolan watched with interest as the tall tough suddenly stiffened, his face turning brick-red. Chee's massive hand gripped the fellow's throat. Just one hand, and the guy was helpless.

The guy lashed out at the Indian, struggling to break loose, but his blows bounced off as if he were hitting a rubber statue. Finally Chee let go and the young tough dropped to his knees.

His friend pulled out a small Smith and Wesson, but his hand shook. The Indian sat motionless while the first young tough climbed up a bar stool to his feet. He felt his neck and twisted his head.

"C'mon," he said to the other guy, his voice surly as he led the way out the door.

Chee resumed staring at the bartender, who bit his lip and turned his back to busily wash clean glasses. He knew when to keep his mouth shut.

Chee still hadn't spoken, but Bolan thought he detected a smile. The man just sat on the bar stool and waited. Bolan stayed in his shadowy corner and waited, too, although he didn't know for what.

At last a young well-dressed man strode in the door as if he owned the joint. He was older than the two toughs, and looked a lot rougher and more sophisticated. His knuckles were big from the fights he'd been in. The way he walked, he'd won them.

"What the hell do you think you're doing!" he snapped at Chee.

The Indian smiled. "Sit down," he said in excellent English. "Join me."

"Not here, you—"

"Shh," Chee said as he put a big hand across the young man's mouth. "Shh. People are dead. Your people. The Feds are in. Guns are gone. The Major wants to know how." He took his hand away from the guy's mouth.

The guy's eyes narrowed as he decided whether to believe Chee. "Okay. My place."

The Indian nodded solemnly, and the two men walked out the door, the dapper guy in front. Bolan followed them.

CHAPTER SIX

High above New York City Chee stepped from the penthouse bathroom, nodded to the man at the door and walked back down the hall toward the living room. The guard followed, his big feet clumping on the hardwood floor.

Inwardly Chee grimaced. His own feet made no sound. He'd grown up on the sandstone ridges of New Mexico, where heavy feet frightened off game and warned of strangers. A heavy-footed man was no warrior.

"I don't give a shit what some nut down in Brazil says!" the young boss grumbled as soon as Chee walked into the room.

The Indian said nothing. Now he would wait. It wouldn't be long.

"You expect me to buy all this crap about trouble?" the New York boss continued. "Look at this guy!" he said to the two young toughs who lounged on a sofa under a window that framed a million-dollar view of the jagged city skyline. "This guy's nuts!"

"Yeah," one of the thugs said, "crazy."

"We'll off him for you, boss," the other said enthusiastically. He was the one Chee had nearly strangled. "Cut him into little pieces. Throw him into the Hudson!"

Chee raised his eyebrows an eighth of an inch. They had tantrums like children. They knew nothing of strength and of how a real man acted. Soon they would learn.

"Whatever it is, it's our damn business!" the boss shouted. He was furious that Chee didn't sweat or even look worried. "Go back and tell your nut that!"

"Perhaps you should tell him yourself, old boy," a cheery voice called down the hall. The footsteps that approached were nearly silent, the Indian noted with respect.

"W-what?" sputtered the boss. "Who's there?"

The boss angrily gestured at the two young thugs and the guard who'd followed Chee from the bathroom. The three guys jumped to their feet and ran toward the door.

"You dumb shits!" the boss said, pacing behind his glass-topped desk. "You let some asshole break in!"

Chee stepped in front of the doorway, arms folded over his broad chest. He smiled.

The three guys pulled their guns and pointed them at his head.

"Move it!" the guard growled.

Chee continued to smile. He stayed put. There was enough time. They wouldn't shoot until their boss gave the order.

"But you probably wouldn't like the climate," the hearty voice continued. He'd stopped out of sight behind the tall Navaho. "A lot of humidity down in Brazil. Makes you sweat like a bloody pig!"

"Who in hell . . . ?" the young New York boss said.

"He must've climbed through the bathroom window, boss," the guard said, figuring it all out at last.

"The Indian let him in!" one of the other thugs offered as an alternative.

"Christ, we're twenty-five stories up!" The boss's face went white. Angrily he swung his arms. "Get him out of the way!" he yelled at his men.

The guys moved their guns closer to the big Navaho's face.

"Your last chance . . ." the guard began.

The Indian ducked, turned sideways and stepped soundlessly back into the room. The thugs turned to look at him, awed by his speed and agility.

Left standing in the doorway was a handsome redheaded man with flushed cheeks, a thick mustache and sideburns. There was a long, ragged scar on his left cheek from eye to jaw. He was slender, of medium height and carried a rappeling rope coiled over his shoulder. "When you know how to use this," he said good-naturedly, dropping the rope to the floor, "no place is secure."

The men in the room stared at him, unsure of what do to.

The New York boss's eyes narrowed. "How . . .?"

"Come down over the top," the new man said. "Name's Miles Haggarty." He walked to the desk and extended his hand across it to the young boss. "Thought it was about time we met."

The New York boss looked at the hand as if it had leprosy.

"Come on, old boy. Don't be a bloody prick. We're all in this together." Haggarty gave a dazzling smile.

"The hand's safe enough. It's the guns you have to worry about!" he laughed. "And there's money in the guns!"

The boss—an arms middleman—frowned, thinking about what Haggarty had said. Yeah, it was a joke. Money in the guns. Actually, it was a pretty good joke. An *in* joke. He liked being *in*. He laughed, and his boys laughed nervously with him. They would keep their eyes on Haggarty. He was too damn good to be healthy for them.

"Frisk him," he told his men.

They ran their hands expertly over Haggarty, who had expected it. He didn't have a gun. When they were finished, the boss shook hands with him.

"You come from Brazil?" the New York boss asked.

"Right from the top. The Major sent me himself. Got any Jack Daniels?"

The boss waved at the bar in the corner. Haggarty strode to it, poured whiskey into a glass, tipped his head back and drank. "Ahh," he said, and wiped his mouth with the back of his hand.

"Why's Brazil so interested in us?" The New York boss sat down behind his desk, his puzzled eyes studying Haggarty. "We make our shipments on time."

"As my friend Zeke told you," Haggarty said, setting the empty glass on the bar, "you have some problems."

"*We* got problems? The only problem *I* got is you breaking in and your Indian pal roughing up my men.

Now I can eliminate my problem very easily." He gestured.

His men lifted their guns and closed in on Haggarty. It was an empty threat, and Haggarty knew it. If anything happened to him, the New York boss would be in deep shit with the Major.

Haggarty laughed. "Kill me and you'll all die!"

The New York kingpin sighed. Haggarty was right. If he had information from the Brazil chief, he had to listen. The man in Brazil seemed to have unlimited firepower...and cash. The New York boss gestured his men back to their sofas and chairs.

"Okay," he said. "Who are you and what have you got on your mind?"

Haggarty snapped to attention and gave a jaunty salute. "Suh! Captain Miles Haggarty, suh! Brit paratrooper and commando, retired. Mercenary, retired! Now working on the side of might, if not right!"

"Get on with it," the boss grumbled.

Haggarty grinned and shrugged. He fell into a leather chair, stretched out his legs and crossed the ankles. He was in a very good mood. Everything was going as planned.

"You remember the Nevada heist?" Suddenly Haggarty's voice was serious.

"The special alloy for making weapons-grade uranium?" the boss asked. He stared at Haggarty. "How did *you* know about it...unless you're the one who..."

"Swiped it," Haggarty finished. "That's it, old boy. MI6, the Yanks and even the Brazilian coppers are after me, and after the source. The Major can handle the wogs. They're easy. They don't require much, just payoffs and a promise that they'll live. We can keep the Yanks and MI6 distracted and dancing. Those blokes are just plodders. They don't have any imagination. But now we've got a joker in the pack." He paused. "A stranger, the Major's sources tell him, skied in and proceeded to wipe out the Japanese at their own Rocky Mountain arsenal. Then he turned the whole cache over to the Yank Feds. Our man's a gent named Mack Bolan."

"I heard about the Japs," the boss said, edgily waiting for what would come next. "But I've never heard of any Mack Bolan."

"You bloody well should have heard! You're the one who sold those Japs the stuff!" Haggarty said, his tone menacing. He cracked the knuckles on his left hand. His face had darkened. His eyes were cold and hard. "Somebody's been feeding this Bolan damn good intel." Miles Haggarty glared at the young New York arms middleman. "How did the joker know about the Red Army in the Rockies? Who leaked it?"

There was silence in the room.

Restlessly Miles Haggarty stood up. He paced like a caged animal.

A COLD WIND WHISTLED around Bolan as he swung toward the penthouse window high above New York City. From below came the faint sounds of traffic— car engines, horns honking, occasional shouts, tires squealing. He'd watched another man come down the side of the building in the same way, a redheaded guy who'd been tailing the Indian and the thugs.

Bolan had gone back to his rental car for some superstrong nylon cord. He'd rigged knots for rappeling and lowered himself over the side of the tall brick building. Now he slid into the same window the redheaded man had used and found himself in a bathroom.

He listened at the door.

Nothing.

Silently he padded into the corridor. At one end was a big steel door with industrial locks, which probably led to the building's elevator. At the other end of the hall was a large living room. People were talking in the room. And just outside the door two deadly MAC-10 submachine guns leaned casually against the wall, out of sight from those in the room.

Bolan felt himself tense when he heard someone mention his name. They knew about him. Somebody had spotted him, or somebody had told the redheaded guy about him. But who? And what was the payoff?

There was a long silence in the room down the corridor. Somebody was up and pacing.

Bolan shook out his tense muscles and moved toward the room. There was no time for his own problems. The door to the room was ajar. Bolan could see five men sitting on sofas and chairs. The sixth—the redheaded guy—was pacing. The Indian was there, the boss man, his two thugs from the bar and a third goon.

"You don't know?" the redhead said, his voice icy as he headed back across the room. "You didn't leak it to somebody who leaked it to somebody else who was paying real good for the intel?''

"Why in hell should we?'' the boss said angrily. He jumped up behind his desk and pounded it. "Why does Brazil always think it's New York's fault?''

The redheaded guy was heading past the corridor door. "Because it usually is,'' he said. He snaked his hand into the corridor and grabbed the two MAC-10s. "Isn't it!''

The redhead tossed one of the submachine guns to the Indian. Chee had been waiting. He caught it with one hand and crouched, preparing to fire.

"Hey!'' screamed the boss. "No! You've got it all wrong! I—''

"We didn't!'' one of the thugs yelled.

The other two lifted their guns, but they were too late. Chee and the redhead opened up.

The MAC-10s thundered, splattering blood on the ceiling and furniture. The air misted pink. The New York arms middleman and his three thugs slammed back against their seats with the impact of the bullets.

Chee and the redhead stopped firing. They looked at each other. The redhead nodded. Obviously he was the leader. The two walked over to the bodies and gave each an insurance blast to the head.

Finished, they strode down the corridor to the steel door. The Indian unlocked it, stood back for the redhead to walk through, and they both disappeared into the hallway.

No need to call the cops, Bolan knew. With all that noise somebody else would. The warrior sped down the hall after his quarry.

"CECIL! It's Miles Haggarty," the woman said. They'd been waiting an hour, sitting outside the apartment building in their rental car. She was tired, cold and hungry. It had been a long day tailing the big stranger. But there was no way she would complain now as she watched Miles Haggarty and the big Indian come out of the building.

"I've got eyes!" Cecil snapped. It had been a frustrating day for him. He started the engine. "Sorry, old girl," he apologized. "Need my distemper shot."

"Our guy's tailing Haggarty!" Marsha said. "Look!"

The big guy strode out of the apartment building's massive front entrance in pursuit of Haggarty. His practiced eyes scanned the street and sidewalks. In the distance sirens began to wail.

"Police!" Olds said.

They watched the Indian and Haggarty speed away from the curb in a Ford Escort. The other guy got into a car down the block and pulled out after them. Olds let him get a block ahead, then moved into the traffic, bringing up the rear of the three-car procession.

TWENTY MINUTES LATER on New York's Lower West Side, Miles Haggarty and Zeke Chee drove around the sleazy warehouse. Weeds sprouted through cracks in the concrete parking lot. Trash littered the ground and collected next to the building where wind had blown it. The burned-out hulk of an old car stood abandoned on the north side of the structure. Spray-painted graffiti colored the gray walls: Fuck Off! Kill the pigs! NY cops suck!

Chee was feeling good. He liked working with Haggarty. He had met the redhead only a few weeks ago when the Englishman had replaced the old underboss in South America. Now Haggarty was the Major's new right-hand man. That seemed good to Chee.

The Navaho remembered their first meeting. As soon as he'd walked into the Houston hotel room to give his secret report, he'd felt the Englishman's power. Strength radiated from the redhead like heat. In South America the Major would know it, too. The Major would like it because now he owned the Englishman.

Haggarty was a warrior, Chee told himself with fierce pleasure. No doubt of it. Haggarty was silent and powerful. There was no need for words between them.

Being with Haggarty reminded Chee of the walks he used to take with his imaginary grandfather across the tops of the sandstone plateaus and mesas of New Mexico. You could see a hundred miles up there, clear into Arizona. He'd never met his grandfather or father, but if they'd stayed on the reservation to raise him, he knew they would be strong, silent and powerful, just like Miles Haggarty.

"This is it," Haggarty said, and nodded at a narrow steel door at the side of the warehouse. It had a big padlock on it.

Chee parked the car next to the door and they got out with their MAC-10s.

"Blast it, old boy," Haggarty said.

Chee stood back and dumped a bullet into the lock. The lock spun away and the Navaho opened the door. Haggarty strode through with Chee right behind.

The warehouse was enormous and empty and smelled of age, dust and diesel fuel. Chee knew that just last week it had housed a thousand boxes of weapons and ammo.

"Let's go," Haggarty whispered.

They jogged up the rickety wooden stairs that led to the mezzanine. Chee had followed other powerful men, but Haggarty was the best. This made Chee happy. At last he had found the most powerful, the best warrior of all.

"Who's there?" a voice yelled.

There were muffled sounds of movement in one of the offices that overlooked the warehouse floor. Silently they passed closed glass office doors but saw no sign of anyone. Nearing the end of the mezzanine, they came to the last office.

Automatically they slowed. As Chee's elbow brushed the wood railing that rimmed the mezzanine, gunfire exploded. Bullets shattered the glass door of the last office and shots screamed past them, the sound echoing like thunder across the warehouse.

Chee and Haggarty dropped to the floor. The Englishman motioned, but Chee already knew what to do. They wriggled on elbows and knees to either side of the door. Haggarty nodded at Chee. The Indian leaned back and felt for a moment the length and power of his big body. In his mind he coiled like a spring. Then he kicked out and the door burst open.

Hugging the floor, they swarmed in together, MAC-10s blasting.

Gunfire hammered thick and deadly just over the heads of Chee and Haggarty. The slugs bit into the walls and streaked out through the doorway. Three Uzis pointed out around a gray metal desk in the office. The warehouse guys were back there. Chee and Haggarty had them cornered and knew exactly where they were, but the targets didn't know where the Indian and the Englishman were.

From the floor the MAC-10s of Chee and Haggarty ate smoking holes across the cheap metal desk front, the bullets popping through easily as BBs through a paper target. Haggarty grunted; it was time to quit firing. Chee nodded and released his trigger finger.

The room was silent. Someone behind the desk moaned—a hopeless, animal sound. Haggarty and Chee stood motionless for a moment, then split up and carefully rounded the desk.

On the far side, wedged between two rows of filing cabinets, sprawled the three warehouse guys. A pond of blood surrounded them, and one of the bodies groaned again.

Haggarty and Chee placed the muzzles of their guns against two of the heads and blasted. The Navaho took care of the third. After the reverberation of the last gunfire, the cold warehouse sounded even emptier.

Chee cradled his MAC-10 against his chest and turned to Haggarty. "That's it," he proudly reported. "Those are the last guys who could've told that broad and the guy Bolan about the Japs and the Rocky Mountain dump. The leak's plugged. Everybody who could've told is dead.''

Haggarty looked at Chee sternly, his face radiating strength and authority. The Indian smiled. Like a sponge, he absorbed Haggarty's warrior power. Everything the Englishman did pleased him. Someday he would take the British warrior home and together they would walk the sandstone ridges of the reservation.

''Not quite *all*, old boy,'' Haggarty said.

Chee frowned. *Not all?* Who could be left? What did Haggarty mean?

Then he saw a new look in the redhead's hard eyes. Haggarty was sad, and the Indian suddenly understood why. He—Zeke Chee, the Navaho—was left. Chee's world exploded, and he slammed back against a wall, a white-hot volcano erupting in his chest.

Pain wrapped around him like a shroud. He thought about the warrior power of Miles Haggarty and smiled ambiguously. Then all he knew was blackness . . . and nothing.

HAGGARTY CROUCHED over the Indian's corpse. He was dead all right. Poor rotter. Then he heard faint sounds—the rickety staircase was creaking.

Someone was coming up.

The Englishman peered through the open doorway. For a moment he regretted killing the Indian. He could have used him now.

The sounds came closer. It was somebody who knew how to stalk. If the stairs and mezzanine hadn't been old and noisy, the guy would have made it unheard.

Haggarty looked at the doorway again. There was a glass shard still in place in the corner. The shard acted as a mirror and allowed Haggarty to see down the mezzanine.

He watched the approaching figure—a tall, muscular gent who moved as lithely as a jungle cat. By the way he walked, Haggarty predicted big trouble. The gent knew what he was doing, and Haggarty couldn't afford to lose time now. He had more work to do for the Major in Brazil, but mostly for his other boss, the one in —

The first shot exploded over Haggarty's head. The new gent was getting his bearings, but Haggarty wouldn't give him time enough to find them. The Englishman shoulder-rolled across the mezzanine, firing down the narrow corridor. On one side of him was the wooden railing and a thirty-foot drop to the warehouse's concrete floor. On the other side was the row of glass-doored offices.

The stranger ducked out of sight into one of the offices. Now their positions were reversed, Haggarty thought, pleased. Now *he* was stalking. Carefully he crept down the mezzanine toward the office where the stranger waited.

MACK BOLAN STOOD pressed against the wall in the warehouse office, maximizing his narrow view of the mezzanine. He barely heard the redhead's approach. The guy was quiet, obviously well trained. He'd known what he was doing when he'd rolled out onto the mezzanine and forced Bolan's retreat.

Now the Executioner waited patiently. Either he was trapped, or he'd get the redhead first. It was only a matter of time....

First Bolan saw the shadow; the black silhouette of the head, shoulders and torso stretched menacingly along the mezzanine toward the office door. His hand flexed on his Beretta as the shadow came closer.

Gunfire thundered in the silence, and the interior wall shook with it. The railing along the mezzanine shattered and pieces fell onto the floor below.

No shots entered the room. It wasn't gunfire aimed at Bolan. The redhead bolted past the office where Bolan waited. As he passed, the gunner dumped a round into the room to keep Bolan there. All the guy needed was a few seconds to get down the stairs. But was he chasing someone . . . or being chased?

Bolan ran out onto the mezzanine. Downstairs a woman turned in the outside doorway and disappeared into the cold glare of afternoon sunlight. It was the woman from the cabin in the Rockies and the warehouse in Houston. Who in hell *was* she?

As Bolan reached the top of the stairs, the redhead vanished out the door after her. The Executioner pounded down the stairs two at a time. He raced across the warehouse to the open door just in time to see two cars tearing away. The redhead was following the woman and her driver.

Bolan's car was hidden out of sight down the street. There was no way he'd ever catch up.

Now what in hell did he do?

He turned to look at the dilapidated warehouse. Why had the redhead come here? It was certainly big enough to house a lot of arms and ammo, but it was empty now.

The warrior surveyed the area. No one was around. This was a place for night people—drug users, pimps and whores. People who lived in the light of day would avoid a place where dirty syringes, sleeping drunks, and excrement littered the alleys.

There were no wailing sirens. No one in this area would ever call the police. Then Bolan remembered the Indian.

He ran inside and up the stairs again. Cautiously he entered the last office. The Indian was sprawled against a wall, head limply forward, his massive hands still curled around his MAC-10. He had an enormous chest wound. Whoever had gotten him must have been almost on top of him. He'd died dirty and fast.

Bolan walked around the desk. There were three more bodies there. Most likely one of them had killed the Indian. No, he thought, there was too much distance. That left the redhead. But the Indian and the redhead were partners. Or were they?

Bolan knelt beside Chee and checked the pockets in his pants, shirt and leather vest. There were keys, a beat-up cowhide billfold with IDs and credit cards under different names, and a roll of hundreds and fifties-probably a thousand dollars—held together by a thick rubber band.

Then he found the real prize. Zipped in an inside vest pocket with odd pieces of business correspondence was a typed letter with a return address in Italy and sent to Zeke Chee in Houston, asking about the location of a lost shipment of ammo.

It was a typical business letter, straight to the point and not terribly interesting except for one detail—it was signed by Colonel Hugo Greenleaf.

Bolan knew the name, and so did the officials of most Third World nations at war. Greenleaf was a notorious mercenary leader renowned for his success in hand-to-hand combat. He read the Italian return address again, folded the letter and put it into his pocket.

Hugo Geeenleaf did business with the death merchants Bolan was chasing. Greenleaf could lead him to the source—the man or men who controlled the weapons and ammo that moved from secret warehouses into the hands of terrorists like the Japanese who had planned to attack the government base in the Rocky Mountains.

It was time to get moving.

CHAPTER SEVEN

Overlooking the icy waters of Lago Maggiore stood the Villa di Cremona, still in Italy but near the Swiss border. In the summer Switzerland was a half hour's walk. In the winter it was fifteen minutes away on cross-country skis. Such proximity to another nation's borders was important to the owner and guests of the luxurious Villa di Cremona.

Snow covered the rugged Alps. The sharp mountain peaks glistened starkly white against the blue winter sky. Pine trees covered the lower slopes.

Inside the great room of the Villa di Cremona a fire blazed. A man and woman who spoke with slight British accents sat in easy chairs in front of the massive stone fireplace. There was a small round table between them. A hand-knotted Oriental rug covered the tile floor of their sitting area. On the table stood two open bottles of Italian wine.

"Ah, yes, the Grignolino," the man said, sipping. "But I don't think it's really up to the Barolo." He was a burly six foot five and had a heavy pocked face and thick-fingered hands that held the tulip-shaped wineglass with great dexterity. A man who knew how to use his hands, he'd learned such urbanity at Sandhurst. Now he thoughtfully eyed the ruby-red wine.

"Not as complex, Hugo," the woman agreed. Tall and slender with short dark hair that framed her beautiful face, she was in her thirties and moved gracefully. She knew he watched her each time she moved, therefore she arranged and rearranged her hips seductively in the big chair. Slowly she crossed and uncrossed her long slender legs, leaning forward occasionally so that the fullness of her breasts would strain against the thin wool of her white dress.

"The Major knows nothing then?" Colonel Hugo Greenleaf asked, returning to the subject they'd been discussing before they'd begun tasting the wine. He watched her with the pleasure of an art collector. There was time enough for what he wanted from her, and waiting would only make it better. "First the Rocky Mountain cache and then the deaths of the Major's people in Houston and New York. And some strange couple spotted nearby during both killings. What were they doing there and who are they?" Greenleaf hesitated. "Perhaps it was this Bolan who eliminated the Major's people. I've never run into Bolan, but I've heard about him from time to time." He sipped his wine.

"It's a puzzling situation," the woman said. "I'm glad you told me about it."

"The Major will let you know officially soon enough about the New York incident, I expect," Greenleaf said. "There was a secret tape recorder playing in the apartment of the middleman. Seems the idiot taped everything, like a voyeur filming his sex acts. Only that poor fellow liked to hear the sound of his own words. Hung up on the power of his little empire, I'd say."

"I'd say," the woman echoed, smiling into Greenleaf's eyes. "Too many people in our business are."

"Estelle," Greenleaf said, "may I say I can't recall an arms middleman, or is it middle*person* as, ah, delectable as you."

"Or a customer as charming as you, Colonel Greenleaf," Estelle Davis replied coyly.

They smiled into each other's calculating eyes, and heat passed between them. They knew what they were, and that made it even more exciting—and dangerous.

Greenleaf continued the discussion. "I wonder whose side this Bolan is actually on."

"Maybe he's on his own side."

"A thought, my dear. Like the rest of the world, eh?" Greenleaf finished the Grignolino and set the glass on the table. He picked up a clean glass and poured in the Barolo. "Yes, that's the basic mistake all do-gooders, idealists, bleeding hearts, socialists and welfare staters make. They forget that self-interest is what counts to all men, and always will be what counts when the chips are down."

"Nature knows only survival of the fittest."

"That's it. The fighters, the unafraid, the doers, the daring risk takers."

"And in the long run, the people with the most guns," Estelle reminded him.

"Power comes out of the barrel of a gun." Greenleaf nodded, sipped the Barolo and sighed with pleasure. "And the one with the most guns wins. In the long run we Europeans are doomed unless we kill off the blacks, browns and yellows before they get too strong. We won't, though. We'll try to deal fairly and be nice guys, and in the end we'll lose to the Third World. Then they'll fight it out to see who's top mongrel." He chuckled. "Well, that's life," he said cheerfully. "I'll stay on top as long as I can."

"For that you need the Major."

"Absolutely, my dear. My old buddy keeps me supplied with matériel, and sometimes men. When we have mutual interests we often work together. That way I can keep my own small, tough, perfect unit. I have a new bunch of recruits coming in now. Would you like to watch me screen them?"

"Sounds boring," she said teasingly over the top of her wineglass. "The qualities you need, and I need, in a man are most probably quite different, thank you!"

He laughed. "Charming! Yes, we must discuss further, at a more appropriate time, these, ah, qualities. Perhaps I have a few of the qualities you search for."

"You're too modest, Hugo!"

He laughed again. "Modest? Never!"

She smiled. "Who is the Major, really?" she asked casually. "I've never met him, only received orders from him through the middlemen who hired me. I don't even know that my orders are *truly* from him!"

"Ah, my dear," Greenleaf lectured good-naturedly, "no one knows for sure. He's reputed to be a former KGB assassin who got in serious trouble for killing a corrupt chief of his without orders. Then he switched sides to our people—the Brits—but he was too hot for us to handle. So he ended up as the most violent and elusive hired gun in the world, after Carlos. Then he suddenly vanished. Everyone thought he was dead."

"But he wasn't?"

"Far from it. He surfaced a few years ago with his, ah, new enterprise. We've worked together for years, before and after his resurrection. His only trademark is that he always insisted on the rank of major. No higher, no lower. I've heard he said it was so that he didn't have to change his business cards, uniforms or code name." Greenleaf chuckled. "A strange one. But he's damn good. Reliable. He's where I get my guns, killers, aircraft, new mercenaries, anything. In fact, I have a meeting with him soon. Why don't you come along?"

"I don't know whether I'd want to meet him or not," Estelle said.

"Probably not, my dear," Greenleaf said. He finished his Barolo, stood and bowed formally. "Now you must leave. My duty calls."

"The interviews with your new recruits," Estelle murmured.

"*Prospective* recruits," Greenleaf corrected. He took her hand; the fingers were long and slender. Gallantly he kissed the hand. "I will see you soon, my dear," he promised as he led her to the door. "Very soon. And our meeting will be, ah, productive. I promise."

IN HIS COMBAT WHITESUIT Mack Bolan lay on a snowy slope and watched the Villa di Cremona through high-powered binoculars. The walls of the building were stone, as was the low wall that encircled the grounds. The villa had the air of a fortress with men carrying hunting rifles patrolling the estate.

The main building sprawled over ten thousand square feet, he estimated. And there were three smaller outbuildings—guest cottage, workshop and garage. Smoke curled up from a dozen chimneys.

Through the tall windows of a first-floor room he watched Hugo Greenleaf talk with a woman. It was the same damn woman again! The one from the Rockies, Houston and then the warehouse on New York's Lower West Side. Was he witnessing a civil war among terrorists? he wondered. Why did they all seem so connected? He could no longer believe the woman had good intentions, not if she was drinking wine and smiling invitations at Hugo Greenleaf.

Greenleaf and the woman stood and disappeared into the room beyond his view. Soon Greenleaf was back, again sitting in the chair beside the fireplace.

Rough-looking men with the sheen of the outdoors and adventure on them filed into the room. Mercenaries, probably. After all, Greenleaf was a renowned mercenary leader. Bolan clipped on his skis and zoomed down the slope toward the villa.

CHAPTER EIGHT

Three dozen unarmed mercenaries stood and sat around the great room of the Villa di Cremona. Refraining from small talk, they waited for Hugo Greenleaf to speak.

Whether the men were big and brawny, or small and wiry, their fierce faces shared traces of the same chilling experience—blood fever. Like any soldier, they had killed and almost been killed. But more than that they knew firsthand what happened when the blood, corpses, gunfire, fear and triumph finally got to a man. It was like hot lust.

"Welcome, gentlemen," Hugo Greenleaf said. He stood before the blazing fire, facing the potential recruits. Towering over most of them, he was a commanding figure, dressed simply in khaki wool trousers and shirt. His black combat boots glistened with polish. He held a glass of the Barolo. "Drinks in a few minutes, but business first. Any of you know why you're here?"

"An interview," said one man.

"Yeah, but for what?" said another.

"Jobs, bozo," said a third, disgusted by the stupidity of the second man.

The group laughed.

"Excellent," Greenleaf said. "You've saved me a long explanation. Jobs. That's what we're here to talk about. Also about the roughest, toughest, meanest team of crack soldiers on the globe!"

"Yeah." Several of the mercenaries nodded approval.

"If a mercenary doesn't have pride," Greenleaf said, "I don't want him. If he doesn't think he's the best damn merc there is, I don't want him. And if he doesn't like money, I especially don't want him."

Some of the men laughed. Others shouted approval. All of them nodded enthusiastically.

"What that means," Greenleaf continued, "is that I want a merc with pride. A merc who thinks he's the best. A merc who thinks he's so damn good that he deserves to be paid well."

"Yeah!" They clapped loudly. "Yeah!"

"How'd you find us?" one guy shouted over the noise.

"Some of your names came on the recommendations of friends of yours I've hired. Others I got out of magazine advertisements or from former commanders. You've already been screened once. Now we need to talk. Everyone here who believes he can fight only for the West, go stand over there."

Greenleaf pointed to the south wall, where an Italian tapestry hung. At first the only movement in the room was of heads turning. Then four men walked over to the tapestry and looked around uneasily.

"Good. Now everyone here who believes he can fight only for the Communists and their bloc, go stand over there."

This time Greenleaf pointed to the north wall, where French doors looked out onto a snowy patio. Three men stood up and went there.

"Excellent. Now anyone here who thinks he can fight only for some other cause—Third World, Indian, Middle East, whatever—go over by the door."

Two black mercenaries strolled over to the arched doorway, where two of Greenleaf's sentries stood, Walthers holstered at their sides. The unarmed blacks cast uneasy glances at the Walthers.

"I appreciate your honesty, gentlemen," Greenleaf said, his voice booming with authority. "Now I'll be honest with you. I deliberately sent you to different sides of the room because I couldn't trust you bloody blokes to stand together without trying to kill each other eventually."

"Hey, man!" shouted a young guy in the West group. "That's crazy!"

Greenleaf cast a cold stare at the fellow, who glared back belligerently. Greenleaf's gaze was icy and steady, and the young fellow dropped his eyes.

The colonel turned back to the group. It was a small, unimportant victory. He drank the Barolo. "As I was saying," he continued, "I respect a merc who has loyalty to his nation or his people, but I can't use that man. I'll ask all of you who've declared yourselves to leave. But to reward you for your honesty, you'll have a free night at the town inn, and all the food and drink you like. Don't cause any trouble, and be out of Italy by tomorrow afternoon. You understand. That's all."

The room was silent as the nine men filed out. The door closed.

"We fight for whoever pays us most!" Greenleaf declared in a ringing voice.

The remaining mercenaries stomped their feet and clapped. They were tired of fighting dirty wars for pennies. They were damn good, and they expected to be paid for it.

"Let's have your names and where you've fought," Greenleaf said. "We'll begin over here."

The mercenary on Greenleaf's right spoke first. "Harry Ochsner. Angola, Zaire, Namibia."

Greenleaf nodded. "Next?"

"I go by Fear Nolan. Nicaragua, El Salvador."

Greenleaf listened attentively as each man spoke. Few of the names were real, Greenleaf was sure. Mercenaries with families wanted the protection of anonymity. And most mercs were loners. When one wanted to disappear for a while, he left no trail behind. Especially not a real name.

At last Greenleaf thanked them. "I'm building up my troops for a big job. If you work out on this, you can count on a permanent salary even when you're not fighting. Until we part company. No contracts. You get tired of me, you're free to go. I get tired of you, I send you away. Okay?"

"Yeah, yeah!" For them this was security. Anything more was prison.

"We have a chain of command. I'm in command," Greenleaf said sternly. "I'm the boss. Anyone who questions that better leave now. Otherwise he'll die. Sooner or later he'll cross me and I'll kill him."

The room was silent and sober. They believed him.

"This is your last chance," he warned them again. "Anyone who has any doubts about working with me can get his tail out of here safe and sound. Go now."

Greenleaf surveyed the room. No one moved. Seconds stretched into a long minute. At last Greenleaf spoke again. "Fairly and Kharkov! Front and center!"

Two of the mercenary recruits strode to the front of the room. Both were of medium height. The guy named Fairly was blond with blue eyes. He had a brown sun-leathered face. The other guy, Kharkov, was prematurely gray. He had small hands and feet and the quick movements of a much smaller man.

"Turn around!" Greenleaf ordered.

The two men turned to face the other mercenaries. They had no idea why Greenleaf had singled them out, whether it was good news or bad. They had reason to fear that it was bad, but their features remained impassive. Neither one showed any nervousness. They were pros.

"I accuse Fairly and Kharkov of being spies," Greenleaf said in a ringing voice as he pulled out a 9 mm Walther to cover the guys.

A flush crept up Fairly's neck. Kharkov, who seldom blinked, now blinked furiously.

"Fairly is CIA," Greenleaf continued. "Kharkov is KGB. Neither knew of the other. Their orders were to infiltrate my operation and report back on my missions. That means *your* missions!"

There was an angry rumble among the mercenaries.

"You're nuts!" Fairly exploded. "I've been a merc all over the world! Panama to Algeria to—"

"Perhaps Fairly is CIA," Kharkov interrupted, "but I left the Soviet Union *because* of the KGB, not *for* them. If they get their hands on me, I'm dead!"

"Silence!" Greenleaf commanded. "This is a tight merc outfit. No appeals, no smart shyster lawyers, no getting off on a goddamn technicality!"

Greenleaf gestured at the sentries. One reached out into the hall. He handed in eight rifles, which the other sentry then passed out to eight nearby recruits. The room of mercs parted so that the eight could trot to the front and surround the KGB and CIA guys.

"The sentence for spies is death!" Greenleaf said. "To be carried out immediately by a firing squad!"

"Wait!" said the man who called himself Fairly. "You're wrong! I—"

"Give me to the KGB and see if I'm telling the truth!" said the guy who called himself Kharkov. "Of course they'll kill me, too!"

Greenleaf ignored them. He had a point to make to his new men. They'd never give him any trouble after this. It was just damn good luck he'd heard about Fairly and Kharkov. He'd make an example of them that his men would talk about for years.

"Bring them," Greenleaf ordered, striding down the center of the room toward the open door. The firing squad hustled after him, four in front and four behind the two spies. The rest of the recruits fell in quickly behind.

Greenleaf led them out the door and down a long, wide galleria hung with paintings on one side and lined with windows on the other. The windows overlooked a flagstone courtyard that had been cleared of snow. The house surrounded the courtyard on three sides, with the fourth side sloping upward into the fir-covered mountains.

The outside air was bitterly cold, but the only way in which the men showed it was in their haste to have the execution over with.

"The KGB first," Greenleaf decided, "then the CIA." He didn't want to give his new men time to think. After they'd been with him a while, they'd learn to obey instantly—and without the annoying habit of thinking.

He gestured at the wall they were to use. Two members of the squad threw the KGB guy up against the wall while others pushed the CIA man aside. There were irregular holes in the stone wall, indicating that it had been used by firing squads before.

"A cigarette?" the KGB spy begged, stalling for time. "I have a pack in my pocket."

"A stupid custom," Greenleaf decreed. "Ready?"

The squad lined up and aimed at the Soviet spy.

"What about a blindfold?" the KGB guy asked, trembling.

"Fire!" Greenleaf commanded.

The spy flinched, and the brittle winter air exploded with the sound. The Russian flew back, crashed against the wall and slid like a rag doll to the ground.

"Now the CIA!" Greenleaf ordered.

CROUCHED BEHIND snow-capped boulders, Bolan watched from the mountainside just above the flagstone central courtyard. First the firing squad executed the guy Greenleaf had said was KGB. Now Greenleaf was ordering another man to the wall. This one the mercenary leader had clearly labeled a CIA man.

The blond CIA man's face was ruddy from the cold. There was determination in his blue eyes. Bolan didn't know for sure what was going on, but he did know he couldn't let them kill the guy if he was CIA.

Suddenly the CIA man slammed an elbow into the belly of the merc who was herding him to the execution wall. Then he spun and let fly with a kick to the chin of another merc. Bolan opened up, the bullets from his G-11 cutting across the firing squad. Completely surprised, they toppled under the steady fire.

Grabbing the rifle of one member of the firing squad, the CIA man ran toward the open side of the courtyard, just below Bolan. The surviving mercs recovered from the surprise attack and scrambled for rifles. Meanwhile Hugo Greenleaf lay flat on his belly and carefully aimed his Walther up the hill at the boulders.

The CIA guy started up the mountainside toward Bolan, but his feet sank into the deep snow as he struggled onto windswept patches of solid rock. Greenleaf turned to fire at him, and Bolan dumped a load around the merc leader, causing him to scramble back.

The blond CIA agent hopped like a rabbit over logs and around trees until at last he reached the Executioner. Bolan had to stop firing to replace his magazine. While he paused, the CIA man turned and fired down on the survivors.

"Who are you?" the CIA guy panted.

"A friend," Bolan said curtly. "What in hell is the CIA doing here?"

"Just following orders."

"This one of Greenleaf's merc groups?"

"Recruits. He's hiring. He's got some big job coming up."

"How'd he make you?" Bolan asked.

"I wish I knew!"

Greenleaf reemerged from the villa with reinforcements armed with rifles and SMGs. The colonel gestured to his few remaining recruits, and they joined the newcomers who swarmed out of the courtyard and up the slopes, SMGs spattering the mountainside with deadly fire.

"Looks like he's called in the experienced troops," the CIA man said grimly.

"Looks like," Bolan agreed as the two men fired down the mountainside.

The veteran troops broke up and fell behind logs, trees and boulders, spreading themselves far apart. Then, cautiously, they moved ahead singly, running from cover to cover.

"This is getting tougher," the CIA man said.

"They're trying to circle us," Bolan rasped. "Time to move."

HUGO GREENLEAF and his troops ran toward the snow-covered mountainside. "A thousand pounds to the guys who kill them!" he promised.

They slogged through the lower snows toward cover. Greenleaf ordered them to spread out in an arc that would encircle the bastards. The colonel hated to lose, and he'd just lost good new recruits. There was no way he was going to miss the CIA guy and the bastard up there who'd surprised him.

Suddenly the two enemies were in sight. They'd left the safety of their boulders and were heading around the mountain. Shots rang out, and the CIA agent went down, causing Greenleaf and his mercs to cheer. When the other guy skied back toward the CIA man, Greenleaf shouted, "Get him! Kill the bastard!"

More gunfire exploded across the forested terrain. Somewhere above snow seemed to shudder. This wasn't an avalanche area, but Greenleaf knew enough about the winter mountains to be respectful. With the right conditions an avalanche could thunder down, wiping out everyone and everything in its lethal path.

The bastard was like lightning, Greenleaf decided, and hard as hell to see in his whitesuit against the snow. The guy paused only a moment over the CIA agent and then was racing off again on his skis.

Greenleaf ordered four of his troops back to the villa for a load of skis, poles and survival equipment, then he slogged onward with his mercs. He had to keep the pressure on. They'd killed one; now they'd get the other. All they had to do was follow his tracks in the virgin mountain snow. There was no way he could get away now.

They pressed on, but the guy was out of sight. With his skis he had the advantage of speed. And then behind him Greenleaf heard shouts. Skiing toward him were his four men, pulling a sled loaded with jackets, masks, ski equipment, ammo and walkie-talkies.

Skiing next to them was Estelle Davis. She moved easily with the terrain, her skis breaking into fresh powder. The mercs crowded around the sled, pulling off equipment and outfitting themselves.

"You were infiltrated?" Estelle asked Hugo, her beautiful face concerned.

"Yeah. CIA and KGB. They're both dead." Hugo snapped on skis and found some long poles.

"I saw the blond one," Estelle said. "Back on the other side of the mountain. You lost so many men. You must be up against an army."

"No," Greenleaf said, disgusted. "One lousy bastard."

Estelle looked ahead at the tracks they were following. "One man," she murmured. She thought about the arsenal in the Rocky Mountains, then reminded Greenleaf of it and described the big stranger he'd identified as a guy named Mack Bolan.

"That's what he looks like all right," Greenleaf said. "You think it's the same guy, this Mack Bolan?" He was thoughtful. "I could use him." He turned to his soldiers. "I want him alive! Two thousand pounds to the soldier who brings Mack Bolan to me alive!"

CHAPTER NINE

Mack Bolan skied among the tall firs. With deep regret he thought about the dead CIA agent he'd left behind. Too many decent men died fighting the evil, greedy barons who lived by ruining ordinary people's lives. The warrior slogged on, feeling the brunt of the rising afternoon wind. As it whistled through the treetops, the alpine temperature dropped dramatically.

Despite the cold Bolan was sweating. The snow was soft, fresh and wet, causing his skis to stick and resist him as he plowed ahead.

He was concentrating on his jogging rhythm, when suddenly he heard shouts behind him. Something exciting had happened to Greenleaf and his men. They sounded happy, and that worried Bolan. He herringboned up a steep slope, stopping between two firs. Sheltered from sight by their branches, he looked back across the mountainside at the trail he'd made.

Hugo Greenleaf and his men had also stopped. A sled had arrived with equipment and provisions, and they were busy putting on skis and bundling up for a long chase.

A long chase to get Bolan.

Then Bolan saw the mystery woman. She had on skis and was dressed for a long, cold trek, just like the other mercenaries. Was she a mercenary, too?

Bolan turned and skied down the other side of the slope. Greenleaf's mercs would follow his trail up the steep slope and down again. If they weren't good skiers, they'd be left behind, unable to follow, perhaps incapacitated with broken legs or arms. And this detour would confuse them, make them wonder what he was up to, for a while at least.

The warrior crouched low over his skis and rode the momentum of his swift descent down the slope and across a clearing. He glanced over his shoulder when he reached the end of the run. His pursuers weren't in sight. He intended to keep it that way.

Humping on, he slogged through the wet snow. He circled boulders, shrubs, logs and trees, pushing his muscular body until it ached. His chest heaved with labored breathing—the high altitude combined with the relentless pace—and his arms and legs throbbed.

Suddenly shots whined past him and plopped into the snow near his moving feet. The crack of the gunfire in the distance sounded like that of a child's cap gun.

He glanced back and saw tiny figures standing at the top of a knoll, silhouetted against the steel-blue sky. Every muscle and tendon in his body screamed with exhaustion. But he increased his speed. He had spotted a stand of brush dead ahead. The leaves were gone, but the naked branches were filled with snow. Once inside he would be out of sight; and on the other side he might be able to escape.

He forced one foot in front of the other. Faster and faster. Shots fell into the snow-covered ground again, but farther away on either side of him. They were trying to get a fix on him.

He pushed on. He knew he could do it. He *had* to do it, even though his lungs felt as if they'd burst.

Bullets rained closer, splattering in the snow on his left. Crouching he sped across the last few feet of snow into the white brush. His heart was pounding, but he was safe, for the moment.

Silence surrounded him; the thick mounds of snow on the skeletal branches probably acted as sound absorbers. Tiny needles of pain pricked his legs as he slowed and his circulation increased, but like an automaton, he kept moving.

Greenleaf was good, he thought. Maybe as good as his reputation. He couldn't outrun the mercenary and his men. Greenleaf had the troops, supplies and firepower to wear him down.

As he skied, he thought about the situation, turning the problem around in his mind. He needed to get away, but he needed information, too—from Greenleaf, or someone close to Greenleaf.

And then he had the answer.

He figured he had about fifteen minutes to accomplish what he needed to do. Maybe longer. Greenleaf and his mercs would move steadily, but they wouldn't bust their guts. They knew they could eventually run him down. But in fifteen minutes at the earliest, the group would have reached the brush.

Bolan inhaled deeply again and again, filling his lungs. Once more he called on his tired body to give him what he needed. He picked up speed, his skis slapping the snow faster as he raced out of the brush and through a stand of birches. Skiing on past fir trees, he headed down a gully, around and then back up. Where the surface snow had melted and refrozen, it was as slick and treacherous as glass. In the shadows of the trees the snow remained soft, wet and resistant.

Bolan dodged boulders, tree stumps and fallen branches. He went all out for six minutes, eating up the distance. With a minute left he slowed to look around and spied a place that might work. He skied across a promontory toward the panoramic view. Ahead the Alps spread in white accordion pleats as far as he could see, while the promontory descended dangerously to a sheer cliff.

Carefully he skied toward the edge of the cliff, dragging his poles to keep his speed from building. It was hard work and sweat blinded his eyes. At last, panting, he stopped at the edge of a sheer thousand-foot drop. The view was breathtaking. Yeah, a guy could even ski off the edge and vanish into nothingness while ogling such beauty. And that's what he hoped Greenleaf and his mercs would figure—he had taken a dive off the cliff.

Crouching, he unsnapped his skis. He couldn't herringbone back because herringbone tracks would destroy the illusion that he'd accidentally skied off the cliff. Backward, he crawled up his tracks, pulling the skis to smooth the prints in the tracks.

At last, on flat ground again, he hooked on his skis and did a perfect jump turn, landing again in his trail. Then he skied back the way he'd come. His secret weapon was surprise. He would do the unexpected and hope the gamble would work.

When he reached the stand of brush, he could hear their skis and chatter. Inside the brush he chose his place carefully. On the far side of a bend, where they would tend to notice less because they'd be concentrating on making the turn, he jumped off the tracks and landed on his back on the side of a snowdrift. Immediately he rolled off and slid beneath the skeletal bushes.

Low to the ground, he could see the first ski-clad feet enter the brush. He had little time. Quickly he swept away any sign that he'd been there. When the snow was smooth, he scuttled farther back under the brush and looked out just as the first feet approached the curve.

Then he saw the buckle.

He'd lost one of his boot buckles, and it reflected the sun like a mirror. They'd have to be blind to miss it. And when they bent low to pick it up, they'd spot him hiding beneath the branches.

"See anything?" said one of the voices coming toward him around the bend. The words were strangely dead from the sound-absorbing effect of the snow-filled bushes.

"Nothin' yet."

Bolan grabbed a handful of snow and tossed it onto the buckle. Part of the metal still glistened. Just as the first ski rounded the curve three feet before his eyes, he threw two more handfuls, burying the buckle. He might never find it again, but, then, they wouldn't see it, either.

One by one Greenleaf's mercenaries skied past Bolan's hiding place mostly silent. Their faces bore the resoluteness of guys with a job to do, a job they intended to do well. Greenleaf hired only the best.

Eventually Greenleaf and the woman passed, too. This was the closest Bolan had been to her since the cabin in the Rockies when he'd found her tied to a chair in the closet. She was a beautiful woman. It was too bad that she hung out with terrorists and mercenaries.

When the last one was out of sight, Bolan got back on his skis, tying his lacings tight around his boots. There'd be no trouble over the missing buckle.

His tidy tracks through the snow were now worn thick and deep. Carefully he got back in them and smoothed away any sign that he'd been hiding. Then he skied back the way he'd come, heading for Greenleaf's headquarters.

A half-dozen mercenaries had been left at the villa to clean up the bodies and blood in the courtyard. When Bolan arrived on the mountainside above the villa, they were finishing up. The CIA agent's body was gone, and so were the corpses of the recruits.

Bolan waited as they shoveled bloodstained snow into a wheelbarrow and rolled it away. Then he skied down the slope toward the side of the villa. Pausing a moment, he rolled over the top of the low stone wall that surrounded the grounds, then skied toward a shoveled flagstone pathway he had seen the sentries use as they walked their rounds.

He figured Greenleaf's gang would be at least a half hour behind him. Taking off his skis, he hid them and his poles behind a stack of logs and covered them with snow. His keen gaze swept the estate, finding it empty for the moment. As soon as Greenleaf returned, that would change. It would be back to complete security.

Bolan opened a French door into the room where he'd seen Greenleaf and the woman sit before the fire. There was a desk in the corner. He opened the drawers and found them a mess, as if someone before him had frantically gone through the papers stuffed inside.

Sitting down, he pulled out a sheaf of papers. There were notes for what appeared to be a speech—about a mercenary's need for pride, confidence and belief that he should be paid well. There were bills, a letter from a Savile Row tailor requesting payment from Mr. Greenleaf, an engraved invitation from another villa in the area... Then, suddenly, his reading was interrupted by shouts and calls outside.

He pushed the papers back into the desk and tried the door behind it. It was a storage room, with files, shelves of paper and office supplies, and a Xerox machine in the back.

After a minute or two, he heard footfalls on the tiled floor. Stomping boots. Husky voices gathering around the fireplace. He opened the door a crack.

"A pity he's dead," Greenleaf was saying. "I would've liked to talk to him."

"I'm not so sure he would've wanted to talk to you," said the woman. "He seemed more a man of action when I saw him in the Rockies."

"I forgot you were there, Estelle," Greenleaf said. "Put the brandy on the table, Roger. You'll have some, won't you?"

A rumble of male voices answered yes.

Bolan filed the woman's name in his memory. Estelle. It wasn't familiar, but he would remember it. She wasn't acting as if she were part of Greenleaf's mercenaries. It was almost as if she and Greenleaf had just met.

"At the cabin, yes," she said. "The Japanese hadn't paid us, and I was sent in as their last warning."

"But you ended up in the closet."

Estelle laughed. "They didn't want to be warned."

"They intended to pay?" asked one of Greenleaf's aides.

"Only if the mission was successful," Estelle answered. "A hazard of the business, I'm afraid."

Bolan frowned. She worked for an arms merchant. That would account for her being in the Rockies, in Houston and then in New York. She must work for the guy—or group of guys—he was after!

The men laughed, but there was a serious undertone in their voices. Through the door crack Bolan watched Greenleaf pour aged brandy into snifters for Estelle and three rough-looking men. The five toasted and drank.

A merc came in and put two logs on the fire. The flames licked high. As the group talked and warmed up from the brandy and fire, they took off their mufflers and jackets.

"I heard some of your men when we were coming in," Estelle said, and smiled up into Hugo Greenleaf's eyes. She was tall, but he towered over her and his aides. "You're getting ready for a new job. Will you be placing a big order with me?"

"Ah, Estelle, always talking business!" Greenleaf laughed. "If I have any orders, my dear, you can be assured I'll give them to you! But, alas, right now I'm getting ready to take a trip and go to work with the Major himself."

"And you won't tell me what this big mission is?" she asked, pouting.

"So you can go to the other side and offer them an arms deal?" Greenleaf grinned. "Don't be silly, Estelle."

"How long have you repped for the Major, miss?" one of the men asked her.

"Four years now," Estelle Davis said.

Greenleaf scowled at the man. "And I can tell she knows her business."

"Thank you, Hugo," she said demurely, and leaned toward him.

Her round breasts pressed against her white mohair sweater. The three aides' faces turned stupid and greedy with lust. A wolfish grin enveloped Greenleaf's broad, pocked face.

"Fortunately for me," she said, and kissed one of Greenleaf's cheeks while she patted the other. "Hugo may not be my biggest customer, but he's already my favorite!"

"You have bigger customers?" Greenleaf said, suddenly less pleased. "Who?"

"What?" she said. This time it was her turn to grin. "If I tell you that, you'll go to them and form a cartel. You'll force prices down. There go my commissions!''

Now they all laughed. Business was business.

Greenleaf poured more brandy. ''To an invigorating day,'' he toasted. The glasses clinked.

''To one less pain in the butt,'' said one of the aides.

''To a dead Mack Bolan!'' said a second.

''To dead spies!'' said a third. ''KGB, CIA, Mossad, Interpol, MI6, all of them!''

''To tomorrow,'' Estelle said, raising her snifter high. ''Tomorrow is always so interesting. Will you be around, Hugo?''

''She's still trying to find out about our big mission,'' an aide said, laughing.

Greenleaf glowered at him. The big mercenary leader turned to Estelle Davis, and bowed gallantly to her. ''Shall we go into town tonight?''

''Tonight?'' she said.

''Dinner!'' announced a voice in the doorway.

They drank from their snifters and put them on the table near the fire, then filed toward the door, Estelle and Greenleaf in the lead.

''I think I'll have a quiet evening after such an exciting day, Hugo,'' she said. ''You go into town with your men.''

''You're tired?'' he asked, disappointed.

She smiled wanly at him. ''I'm not used to so much exercise,'' she said, disappointment also in her voice. ''And now the brandy. I've been traveling all day, and I'm exhausted. I'm afraid I wouldn't be much fun. You do understand, dear Hugo? Tell me that you do!''

The colonel nodded numbly at her.

Bolan figured Greenleaf wasn't too happy, or understanding. He watched them leave through the door, and slowly he began to smile. Estelle—or whatever her real name was—was beginning to make sense to him. She wasn't a terrorist; she claimed to be an arms rep. And the little lady got around. Tonight he'd find out exactly who and what she got around with.

CHAPTER TEN

Beretta in hand, Mack Bolan stepped from the dark storage room into the Villa di Cremona's empty great room. Darkness had fallen, and in the fireplace a fire snapped and crackled. The brandy bottle and five snifters still stood on the round table in front of the fire.

The villa was quiet.

The warrior padded across the tiled floor to the door and listened. Nothing. He moved into the long gallery and found a wide central staircase rising to the second floor. Next to the stairs a covered cart on gold wheels stood outside massive double doors.

The galleria was filled with the heady aroma of hot food—roast beef and potatoes, he thought. He smelled and salivated. He was hungry. He'd had a big breakfast in the village before starting out, then cold rations as he'd skied. He was ready for real food.

When he got to the food cart, he helped himself to some of the rare beef. One of the massive dining-room doors stood ajar. He peered through the door crack and saw Greenleaf, the woman called Estelle and the three aides finishing up their meal at a long trestle table. They were engaged in an animated conversation and would be there for a while, which was just what he needed.

He sprinted up the stairs and crept silently along the second-floor corridor, opening one door after another and peering inside the dark, empty rooms. At last he found what was probably Greenleaf's suite. It was the largest and most imposing—characteristics Greenleaf would demand.

Bolan closed the door and switched on the light. The huge room was panelled in mahogany. Like a throne, a big four-poster stood on a platform at the opposite end of the room. Khaki wool trousers were thrown across a leather chair; the pant legs were so long that the pants had to be Greenleaf's. Adjacent was a private bath with steam room, shower and Jacuzzi. There was no desk; it was unlikely he would find business papers here.

Looking around the room, he noted paintings of forests, jungles and wild animals. Greenleaf was an outdoorsman. Even indoors he surrounded himself with the wilderness and animals he loved.

After looking around a bit more, he switched off the light and slowly opened the door, an action that almost proved fatal. Just as he was about to step into the hall, he spotted a white-jacketed mercenary carrying towels out of the next bedroom. Beneath the white jacket, he caught the outlines of a holstered revolver.

Silently he closed the door, listening as the footsteps retreated. There had to be a real office somewhere in the villa. He continued down the hall, opening doors as he went. All told he found seven bedrooms, a linen closet, three baths and a billiards room, but no office.

That meant the office had to be downstairs, or in one of the outbuildings. As he headed for the stairs, laughter and talking burst out from below. The five had finished their dinner and were walking into the galleria.

"Good night everyone!" the woman called. "Good night, dear Hugo!"

Steps sounded on the stairs—she was coming up. Bolan opened a door and quickly moved inside. Her footfalls were quiet on the carpeted hall. She was alone. The door next to his hiding place opened and closed. Below, the voices and laughter continued and then faded. Greenleaf and his aides were going somewhere, probably back to the great room for cigars, coffee and more brandy. That was the routine of a gentleman, and Greenleaf liked to think of himself as a gentleman.

Bolan was restless. He was getting nowhere fast. If he didn't get some answers soon, he'd blast this place and get out. He listened again, then moved out into the hall and to the door the woman had disappeared behind.

Steps sounded up the stairs. Someone else was coming. He opened the woman's door and slipped in just as she was pulling back the covers to her bed.

She stood there, leaning over slightly, her short dark hair falling forward against her cheeks. Turning, she stared at him and then at the Beretta, her eyes widening with astonishment. "You're dead!" she whispered in a shaken voice.

"Not yet," he growled.

All she had on was a military shirt. But she'd have been sexy in a burlap sack.

"I thought you went off the cliff," she said.

"That's what I wanted you to think. And Green-leaf."

"Oh." Dazed, she climbed into bed as if she needed the comfort of finishing something she'd started. As she got in, the top of her long, smooth thigh showed.

"You want to tell me what's going on?" Bolan asked her, the memory of the perfect thigh burned into his brain. "You're not a terrorist, and I'm beginning to think you're not even an arms rep. Arms reps don't turn down the favors of a powerful customer like Hugo Greenleaf. And they don't try to save my life, which is what you were trying to do in that warehouse in New York. Were you tailing me?"

"Yes," she said in a small voice, leaning back against the headboard and wrapping her arms around her knees like a little girl. She was trying to readjust to the radically changed circumstances of not only having the dead come back, but having the dead man hold a Beretta on her. "You didn't fall off the cliff?" she asked, still puzzled.

"I backtracked," he said. "I waited for you guys to go by me, then I skied back to the villa. Who's the guy who's been helping you?"

"Who?"

"The man—or woman—in the snowmobile, in the car in Houston, in the car in New York."

"Oh, him. I can't tell you."

Now Bolan at least knew that the other one was a man. "Where is he now?"

"I can't tell you that, either."

"Why have you been following me?"

"I'm trying to find—" She stopped and stared in dismay at him.

"Maybe I can help."

"No one can," she said grimly.

"Tell me what the problem is. It must have something to do with illegal weapons dealers."

She shook her head.

"You and your friend don't seem to be making much progress," he told her.

"No," she agreed. Then she bristled. "I don't know a bloody thing about you, Mr. Bolan. Why should I trust you?"

"Because you need help. Because you know whose side I'm on. Because you know I *can* help you."

She lifted her chin stubbornly. "I don't know any of those things."

"I got you out of that Japanese terrorist mess," he told her.

She looked away and pursed her lips. He was right, and she knew it.

"I helped you and your friend escape those Houston thugs at the warehouse."

She said nothing.

"I almost saved the CIA guy today," he said.

She looked at him with troubled eyes. "I'm sorry about that. I had no idea he was here...." Again she looked away.

"I could make you talk," he said.

She smiled sadly at him. "If you made me, then you wouldn't be the kind of guy I need to help me."

She had him. She knew he wouldn't force her.

"Seems to me you just put yourself in a box," he told her.

She looked glumly at him.

"Has Colonel Greenleaf talked about a big arms supplier down in South America?" Bolan asked, his voice hard and cold.

"You don't know?"

"Why don't you tell me," he said.

She stared worriedly down at her hands as if they could do something about the mess she was in. She wanted to talk, but something—distrust, probably—was holding her back. Or maybe it was fear. What was she afraid of? Or maybe she was afraid *for* someone?

"Where's the base in South America?" he demanded.

"No."

"Who's the Major?"

"No."

"How'd you get onto his trail?"

"No."

"How'd the Japanese terrorists capture you?"

"No, no no!" She shook her head. "I won't tell you anything." She raised her eyes angrily. Bolan knew she was scared to death about something. "Why don't you be a good fellow and just go away?"

"Innocent people are being hurt by these terrorists."

"There's nothing you can do," she argued. "You only make things worse."

"You think you can take these guys alone?" he asked, astounded. "You're crazy!"

"Not crazy," she said, glaring back at him. "Determined. I know what I'm doing. You're just mucking things up. I'm warning you—"

"*You're* warning *me*!"

"Yes, you bloody bastard," she hissed. "I'm warning you! Get out of here. Get out of my business! Next time *I* may have the Beretta, not you. I can't have you ruining this mission!"

"Mission?" he echoed. "You're an agent . . ."

"No! Goddamn it! Will you get out of here before I have to call Hugo to get you out!"

Suddenly there was a shout in the hall, and the door next to her room banged shut.

"Hugo's room!" she said. "That sounds like Roger, Hugo's orderly."

The shouts continued down the hall to the stairs. Bolan stood and scanned the room for an exit. "Is Roger a guy in a white jacket with a revolver holstered underneath?"

"Yes. He adores Hugo and watches over him like a mother hen."

"Looks like I just outsmarted myself," he said, disgusted. Somehow the orderly was wise to him. Now they knew someone was in the villa and they wouldn't stop searching until they'd found him. "How do I get out of here?"

"The balcony," she said, pointing to the French doors next to her bed. Footsteps pounded up the stairs. "Quick!"

"Keep quiet about this," he said.

She smiled and walked across the room to open the door. She had him. If he shot her, he would reveal himself. And anyway, he didn't want to kill her. He wanted her intel, and he wanted intel from Greenleaf, too.

Bolan ducked out onto the balcony and felt the freezing alpine air cut into his face. Flipping over the side, he found handholds in the ornate grillwork that covered the rail and decorated the balcony's underpinnings.

Expecting bullets to fly around him any second, he dropped to the ground, practically on top of a sentry. The guy spun around and opened his mouth to shout, but Bolan slammed the Beretta down on his head. Blood poured out of the wound, and the guy dropped to the ground.

Grabbing him under the armpits, Bolan dragged him off the walkway and behind a low stone building. In the distance at some faraway mountain farm dogs barked. He could hear quite a commotion in the house, and shadows and figures wavered back and forth upstairs in Greenleaf's room, then in Estelle's room.

Not long after, the light in Greenleaf's room went out. A few minutes later there were no more shadows in Estelle's room, and the lights went out there, too. Bolan was puzzled. Then, on the other side of the villa, car engines roared to life. One after the other the cars drove away. Their headlights swept the rolling white terrain as they moved down toward the village on the lake.

Silence draped the dark villa. Bolan stood. He listened, but the estate was as quiet as a tomb.

He waited out in the snow for another hour, and then he was sure. Slowly he slogged through the snow until he reached the windows of the villa. No one and nothing moved inside. He circled the great house and found the garages empty. Damn!

Estelle Davis had saved him, but she had also escaped from him. Not to mention Greenleaf and the rest. Whatever story she'd told Greenleaf had gotten the mercenary leader and all of his troops to leave the villa. He had been helped and outfoxed at the same time. Estelle Davis was some woman.

But she hadn't gotten rid of him yet, and neither had Hugo Greenleaf.

Bolan slipped into the now-empty villa again and resumed his search for Greenleaf's office. Finally he hit pay dirt. He found a room with a big desk. Turning on the desk light, he discovered maps on the walls—Europe, Africa, South America, Central America and the Far East. Colored pins stuck out of the maps, metal filing cabinets stood in one corner, and there was a computer, an electric typewriter, a telex, a photocopy machine and four clocks set on different time zones.

He went through everything in the office, but he found nothing about the Major, or any hint of what Greenleaf's "big" new mission could be. Nor did he find anything to tell him where Greenleaf was meeting the Major, or when.

He pondered the situation in the dim office for a while, then went out and climbed the stairs to the second floor and Estelle Davis's room. At first he found nothing there, either. Then he spotted a notepad on the table next to the telephone. An address in Vancouver, British Columbia, Canada, was written on it in a woman's flowery handwriting.

Estelle Davis's handwriting? He didn't know or care. Ripping off the note, he strode to the door; this time he'd get there first.

CHAPTER ELEVEN

On one of the endless small islands in the Strait of Georgia north of Burrard Inlet and the city of Vancouver, the boathouse stood silent behind a secluded mansion. The mansion appeared deserted, and inside the boathouse there was no sound except the quiet voice of the man who sat alone in a large room packed from floor to ceiling with electronic equipment.

"Make your report, Jakarta."

An indistinct voice crackled and faded in and out from the speaker in the computer-controlled short-wave console in front of the man. "Government has okayed hiring a special strike team to hit and run on the ethnic rebel villages. We're negotiating terms. Our weapons supply to the rebel guerrillas is proceeding smoothly again after the unfortunate setback last month. In Timor we have..."

The voice droned on, alternately fading and strengthening until it signed off. The man in the boathouse made some notes in a large ledger. When he finished, he entered a series of code letters on the keyboard before him.

"Come in Fiji."

A heavily accented voice from those distant islands crackled from the speaker. "Training contract for Fijian army secret expansion is close to finalization.

Minister Baraka wishes to speak personally with you in Suva. Is that possible, Major?"

"Will he accept Haggarty or one of our field commanders?"

"I will ascertain and return to you."

"The other side?"

"The Indian leaders are cool to any use of force, but they are listening. I believe we have an excellent prospect of convincing them that a well-trained mercenary unit would be most helpful to protect their interests against the ethnic Fijians while they consider their future course of action. It is even possible we can get a contract to train an ethnic Indian peacekeeping force in the islands."

"Good. Get back to me on the meeting with Baraka."

"As soon as possible, Major."

When the shortwave went silent this time, the man in the empty boathouse leaned back in his chair, rubbed his eyes and stretched. Known to his associates and the world as the Major, he was a tall man, well over six feet, and muscular without being heavy. Lean and rangy, with the smooth movements of a cat despite his almost white hair, he wore camouflage fatigues, highly polished combat boots, and a heavy Colt .45 holstered on his hip. The white hair was cropped short, and his craggy face was deeply tanned. When he stretched, the muscles seemed to ripple under his camouflage shirt like those of a man half his age.

He lit a thin cigar, smoked contentedly for a moment, then leaned again over the computer keyboard. But before he could enter his next series of coded commands, the speaker began to talk again, louder and clearer this time.

"Major? I have an Abdul al-Krim on the private line. He's calling from Tripoli via the Malta-Toronto relay satellite. He says he has a business proposition and has been cleared by our London rep to get the number."

"Put him on," the Major said. He remembered al-Krim, a Middle East warlord—part patriot, part terrorist, part drug kingpin and part wheeler-dealer politician. He wondered which hat al-Krim would be wearing this time.

"Ah, Major?"

The voice was as smooth, soothing and devious as a Texas Republican talking to the Daughters of the Confederacy.

"Been a while, Krim," the Major said dryly. "What's your hobbyhorse this week?

There was an oily chuckle. "The Major has his jokes eh? So we get to business at once. I need a job performed that only you can do—quick, certain, discreet, invisible."

"I have a hundred men who can do that. What's the target?"

"Ah, a man of directness. An English trait, perhaps? A man after my own heart, Major, as always. But it is not one of your hundred men I want, excellent as I am sure they are. No, this is a delicate, ultimate job. A job for the Major himself."

"I don't do jobs anymore, Krim," the Major said, cold and flat. "If you know enough to have this phone number, you know that. Don't waste my time."

"The fee will be a hundred thousand, but I must be certain of success. There can be no mistakes."

"You'll pay two hundred thousand," the Major said, "for one of my top men. I teach, train, plan and supply now. I handle the whole affair, big or small. I guarantee success. Totally. No slipups, and the client can't be named or traced."

"I do not pay such money for an unknown skill!"

"Take it or leave it, Krim."

Silence, and when Abdul al-Krim spoke again, his voice was as flat and cold as any desert wind. "I will think on it."

The Major clicked off. In the silent boathouse he smoked his cigar and leaned back in his crisp uniform. He closed his eyes as if suddenly tired. This happened to him when, unexpectedly, he was reminded of his life. Al-Krim had called him an Englishman. He smiled in the empty room with its low humming and bright flashes of the electronic equipment that kept him in touch with his worldwide agents, contacts and installations. He smiled and remembered the snow and frozen land of his birth.

The first man young Lavrenti Semenov killed was his father. He hadn't known it would be his father. The fuel oil that was the lifeblood of the Siberian installation where his father and uncles and almost everyone in the remote settlement worked seemed to "leak" a great deal. The trucks were always in the shop to have "worn-out" parts replaced. The managers from far-off Moscow grew suspicious of so much bad luck, but the isolated community on the

Soviet frontier was too close-knit for them to get any real information.

Until the militia detectives from Yakutsk gave up and sent for the KGB. No one ever knew just when the KGB man showed up. Or, for a long time, exactly who he was. Lavrenti was one of the first to learn. It was the KGB man who hired him and two other local boys to infiltrate and find out why the station was having so much "bad luck." He was twelve then. A big boy, dark and silent under the gray sky of the vast, snowy landscape.

The KGB man was small, pale and quiet, with rimless glasses and a thin voice. He had come to the installation as a replacement clerk in the accounting office.

"So much bad luck is not normal," the KGB man told Lavrenti.

"No," the boy had agreed.

"We need someone who loves his country, who knows that for Mother Russia to survive such bad luck must stop."

"Yes," Lavrenti said.

"Love of country is a great thing," the little KGB man said, "but a man has other needs. Life is short and money will buy many needs."

"How much?" the twelve-year-old Lavrenti had asked.

Even now the Major smiled through his cigar smoke in the silent British Columbia boathouse as he remembered the KGB man's offer, his demands and the final compromise that was far closer to his demands than the KGB's offer. He had driven a hard bargain even then—to become a spy and informer on his own village and the fathers and mothers of his friends.

He had not counted on his own father.

The three boys had made their plans under the silent watch of the gray KGB accountant. The KGB man said nothing unless he felt something wouldn't work, then he corrected the error. There were no arguments. It was a lesson Lavrenti never forgot. You listened to a man who knew more than you, and did what he told you. You told a man who knew less, and he did what he had to.

Their plan had been simplicity itself. All three boys, who had previously shown little interest in working hard at anything, had suddenly volunteered to help their families by taking low-paid employment at the installation. Menial jobs. Hard work. But on the spot. Who noticed boys sweeping up in a corner? A boy washing dishes in the mess hall kitchen? A boy carrying steaming coffee from mess hall to outer offices across the snowy yards?

At first, some. After a month, no one.

It was two months later, on a moonless arctic night so dark even the trees could barely be seen against the snow, and so cold the breath of police and conspirator alike hung like a thick fog before their hidden faces, that the militia, led by the three clever boys and the silent KGB man, surprised the thieves in the act of helping the fuel oil to leak and the truck parts to wear out rapidly. One boy, two militiamen, three thieves, including one of young Lavrenti's uncles, and his father died in the battle.

Lavrenti, safely on the edge of the action, and armed with a pistol stolen earlier from the militia supply, happened to be in the right spot at the right moment. One of the gang of thieves slipped away toward the safety of the forest shadows. Lavrenti saw him and met the hurrying man at the edge of the shadows. Only when he had the pistol aimed, when he was already counting the bonus he would demand for this extra effort, did he see the face of the thief.

His father stared at him there in the dim forest, the fog of their breath like a cloud between them. Though his father held a pistol, he didn't raise it. Lavrenti hesitated for the first and last time in his life—a full five seconds before he killed his criminal father with a single shot to the heart.

"So?" the KGB man said when he looked down at the body.

"A thief is an enemy of all of us," Lavrenti said.

The KGB man was impressed. When he left after the surviving conspirators had been sentenced to prison camps in even less pleasant areas of Siberia, where they would do useful work for the state as long as they lived, he took Lavrenti with him. The KGB man's superiors were equally impressed with what they heard and saw and decided the young killer had a future in the service. What future they had in mind quickly became clear—Lavrenti Semenov, at fourteen, became one of the most prized assassins of the KGB.

The crackling voice from the Major's speaker brought him out of his reverie.

"Colonel Greenleaf and his party have arrived in Vancouver, as arranged, Major," the hard, clipped voice said. "Should I bring them out?"

"Party?" the Major said, slowly stubbing out his cigar in an ashtray. "Who the hell has he brought with him, Haggarty?"

"One of those Texan arms dealers you work through in the States."

"Who?"

"A woman named Estelle Davis."

"Estelle Davis? She was one of the reps who supplied the goods the American Feds grabbed from the Japanese in the mountains."

"That figures. Probably wants to explain, eh?"

"How'd Greenleaf get involved with her?"

"Haven't a clue. Mutual interest, I suppose. She's probably trying to cut out one of your other middlemen with the colonel. Free enterprise, what?"

"Yes, probably," the Major allowed. "All right, take them to the hotel in Vancouver and call me again. I have a few things to do before I meet Greenleaf."

"Roger," Haggarty's voice said cheerfully. "Will do."

Silent again, the Major frowned. Caution at the right moment was always the key. Too much caution was the end of any agent. Risk was the game. Boldness. Daring. But lacking caution when it was needed could also spell the end. His judgment had always been spot on. Probably as much an accident of nature as the ability to paint or act. The razor edge of knowing when to strike and when to disappear.

Again his thoughts spanned the years.

"Ten years," the KGB control in Moscow had written in the curt memo to Lavrenti Semenov's KGB master in London, "is enough for an assassin to be based overseas. Beyond that, our analysis and statistics tell us a man becomes a risk to himself and to us. Order Semenov home for debriefing and internal assignment."

Lavrenti thought it over and came to the conclusion that a desk job back home would be unlikely to pay what he had become accustomed to as an assassin. He came to the second conclusion, that an ex-assassin who had lived ten years overseas would be of little use to the internal operations of the KGB. At home he would be unnecessary or even a problem, and the KGB had only a few ways of dealing with problems. His third conclusion was that his skills would almost certainly command the highest price where they would be of greatest value—the other side. But it would be necessary, first, to demonstrate both reliability and need.

On the day he was to fly home as the only passenger on an Aeroflot jet, he walked into the office of his London master and shot him with the same efficiency, and a lot less noise, than he had used on his father so many years before. An hour later he was smoking a cigarette with a high-ranking member of MI6. A month later he made his first kill for his new masters.

They paid much better than the KGB. He lived much better in England and on the road. But they didn't pay the best, they were much more squeamish than the KGB and they had nowhere near as much work for him. He was, after all, a specialist. He wasn't a spy, he wasn't a terrorist; he wasn't even in the larger sense a counterterrorist. He was a killer. And even with loan-outs to the CIA and Mossad, he couldn't keep busy. So Lavrenti—who by now had so many names, including the cover the Major, that he sometimes wondered who Lavrenti Semenov could have been—began to free-lance on the side.

This was far too much for the British to handle, and the Major became independent, the most efficient and elusive hired assassin after the legendary Carlos. He had the money, scope and freedom he had always wanted; in short, an ideal life.

Until he found an even better one.

The Major sat another long minute in the boathouse, where nothing moved but the blinking lights on the electronic equipment. Then he stood up and punched some computer keys. The clipped voice answered at once.

"Haggarty."

"They're at the hotel?"

"That they are, Major."

"Keep them there." He switched off the computer, watched the lights go dark, then strode out, locking the boathouse behind him.

MACK BOLAN LOOKED out the small window of the speeding Concorde at the clouds below. He thought about Estelle Davis. He didn't believe that was her name, but it would do until he had more to go on.

She'd saved his butt and outfoxed him at the same time. There weren't a lot of people, man or woman, who could say that, and he had admiration on his craggy face as he thought about her. She was one hell of a woman. Because of her, and because a quick call to Hal Brognola had added some interesting, vital intel, he was on his way to Canada.

Bolan thought about the Major, and what Brognola had told him. The guy had once been the most successful, violent and elusive of the world's top political killers for hire. He'd worked for the Communists, and a ton of other governments East and West, North and South. He'd gunned for terrorist groups and the Mafia, drug dealers and slave traders, guerrillas and death squads. And his killings weren't always so political, either, the way Brognola had told it. "We got the idea the Major would kill just about anyone or anything if the price was right," the big Fed had told him.

But Brognola and the world had thought the Major was dead. It had been a lot of years since any killing had been pinned on him or anyone had heard about him. He'd just stopped and vanished. In the no-man's-land of international killers, you didn't just retire and go sit in the sun. No way. Someone who could never trust you would find you and blow you away if you didn't blast them first. Death was the only retirement, so the shadowy underworld of intrigue gave its verdict—the Major was dead.

Now it looked as if the Major was alive and back in action, and Bolan would have to find him and stop whatever hellish evil he was up to now.

The warrior studied everyone on the jet for the tenth time. He was pretty certain no one was tailing him.

Estelle Davis, or whoever she really was, had left the note and not been observed. All he had to do now was change planes in New York, reach Vancouver and find the Major.

IN THE VANCOUVER HOTEL Colonel Hugo Greenleaf and the woman who called herself Estelle Davis sat facing the ruddy, scarred and smiling Captain Miles Haggarty.

"What's the holdup, Haggarty?" Greenleaf demanded.

"Haven't a clue, Colonel," the English mercenary said cheerfully. "The Major probably had some tidying up to do before he meets you."

Estelle Davis glanced at her watch. "I've got to contact some overseas buyers, Hugo. There may not be another chance after we start dealing with the Major."

Haggarty glanced at her. "If the Major contacts us while you're gone, Miss Davis, you'll be left out of the meeting. That's a strict MO—everyone arrives in a single unit at any meeting with the Major."

The woman stood. "I'll have to risk it. My contact must be made at a precise time, too, Captain. We have our security rules. If I'm not here, Hugo can fill me in on anything that might concern me."

Haggarty nodded. "Suit yourself."

Greenleaf stared with puzzled eyes at the woman. "It's a long way to come to risk missing the meet, Estelle."

"I really expect I'll be back in plenty of time, Hugo." She smiled at the two men, who continued to watch her with a kind of wary surprise.

THE MAJOR SAT in front of a small television monitor in a room almost directly across the street from the Vancouver hotel. He watched and listened to Greenleaf, Haggarty and the woman, Estelle Davis, who waited for his contact.

On the monitor the woman smiled and told the two men she would be back in plenty of time. Reaching for the telephone, the Major dialed and saw the three faces in the hotel room turn sharply at the ringing of the instrument in their room. Haggarty picked it up.

"Haggarty here."

"Listen and don't react," the Major said.

"Of course." Haggarty smiled on the monitor screen.

"Shut down our entire Vancouver operation at once. Move everything out, and abandon the HQ. Close up shop permanently."

"Right. No problem." Haggarty nodded cheerfully on the screen.

"Then take Greenleaf and the woman to the island at once."

In the room on the screen, Haggarty nodded, then looked toward the woman and Greenleaf. "Of course, Major, no problem. We'll be there in an hour."

"That woman isn't Estelle Davis. Kill her before you evacuate."

"No problem," Haggarty said, smiling directly at the subject of their conversation.

CHAPTER TWELVE

Mack Bolan cut the skiff's engine, and it seemed to glide across the icy water of the Strait of Georgia into a small cove. The warrior sat at the helm, steering across the dark water, alert to any sound on water or land.

He heard nothing.

He saw the shadowy outline of the two-story boathouse on the shore of the isolated cove, and the massive silhouette of the great brick-and-timber mansion up the slope behind. There was no light in either of them or anywhere on the island as far as he could see.

But this was the address Estelle Davis had left in her room back in the Villa di Cremona. In his black combat suit he slid silently over the side into the freezing water as the skiff glided into the shallows. Walking the boat ashore onto a tiny pebbled beach without making the faintest sound, he listened again in the night. There was nothing.

The soldier secured the skiff and holstered his Beretta 93-R under his arm, then slung the short and deadly Colt Commando and trotted up the dark slope through the tall pines to the silent mansion. After circling the perimeter like a ghost and seeing no sign of the enemy, he moved in.

The rear door of the big house yielded to the soldier's commando knife and he found himself in the shadows of a vast kitchen. Cautiously he cat-footed across the deserted kitchen and out into a long rear hallway, lined with almost invisible portraits of the hard-faced businessmen who had built the west coast of Canada.

But he found nothing. The house looked as if no one had lived in it for years. The furniture was draped with dustcovers and everything was wrapped in plastic. Bolan wasn't fooled, though. He found a single cigarette butt swept into a crack of the floor and missed by whoever had evacuated the mansion. It was a recent evacuation—the toilet bowl in an upstairs bedroom was still wet along its porcelain interior; a fly trapped between a storm window and an inner window was still alive.

Whoever had been here had moved out very recently. He searched each room on every floor for any data that would tell him who the recent occupants had been. But he came up empty, with only the live fly and the dead cigarette to prove there had ever been anyone in the mansion.

Out in the clear, cold Canadian night again, the big soldier moved with expert stealth down the slope to the boathouse. Then he heard a sound and froze. In a split second he dropped to the dirt. As invisible as part of the landscape itself, the warrior listened. Above the faint lapping of the water against the rocky shore, the cries of night birds and the sudden scurrying of small animals, it came again: a faint, widely spaced but steady thump, like an open casement window banging in the wind or a door, forgotten by someone leaving in a hurry, slowly swinging open and closed on the sea breeze.

With the radarlike hearing of the trained combat soldier, Bolan homed in on the sound. It came from the dark boathouse itself. Was it nothing more than a loose window, a forgotten door?

He stood up. There was only one way to find out. Unslinging his Colt Commando, he moved out through the tall pines to the edge of the cove and the dark but no longer silent boathouse. He circled the heavy shadow of the rugged boathouse but saw no banging shutters, no open doors.

The thumping persisted. What the hell was it? He didn't have to ask where anymore. It was clearly coming from inside the boathouse. A trap? Someone who had seen him land and reconnoiter the grounds and mansion?

Well, one thing was certain, he thought: idle speculation wouldn't give him any answers. If someone was waiting for him in there, he wouldn't disappoint him. But he'd go in his way, the way the guy would least expect—by water and without a boat.

He slid the Beretta up inside the blacksuit, held the Commando flat on his shoulder and waded back into the icy water of the cove. Without a ripple to reveal him, he moved like a silent sea animal into the open maw of the boathouse dock area.

His eyes grew accustomed to the deeper dark under the building as he quickly scanned the deserted docks. The thumping continued, like a malignant heartbeat now, or maybe a death knell.

Part of the dark water itself, he flowed up onto the dock and cat-footed into the boathouse's lower floor. The thumping was coming from the second floor. Bolan found the stairs and went up, the noise getting louder and louder. It came from behind a door directly ahead at the top of the stairs. With a single kick, he smashed the door down, and shoulder-rolled in, Commando primed and ready.

The woman was tied in the chair. Slowly she raised it with great effort and thumped the single leg down against the floor. Again and again, unaware of the door bursting in, of anyone being in the room.

She sat in the chair with thick rawhide thongs tight around her throat, so tight they bit deep into her flesh and a thin trickle of blood flowed from under them. Wet rawhide, and the almost invisible red rays of a heat lamp in front of her focused on the drying rawhide that tightened more and more as it dried. Tightened and slowly strangled her.

It was the woman from the Rocky Mountains, from Houston, from New York, from the villa in Italy. Estelle Davis, of course.

Bolan acted fast. He strode across the dark room and hurled the heat lamp aside, wincing when he saw agonized eyes stare almost sightlessly up at him. She raised up once more to thump the chair leg against the floor, seemingly unaware that he was there.

The warrior found the light switch, then kneeled to gently cut the rawhide from her bloody throat. The thongs had bitten so deeply into the soft white flesh of her neck that he had to work the point of the knife carefully until he could finally cut through. Deep, raw, bloody grooves were etched into her throat. When Bolan finally cut the ropes that held her to the chair, she slumped unconscious into his arms.

Lifting her as lightly as a child, he looked around. The large room was totally empty except for the single chair and the now-smashed heat lamp. But Bolan's experienced eyes told him that until recently the room had been full of sophisticated electronics equipment. The special electrical outlets were still there, the marks of heavy metal cabinets still on the wooden floors.

Carrying the unconscious woman as easily as the Colt Commando now slung over his shoulder, he opened other doors until he found the sail loft. The piled sails were as good as a bed, and he put her down. She stirred and groaned, but the shock was too much for her to come out of it so fast.

He bandaged her throat, using fabric from the sails, and tried to revive her. Finally she gagged and coughed, and at last sat up, pale as death. She didn't speak, as if not sure she could, afraid to try. Confused, she put her hand on her bandaged throat, watching Bolan with wide eyes.

"We've got to get you out of here and have those wounds treated," he told her. "Understand?"

She nodded, and tried to smile.

"That was damn close," he said, giving her some water from his canteen. "How long were you tied up like that?"

"It seemed like forever," she rasped, choking a bit on the water. Her eyes went distant, vague, as if seeing herself as dead as she would surely have been if Bolan hadn't arrived. "I lost track of time. I suppose I lost track of consciousness really. How did you find me?"

"You were lifting the chair with your legs and banging the chair leg down on the floor."

"Was I?" She shook her head in a kind of amazement. "I have no recollection of that at all. Reflex, I suppose. The old training. Must get through and all that, eh?"

"You know who left you like that?"

"The Major, I suppose," she said, coughing. "Do you have any more of that water? I'm beginning to shiver. Shock, I'm afraid. God, I could use a drink. Brandy's pretty good when it comes to reviving the dead."

A joke to reassure Bolan, but he could see the hollowness behind her eyes and the trembling of her hands that could easily become uncontrollable. He gave her some more water. She drank greedily.

"The Major had to be behind it," she went on, as if she had never stopped. "But a renegade British mercenary, Captain Miles Haggarty, did the actual job. I think the Major would have shot me and have done with it, but Haggarty persuaded him that spies should die slowly."

"Nice guy," Bolan said.

"Yes…" The color was slowly returning to her face.

"But stupid," Bolan said. "It's a pretty damn inefficient way to kill someone. It takes so long there's a good chance of rescue. Just the way it happened."

"Well, I suppose I'm very lucky Haggarty seems to be a sadist, eh?"

"Yeah," Bolan said. "Lucky. Now let's get you back to civilization."

Outside, the faint light of dawn was beginning to silver the black. "Please," she said, a wan smile tickling her lips. "Let me rest a few more minutes."

Bolan shrugged and sat down facing her on another pile of sails. "You ready to tell me the whole story, then? Who you really are? What you're doing in this? Why the Major would want you dead?"

She shook her head. "No, I don't think I do."

"You were a threat to those terrorists in Colorado. You've been backtracking on the weapons. You infiltrated Greenleaf's operation. You know my name. You're in this up to your eyebrows, and I want to know why, and when and who and how."

She stared at Bolan, unflinching. "I still have the same problem I had in Italy. I know your name, but I don't know what you are, or who you work for, or why. For all I know this rescue could be all part of some scheme by the Major to find out what I'm doing. You could as easily be part of the Major's gang as anything else, and—"

Bolan put a finger to his lips. Soft but heavy footsteps were coming up the stairs. Sweeping the woman to the floor in a single motion, the warrior turned to face the door in a crouch as a man crashed through, an Uzi in his hands, eyes searching for a target.

The guy took two steps into the loft, turning his Uzi toward Bolan, who had no time to unsling his Colt Commando. The Executioner hurled himself through the air, hit the gunner high, and slammed him back and into the wall. The Uzi flew across the loft and clattered into a corner. But the guy was up immediately, clawing inside his jacket for a pistol.

Bolan kicked the Browning Hi-Power away and smashed his fist into the guy's jaw. He went down as if felled by an ax. The warrior retrieved the Uzi and aimed it at the fallen man's head.

"No!" Estelle cried. "Don't kill him. I'll tell you what you want to know."

"Who is he?" Bolan rasped. He'd play it tough; it was time he got some answers.

"His name's Cecil Olds. He's an agent for MI6. He's my partner."

Bolan kept his finger on the trigger. "You're MI6, too?"

"I was."

"Now?"

"Now I'm a woman looking for her man."

Bolan looked at her, but the Uzi remained steady on the unconscious MI6 agent. "You better explain that fast."

She stared at Bolan, probably wondering what he might be capable of. "Steve is an MI6 agent, too. Steve Barr. My name's Marsha Barr. I retired from the service when we were married. We had two children. Steve went on working for the service in desk jobs. Two years ago our children were killed in a car accident. A drunken driver. Steve took it hard. So did I. Our life went to pieces. We separated. Then Steve disappeared. I realized I'd been a fool. I went to talk to him and MI6 told me he'd volunteered to go back into the field on a vital top-secret mission that no one would tell me about."

On the floor Olds groaned and began to move. The woman stared at him as she talked. "In the old days, when either of us was in the field, we always sent each other notes in a code only we knew. During the past six months I received two notes, both from São Paulo. He told me he loved me and that when he got back from Brazil we'd start over. I realized Steve was all I had left, so I waited for his next message." She stared down at the man on the floor. "It never came. No one at MI6 would talk to me. They acted as if Steve were dead. But I know he isn't! I know it!"

The man on the floor suddenly stopped groaning. His eyes opened and were as alert as if he'd never been unconscious. Bolan watched him. The guy hadn't been as helpless as he'd made out. He'd fooled Bolan, and that wasn't easy.

"I don't think Steve's dead, either," the MI6 agent said. He sat up, revealing a tiny boot gun he'd had under him the whole time. Now he tucked it back inside his boot. It wasn't much against an Uzi, but he wouldn't have given up without a fight.

"The high brass thinks Steve's had it, but I don't," Olds continued. "He's too good to be taken out without some sign to his control. No, he's gone way underground. I owe Marsha and Steve, so she came to me, and when they decided to send me to check on Steve, I took her along. She wanted to go to São Paulo, but I convinced her that's the last place to look. Steve would have had his messages sent as far from where he really was as possible. We got reports that took us as far as Nevada and then to the Red Army in the Rockies. After that we've been tracking the weapons."

"This Steve Barr's assignment was the arms supplier?" Bolan asked.

"Right," Olds said. "Only we think it's a bit more now than simple arms supplying." He told Bolan about the fissionable material, the missing scientists, the special alloy for weapons-grade manufacturing stolen from Nevada. "If it's all the Major's operation, it looks as if he's decided to go into a higher grade of weapons to sell his terrorist and mercenary customers."

In the silence of the sail loft they let the implications of that sink in. A totally amoral killer and terrorist selling nuclear weapons on the open market!

"I think," Olds said, "we might join forces. If there isn't a lead here, we've hit a dead end. We'll need all the help we can get."

Bolan lowered the Uzi and handed it back to Olds. "There's no lead here. We'll have to go back to square one and pick up intel on the route of those mining tool crates to the Red Army's Rocky Mountain hideout."

"But that could take months!" Marsha cried.

"It could," Bolan agreed. "But it's all we've got."

CHAPTER THIRTEEN

The hot, lazy mining settlement and river village of Miradora was a collection of shacks on both sides of a single dusty main street. Named Avenida de los Angeles by some forgotten official from Caracas, the dirt street ran from the edge of the towering green jungle to the fast-flowing tributary of the Rio Negro. There was a town hall in a large Quonset left by some forgotten American mining company, six cantinas of poles and thatch open to the heat, a brothel and 120 people.

Northeast of the Brazilian river "metropolis" of Içana, between the jungle and the Serra Curupira, the village existed to serve the miners in the mountains and the traders, explorers, hunters, prospectors, anthropologists and assorted adventurers who came up the Rio Negro from the Amazon. It also served the young and bad-tempered officials who came up the rivers from distant Rio de Janeiro nearly three thousand miles away by the shortest route. Or from Caracas, a thousand miles by the only route. Or from Bogotá, a short five hundred miles by air.

From Rio, or Caracas, or Bogotá, because the remote, half-forgotten village was at that exact spot of trackless jungle where Brazil, Venezuela and Colombia meet, where the borders were only lines on a map and no one was quite sure what country the village actually belonged to. Over the past few hundred years haphazard patrols of all three armies had claimed Miradora, but now none of the distant capitals cared very much. At the moment, most international maps said it was in Venezuela; Brazilian maps had it a hairline in Brazil; and Columbia didn't even have it on their maps.

It was this obscurity that had attracted the Major to the godforsaken dirt village near the treacherous jungle and inhospitable mountains. Land was cheap. Only the mayor and his relatives and cronies had to be paid off to forget the Major was there. No one who might ask questions ever came from outside, and in an emergency his entire operation could be in another country in half an hour.

It was the perfect location for training and supplying terrorists and mercenaries from all over the world. The village itself was patrolled and controlled by his own mercenaries, and the warehouses and training center were invisible under the jungle canopy. It was a location the Major enjoyed returning to, landing on the camouflaged airstrip carved at the edge of the camp just where the mountains began.

This time the Major wasn't as pleased as usual. He'd had to close down his entire British Columbia installation because of the bogus Estelle Davis, who had been left to die by Miles Haggarty's improvised garrote as a warning to others. He considered this problem as he stepped out of his small jet with Haggarty and Greenleaf.

"Colonel, go and check on the recruits you've come for," the Major snapped. "I want them out of here as soon as possible. Miles, you make sure we're running smoothly, then start working out a report on the best place to relocate our North American operations."

Both men nodded, then climbed into waiting Land Rovers to be driven to the installation itself, where barracks, training fields and warehouses were all hidden under the thick canopy of the jungle along the river. When they had left, the Major turned on his heel and strode across the metal grids of the strip to a helicopter pad. The pilot of a waiting chopper opened the door.

"I'll handle it myself," he told the pilot. "Go get your lunch. I'll send word when I'm back."

The pilot hopped out and went off to the nearest mess hall. The Major climbed in and started the rotors. Seconds later he lifted off and banked in a steep, sweeping turn as if he were heading south down the river. Once out of sight from the airstrip, he turned the chopper a full 180 degrees and settled into a course steadily east, away from the river, flying over the Serra Curupira until he reached a high mesa.

He touched down on a flat spot that was like a small plateau of its own. Up close the plateau wasn't a plateau at all, not even a mountain. He got out of the chopper onto what was actually the roof of a camouflaged building set into a barranca at the edge of the mesa.

There was no sign of life anywhere. The Major waited. Then a fake boulder rose to reveal a circular metal staircase descending into the mesa. The Major went down the staircase and the "boulder" closed behind him.

MACK BOLAN STRODE along the Galveston, Texas, docks. His intel call had brought him, Marsha Barr and Cecil Olds this far. Then his Galveston contact had zeroed in on the shipping outfit that had slipped the "mining equipment" crates through. The Galveston agent was one of Hal Brognola's men who'd helped him before.

"The guy I got to talk is the first mate of the container ship *R. V. Dunn*," the Galveston Fed had told him. "He's an old swabbie, a real patriot. He hates all terrorists and wants to cooperate. But he has to give the details to my top man. Says no offense to me, but the way things are now in Washington he doesn't trust anyone. Here are your fake Justice credentials."

Now the warrior walked into the busy office of the shipping line and asked for First Mate Karl Sipper. A clerk pointed at a saloon across the street, and Bolan headed over to it. Even at midday the dive was dim. At the bar a sullen bartender directed him to the rear, where a small, scrawny man in gaudy civilian clothes sat alone, nursing a shot and a beer.

Bolan was dressed in a dark suit, the bulge of a big regulation pistol visible under the jacket, a snap-brim hat perched on his head. He sat at Sipper's table and said nothing, just stared at the man the way Feds do when they want to throw their weight around.

"Who the hell are you?" Sipper growled nervously. He was a man with more than ships on his mind.

Bolan took a billfold and flipped it open to reveal his badge and identity card.

Karl Sipper grinned. "Hey, all right. You're the big Fed around here, right?"

"You wanted to talk, Mr. Sipper," Bolan said. "Here I am. Start with who shipped those crates and from where."

The weasel-like man looked quickly around. "Hey, not here, right? I ain't supposed to tell you that stuff. It could cost me. Know what I mean?"

Bolan nodded. "Where?"

"Pick up my tab and meet me out front. We'll take a ride."

Sipper stood and scurried out a back entrance. Bolan paid the little man's tab and walked out of the dive. Minutes later a red Corvette glided to the curb, and Sipper opened the door. Bolan got in. They drove three blocks to a small building on a back street. The Corvette cruised in through open double doors. Sipper got out and beckoned for Bolan to follow him.

Two goons appeared from the shadows and followed Sipper and Bolan into a windowless office. The first mate sat on the edge of a large desk, motioned his two hulks into the corners behind Bolan, then smiled wolfishly. "Okay, I've got the goods. Now let's talk about the money."

Bolan looked back at the two goons, then at Sipper. "I thought you loved America and hated terrorists."

"That, too." Sipper laughed. "But cash on the barrel head makes me love my country even more."

Bolan didn't laugh. "That's not the deal."

Sipper stood. "It is now," he snarled, "and you better start talking real money if you want to walk out of here in one piece."

"You didn't mention money, so I didn't bring money."

"Make a phone call. One of the boys'll be glad to go pick it up. Let's say, ten grand?"

"How do I know it's worth that?"

"Because I say it is." The scrawny first mate sat down again, then leaned toward Bolan. "Look, buddy, I've got where those crates came from, the place they was loaded and how they got to that place. It's what you want, and it'll cost ten grand."

Now Bolan smiled. "No, buddy, I don't figure it will."

"Why, you—" The weasel was up again.

The two goons stepped toward Bolan. The warrior let fly with a punch to the first guy's jaw, and he crashed into a wall and fell flat on his face, out cold. The second goon tried for a gun, but a single high kick under the chin snapped his neck with a sickening crack. Then the first guy staggered up, this time with a knife. Bolan caught his thick wrist, twisted it back on itself and shoved the guy's knife in under his rib cage and up into his heart.

By this time Sipper had his gun out. The sailor fired straight at the Executioner, who lunged sharply right and felt the bullet crease his side as he caught the first mate by the throat. He tore the pistol from Sipper's scrawny hand, lifted him up until he dangled, choking, his feet a foot off the floor.

"Tell me," Bolan said. Sipper choked and gasped. Bolan tightened his grip slightly. "Now."

Gagging, Sipper croaked out, "Puerto Ordaz...Icato Mining warehouse...Ciudad Boliívar. All...I...know."

Bolan dropped the weasel on top of his dead goons and walked out. He drove Sipper's Corvette back to the hotel where Barr and Olds waited for him.

"Not Brazil," he told them when they were together. "Venezuela."

THE MAJOR STOPPED at the bottom of the circular metal staircase. He was in a long, lit corridor where two armed men hurried to meet him. Behind them a heavy, bearded man in a white laboratory coat looked worried.

"Well?" the Major snapped.

The bearded man shook his head. "Not yet. He's a tough nut, Major. I told you he would be."

"You saw the advantage of working for me, Tellford."

"He's not as easily lured by money as I am," Eugene Tellford said. He'd been a rising young scientist under Hitler, and later a key man on Wernher von Braun's American rocket team. Half-forgotten in a dusty faculty position at a second-rate university, the Major had scooped him up and made him his science chief.

"What the hell will make him work with us?"

"I'm not sure anything will."

"Everyone has a price, Tellford." The Major smiled. "It's just not always money."

"So they tell me," Tellford replied. "But I can't find it for Lev."

They had been walking along the air-conditioned corridors and down the stairs all the time they talked. Laboratory doors lined the corridors, and behind the glass other white-coated scientists worked. On the ground floor the doors were all solid and closed. These were the living quarters of the various scientists the Major had brought to his secret jungle center. Not even the mercenaries and terrorists training and practicing with new weapons at the base camp knew it existed. Not even Haggarty knew where the laboratory was. Only the scientific staff itself, and the guards at the lab, knew of this work.

"Are they all in the dining hall?" the Major asked.

"All of them."

It was a rich, comfortable dining hall for the entire elite staff of the scientific center, but now only six men sat in it, and they were neither eating nor comfortable. They were older men, all with that nervous, flabby, owlish look that comes from having spent lives exercising minds and not much else. Five of them sat close together, sullen and beaten, afraid. The sixth was a little apart, neither sullen nor afraid, and a long way from beaten, judging by the fierce look in his eyes behind rimless spectacles.

The armed men behind them in the corners of the dining hall left little doubt that the scientists were here against their will. Despite comfortable rooms they were still prisoners.

The Major went to the front of the hall and smiled at them. He sat easily on the edge of a table, his polished boots catching the artificial light. "First, let me apologize for not coming to talk to you all earlier. I've wanted to since you got here, but business detained me. I do hope you're all comfortable and that you find the facilities we've provided adequate for your needs. Does anyone have a complaint?"

The Major looked slowly at each of them, still smiling. The five who sat together cowered as if his smile were something lethal aimed at them. The one apart snorted, but said nothing. He just glared at the Major and Dr. Eugene Tellford beside him.

"I have a complaint, Major," Tellford said. "The work is going far too slowly. I think our friends may not be giving their best efforts."

"So?" the Major said softly, fixing his eyes on the pale five. "Why would that be? You're all being paid well. The money's being sent to your families as I promised. You have good facilities. I regret it was necessary to bring you here by force, but I knew that I couldn't convince you of the importance of our work until you saw it. I want to try to save this insane world from itself. You see that. Your work here will protect the world from its own hatreds and rivalries that have no place in a modern nuclear society. We have the fissionable material, the special alloys, the missile capability, and we *will* have the bomb sooner or later, so why not get it done as fast as possible? Then perhaps we can make the super-powers really sit down and talk peace. What we're doing here is the greatest hope of world peace ever, and I'm going to finish it!"

The five shrank back and nodded as if agreeing. Only the one man who sat apart had a different reaction. He laughed and said something in Hebrew.

"You know we don't understand Hebrew, Dr. Lev," Tellford said.

"And we know you speak English," the Major said. "So why play this game?"

Dr. Claudius Lev answered again in Hebrew, his voice mocking.

The Major stood. "You'll work for us, Doctor. I know that, even if you don't. A man like you isn't hard to persuade by more direct methods, but I'd rather avoid that. It's messy and might even kill you after a couple of weeks, and then we'd have to go and kidnap someone else in your specialty. I'll give you another two days, then I'll have no choice except to send in *my* experts."

The Major smiled at them all once more, then he and Tellford walked out. Even the defiant Lev seemed pale now as they left.

Outside, the Major lit a cigarette. "Well?"

"I don't know," Tellford said. "He's a tough nut. Even the Gestapo couldn't break him when he was younger."

"Okay, start working up a list of others we could get if we have to kill him," the Major said. "I'm going to have those bombs, Tellford. The ultimate terrorist weapon, eh? They'll pay anything to get nuclear weapons, and the big powers will pay anything to stop them from getting them. A gold mine."

"Platinum," Tellford said, and laughed.

THE WAREHOUSE in Puerto Ordaz was on the bank of the massive Orinoco, as broad as a lake and deep even this far from the ocean. An oppressive heat hung in the twilight air as Bolan, Marsha Barr and Cecil Olds talked to the jovial Englishman who operated the transfer warehouse and sighed now as he drank the English ale Olds had brought for him.

"Bloody Hispanics can't make anything close to a proper beer, and in this godforsaken backwater you can't even buy it. Well, cheers, eh?"

They all drank and watched the jolly little man wipe his mustache.

"So, those mining equipment crates, eh? You won't actually believe where they came from." He looked around at them all as if daring them to guess. "Upriver!"

"Ciudad Bolívar?" Olds asked.

The Englishman waved his glass. "No, no! That's the beauty of it. Farther inland, you see. Much, much farther! The first loading label on the crates read Maroa!" He looked at them, triumphant. "Maroa! That's seven hundred miles upriver over the mountains and on the Rio Negro! Not even in our watershed, eh? In the Amazon basin!"

"Mining equipment being shipped *out* of the jungle and mountains?" Bolan said questioningly.

"Exactly! Can you imagine it! Why in the name of all that's holy would someone ship crates of mining equipment *out* of a mining area to the States?"

"Yeah," Bolan said, "why?" He nodded at Olds and Barr.

Olds thanked the Englishman and gave him the rest of the case of British ale.

"That's awfully decent of you. I hope I was of some help."

Outside the warehouse Bolan, Olds and Barr got into their rented car.

"A charter flight's the fastest way to Maroa," Olds said.

"Let's go," Bolan agreed grimly.

At the window of the warehouse office, the Englishman, drinking his ale slowly, watched them go. When they were out of sight, he turned, walked to the telephone and dialed.

"You there? Yeah, I gave them the whole story, Maroa, right. Only one way to get there fast—charter flight. I'd say a half an hour from here. Put the cash in the mail."

The Englishman hung up, grinned, then laughed out loud.

CHAPTER FOURTEEN

Alone at the controls of the helicopter, the Major flew back to his main base. He was angry. The Israeli physicist was the key to making the small, powerful nuclear bombs he had to have. He wanted a strategic bomb just for the threat of it, but the market was in the small, tactical weapons that could be used by two-bit countries and terrorists without blowing up their own people in the attack.

There were billions in tactical A-weapons, and Claudius Lev was trying to screw him out of them. But the scientist couldn't hold out forever. There were ways.

The Major came in low over his installation. He surveyed it critically but proudly. It was the creation of a lifetime. He'd put into it everything he'd learned since that first killing of his father, who had been worse than just a half-assed thief—he'd been dumb enough to get caught at it. That had been the start, and he hadn't looked back, and the big but almost invisible installation below was the culmination. Everything was state-of-the-art for terrorists and mercenaries. He turned out the best fighters, offered the best weapons, had the most reliable services.

Soon he'd be the richest man in the world, and then he could retire and turn it over to a man like Haggarty. That was the main reason he'd welcomed the renegade Briton aboard so eagerly. He'd been after a man like Haggarty for years, and now he finally had him. A man almost as good as he was, almost as smart and, most important of all, almost as ruthless. He'd thought about Greenleaf, but the big colonel lacked the cold ruthlessness. He was still too much the officer and gentleman. Too much by the book, too many good manners. Sooner or later that would cost Greenleaf.

The Major wouldn't put the future of his perfect violence-for-profit organization in the hands of a man who might hesitate at a critical moment because of some stupid moral code from the past.

As if his thoughts had conjured the two men up like voodoo, they were both waiting for him at the helicopter pad as he brought the chopper in. Greenleaf was sharp and neat in the combat fatigues and maroon beret of his former British regiment. That weak, sentimental streak of patriotism and loyalty would ruin Greenleaf someday, despite his pretense at being above national affiliations.

Not Haggarty. The turncoat captain was relaxed and leaning against a tree in the efficiency-designed basic gray coveralls the Major had developed for jungle warfare. Haggarty wanted no part of his old uniform, country or useless loyalties that only got in the way of what had to be done to win.

But both of them looked a little anxious now. Something had happened.

"What's the problem?" the Major snapped as he jumped down from the chopper even before the rotors had stopped turning.

"Someone's backtracking that weapons shipment the U.S. Feds picked up from the Red Army in the Rockies," Haggarty said.

"Backtracking? You mean trying to trace us?"

"They're not looking for a Venezuelan vacation."

"Who?"

"An MI6 agent," Haggarty said, "and that freelance Yank, Mack Bolan."

"A British agent? You know him?"

Haggarty nodded. "Guy named Cecil Olds, a top agent. Probably looking for me. MI6 doesn't give up. They could never believe a real Englishman could change sides." He laughed. Then his face became serious. "They've got someone else with them—that woman we left in the garrote up in Canada." He shrugged. "I blew it. Olds must have rescued her. Should have shot her right then."

The Major frowned. "Tell me more about this Bolan."

"Ask Greenleaf."

The mercenary shook his head. "No one actually knows. We do know he served in Vietnam and has been death on the Mafia and terrorists ever since. He's a one-man army."

"But he's about to meet his Waterloo," Haggarty said.

The Major looked at both of them. "You're sure? You've got it covered?"

Haggarty grinned. "All the way."

Greenleaf only nodded. Always the ramrod soldier.

THE TWIN-ENGINED CESSNA climbed to fifteen thousand feet to fly above the mountains of the Cerro Bolívar. From the copilot's seat, Bolan saw the thin, towering plunge of Angel Falls off to the far left. The highest falls in the world, it fell in two mist-enshrouded stages from its plateau to the tributary of the Rio Caroní thirty-two hundred feet below.

Marsha Barr and Cecil Olds sat in the rear seats as the charter plane flew on across the Sierra Maigualida toward their destination of Maroa on the Rio Negro. Below, the dark forested mountains showed no signs of life, nothing but the trackless, remote land itself. After the mountains would come the jungle, the distant Colombian llanos, the endless rivers of the Orinoco and Amazon watersheds, a land as empty of civilization as any left on earth, with thousands of square miles without a town, a village, a house, only Indians so primitive that many had never seen a European. Then, far ahead, they saw the ribbon of lighter green in the jungle beyond the mountains that indicated a river.

"That the Rio Negro?" Marsha asked.

"Upper Orinoco," the pilot said. "The Negro's another fifty miles beyond it. Funny, they flow in opposite directions."

And then the engines stopped, both at once. An ominous silence followed, punctuated only by the rush of wind.

"What is it?" Olds asked quietly.

"Pilot?" Marsha queried.

Bolan grabbed the copilot controls and felt the heavy, sluggish plane begin to tilt downward toward the distant ground. The pilot checked dials, turned switches, his face now chalk white.

"The electrical system's gone! All of it!" Terror shook his voice. "We're finished! We've got to get out! In the back! The chutes! Hurry!"

In complete panic the pilot abandoned the controls and began to claw his way toward the rear over Olds and Barr. The plane tilted, rocked and swayed high in the sky as Bolan fought to keep it steady. At any moment the pilot's wild thrashing could flip the whole plane over and send it crashing to the ground.

Olds hit the panic-stricken pilot with his pistol, catching him as he fell unconscious. Meanwhile Bolan steadied the plane, which had now begun a slow, gliding descent. As he grappled with the controls, Marsha went back to the locker and opened it. She was silent a moment, then turned to Olds and Bolan.

"It's empty. He forgot the parachutes."

"So?" Olds said, shrugging. "You'll just have to bring us down in one piece, eh, Bolan?"

Bolan smiled. "With a little bit of luck."

"You, er, do know how to land this thing, Mack?" Marsha asked nervously.

"In this terrain? I guess we'll find out," Bolan replied.

His voice was light, but inside he knew the odds. The conditions below were less than ideal for a crash landing. He could take his choice—the mountains or the jungle. Talk about a rock and a hard place... Well, it was a choice fate would make for him, and whatever it was he'd face it open eyed, as always.

Meanwhile, the problem was to keep the plane airborne and in a safe, steady descent. Let it go down at too sharp an angle and it would accelerate into a death dive no one could pull it out of. Keep the angle too small and the plane would lose airspeed to the point where it would stall and go into a spiral as deadly as the dive or start dropping like a rock.

It was a hell of a narrow margin of error for a guy who didn't fly all that often. Bolan felt himself sweat. It was one thing to go up against the hounds of hell in human form; that he could handle. But how did you fight the air? The wind? A simple, intangible thing like the angle of descent of a dead airplane?

Marsha was suddenly beside Bolan. She reached out and wiped the sweat off his forehead with her head scarf, keeping it out of his eyes. He smiled at her.

"You okay?" She searched his eyes.

"All systems go," he said. "We'll make it."

"I know we will," she said quietly.

They were down to a thousand feet now. Marsha sat close to Bolan and kept the sweat from his eyes as he stared straight ahead, searching for a landing spot, somewhere that would give them a fighting chance. But all he could see were the raw peaks of craggy mountains or the thick jungle cover that hid treacherous barrancas and ravines. He had to find a meadow, a clearing, even a river, where he could see what he was coming down into, something that wasn't rocks or cliffs.

But he saw nothing, only the remote jungle-covered mountains rushing past, now almost close enough to touch. Then a bare rock peak flashed under the wing, and a ridge came up at them.

"Hang on," he gritted through his teeth as he fought to clear the dropping plane over the ridge. With all his strength, he fought to keep the nose up, felt the edge of a stall and had to lower the nose again, then cleared the jagged rocks of the ridge and made it over a flat river valley another thousand feet below. The ridge had been the tip of a cliff that dropped a thousand feet to the river jungle.

"That," Olds said, whistling, "was close."

"Piece of cake, as you Brits say." Bolan laughed as Marsha wiped more sweat from his face. "Now all we need is an opening."

The Cessna glided on, swept lower and lower, as Bolan searched for the one opening in the jungle roof that would give them a chance. He needed a stretch of river where he could ditch the plane in deep enough water and take their chances with the caimans and piranhas.

"Bolan!" Olds pointed. To the left, like a highway in the endless green of the jungle, the river ran a straight course for nearly a mile. And the river was low! A long, barren, gravel bank lay uncovered between the shallow water and the jungle wall.

"That's it!" Bolan cried. "Hold on to your teeth! We're going in."

The warrior took a deep breath and turned the wheel. The gliding plane went into a bank that slowed it and sent it down in a long, sweeping curve. This would have to be it. There was no way to get the plane on any other course now. It was down on the gravel, or down into the big silence.

Bolan fought to keep the nose up, struggled to keep the long glide in the curve that would bring it to the straightaway just as he hit the river opening. One more turn back to the right, then straight down and in.

"You're gonna kill us! We're dead! Pull it up! Pull—"

Forgotten, the pilot had come awake just as they swooped in for the final drop to the gravel bank. He staggered up and stared ahead at the water and gravel, totally out of his mind with fear. Lunging he groped for Bolan and the controls. The plane yawed, tilted and shuddered as Bolan battled to keep it up, and moving, and gliding into the straightaway of the riverbank. Olds tried to grab the pilot, but a sudden yaw flung him aside. Then Marsha attempted to block the crazed pilot.

In another twenty seconds they'd be down, but in ten seconds the mindless pilot could destroy them. Bolan half turned, his Beretta in his right hand. Without thinking, he smashed the gun against the guy's head, sending him back against the rear wall of the Cessna. Then the warrior dropped the pistol, held the wheel in both hands and brought the Cessna down, hitting the gravel hard.

The plane bounced up and tilted, dipping a wing dangerously. Cool as ice, Bolan made a slight correction, then touched the brakes. The Cessna hit again, slithered, bounced around, skidded sideways and finally came to a bone-crunching stop as it slammed into three feet of river water.

Birds rose in a flapping cloud that darkened the sky, small animals scurried and crashed through the thick green, caimans slithered off into the river and larger animals froze, listening in the jungle shadows. The Cessna's tail tilted up and its nose buried itself in the water. One wheel had crumbled, while a wing lay a hundred yards back. Bolan climbed out the side window and reached back inside. "Grab my hand."

Marsha, blood on her short black hair, took the warrior's hand. He pulled her out and lowered her into the shallow water, where she sat down, her head in her hands.

"Olds?" Bolan said, looking back into the Cessna.

"All in one piece, old chum," the MI6 man said. "Just checking on our ex-pilot and seeing what supplies we have in case this thing decides to blow. I'm afraid the poor bloke's quite dead. Too bad he had to get caught in our war."

Marsha raised her head. "Sabotage?"

"Of course," Olds said. "Our dear friend at the warehouse, I should imagine. In the Major's pay, no doubt. Explains why he was so bloody cooperative."

"It sure wasn't an accident," Bolan agreed. "What about the supplies?"

"Not much better than the parachutes, I'm afraid. I'll bring out what we have."

With what Olds carried from the plane, they waded the few feet to the gravel bank and laid it out. Using a half-empty first-aid kit, Bolan bandaged the cut on Marsha's neck. Miraculously that was their only real injury, outside of assorted bruises.

"Pretty damned good landing for an amateur, I'd say," Olds said, smiling.

But Bolan wasn't thinking of the past; he was thinking about the future. It didn't look all that hot. After the first-aid kit, what they had from the plane was three candy bar emergency rations, a rifle with one box of ammo, a tarpaulin and tent in bad shape, mosquito netting, a machete and a Coleman stove with no fuel.

"I've got my Browning, Uzi and sleeping bag," Olds said. "And a flask of Scotch."

"MAC-10," Marsha said, "a survival knife and water purification tablets."

Bolan had all his weapons, his commando knife and the lightweight thermal blanket he carried in his jungle fatigue pocket. "If we don't run into any trouble, we should be able to follow the river to some civilization."

"I wonder what kind of river it is? Orinoco watershed or Amazon?" Olds speculated. "Let's hope it's Orinoco. The Amazon would be a rather long trip."

The sun was low in the sky now, and the three stranded adventurers began to look for a campsite. They soon found a sheltered backwater clear of the jungle, and Olds started a fire. Marsha took her fishing line and hooks from her survival knife and set to work on dinner. Bolan worked on the tent.

"Well," the soldier said after he got the tent up, "I guess it could be a lot worse."

LESS THAN A HUNDRED MILES southwest, the Major sat at his desk as the tropical sun set over the rim of the jungle wall around his secret base. He sat with his eyes closed, his face impassive. He was working on how to make Dr. Claudius Lev do what he needed.

The heavy knock on the door interrupted him. He frowned, but opened his eyes and spoke into the falling darkness of his office, saying, "Come in."

Haggarty entered the office, with Greenleaf right behind him. "We got 'em," the renegade captain said.

"Crashed in the jungle," Greenleaf added.

"You're sure they're dead?" the Major asked.

Haggarty laughed. "What difference does it make, Major? They're down, and that's Yamano territory. If the jungle doesn't get them, the Yamano will."

Greenleaf looked uneasy. "I don't know. We better hope the crash killed them. If they survived, that Bolan is pretty damn tough.

"So are the Yamano," Haggarty said. "And it's their turf."

CHAPTER FIFTEEN

Bolan jerked awake, opened his eyes and listened. Someone was talking, low and urgent. Morning light filtered through the patched tent and its mosquito netting. Then the voice spoke again, almost desperate.

Bolan raised himself on his elbow under the thin thermal blanket and put his big hand on his Beretta. The voice was Marsha's.

"Where are you, Steve? I'll find you. I will!"

She was talking in her sleep. Bolan looked around the tiny tent. Olds was gone. The guy was good. There weren't many men who could sneak out of a tent and not wake him.

The warrior lay back and watched Marsha. She was one hell of a good-looking woman, and tough, too. Brave and tough. The kind of woman he liked. But she was searching for her husband, and that meant hands off. A lot of guys would call him old-fashioned, but sometimes the old-fashioned ways were the best. Then he found himself looking into Marsha's eyes.

"Hello," she said.

"Sleep well?" Bolan asked.

She nodded, but her eyes continued to stare at Bolan, and he knew she was thinking the same thing he'd been. He liked her and she liked him. Maybe more than like, but her husband stood between them, as well as where they were and what they were doing.

"Where's Olds?" Bolan asked.

She sat up and saw the empty sleeping bag. "I don't know."

"He slipped out pretty quietly," Bolan said. "You got your weapon?"

Marsha indicated the MAC-10 alongside her. Bolan nodded, and they both rose slowly and silently into a crouch. The warrior put one hand on the netting and the tent flap, holding his Beretta in the other. "Now." He pulled the tent flap and netting back and they both jumped out, their guns sweeping right and left.

Olds sat in front of a small fire, and turned to grin at them. "Care for a bit of breakfast?" The MI6 man was roasting three plump birds impaled on three long sticks. "Not exactly pheasant, or even chicken, but they'll be quite tasty. A kind of pigeon they have down here. They weren't at all used to a snare. Practically walked into my hand. And we've got some river water, some cooked plantain, hell, practically a bloody feast."

"You should've gotten us to help," Bolan said.

"Only takes one man to snare birds," Olds said. "You can do KP." He looked toward the sun, which was just barely above the river in the narrow opening between the rain forest walls on either side. "I thought it best we start moving as soon as possible. I'm afraid this river looks like a Rio Negro tributary, and that means quite a trek before any hint of civilization."

"It also means the first civilization would be our original destination at Maroa, doesn't it, Cecil?" Marsha asked.

"Yes, my dear."

"And sabotaging us means the Major knows we're coming after him," Bolan said. "We'll have to move carefully."

"Very," Olds agreed. "They undoubtedly think we're dead, and we'd do well to keep them thinking that."

"We'll use the river as much as we can to make time," Bolan said. "The Major's sure to have aerial surveillance, so that means we'll have to travel mostly at night when we get close to Maroa."

"We'll have to build a raft, then," Marsha said.

"Or commandeer a canoe if we can find a village," Bolan said.

"So let's eat and get the show on the road, as you Yanks say," Olds suggested.

The roasted pigeons turned out to be delicious, the water safe with the addition of some purification tablets, and the cooked plantain filling. They wrapped the leftovers in leaves for later, and while Marsha struck the camp, Bolan and Olds used the machete from the plane to hack down small trees and tough vines for a raft.

That was the plan, anyway.

The camp had been struck and packed, the raft was half-finished and Marsha was getting the maps from the plane, when she turned and saw them. "Mack."

Bolan and Olds looked up. Slowly they stood and began to walk casually toward her. The Indians were at the edge of the rain forest, in front of them, along the edge of the open gravel bank and behind them. Maybe twenty all told.

They were short, dark, muscular, naked men with bows and long arrows and spears at least three times as tall as they were. The arrows and spears all had their wooden tips sharpened and hardened by fire. Their coarse black hair was cut in an upside-down-bowl shape like the thatch on a conical roof. Black arm-bands circled their biceps. A few men, probably the leaders, carried machetes across their backs, the prized importations from traders. Paint in many colors wriggled on their chests like snakes, while earrings dangled from their earlobes. All had arrows fitted to their long bows, arrows that were aimed ominously at the three white people.

The natives' eyes were black, fierce and deadly. Bolan and Olds, and even Marsha, towered over them, but that didn't seem to worry the powerful-looking little men. One of them stepped out and motioned with his arrow for them to come along.

"Amigos," Olds said as he smiled and held his open hands out. The instant Olds moved, every man in the band pulled back his bowstring, ready to fire. Spanish obviously wasn't one of their languages.

"Friends," Bolan said, trying English.

The Indian leader made the same threatening motion with his bow and arrows, so Olds tried his limited Portuguese, but to no avail.

"What Indian dialects do you guys know?" Bolan asked, not taking his eyes off the drawn bow of the leader.

"Quechua," Olds said, and tried it.

The Indians looked at him. Something about the Peruvian Indian language reached them, but not enough for them to act as if they understood it.

"That's my whole language bank," Olds said, smiling at the Indians as he spoke to Bolan and Marsha. "What do we do? Try to take them? We've got the guns."

Bolan smiled, too. "One, we'd have to be damn lucky. They look as if they can handle those bows, they look trigger-happy, and I'd say they like to kill people. Two, there's got to be more of them around. We don't want to have to fight our way through the whole rain forest with the Major watching. Three, they have a reason to want us to go with them, and we better see what it is."

"Four," Marsha said, "we don't want to slaughter innocent Indians unless we really have to."

"Okay," Bolan said, "we do what they want. Stay sharp. They could get ugly anytime."

"We better take all our stuff," Olds said.

The trio picked up their packed supplies, ammo and guns, slinging them over their backs. The moment their hands were full, the Indian leader grunted out a sharp order, and instantly three of the small natives had their arrows touching the necks of the three anti-terrorists.

The leader came up and collected all their weapons except their jungle knives. He even took the machete. Then he motioned for them to walk into the forest wall as the other Indians closed around them.

Under the towering trees, thick vines and lush vegetation of the rain forest, they marched through shadows as dark as night. Shafts of sunlight reached from above like great pillars that seemed to hold up the thick canopy overhead. Thousands of birds flapped, cried and chattered, while monkeys swung, swooped and screamed.

The forest floor was so thick with fallen and decaying vegetation that their feet sank in up to their ankles. Bolan marched ahead, ever alert, his eyes never losing the broad, powerfully built leader whose face and torso were a mass of scars from countless wounds. All around the three strangers the other warriors moved as silently as the shadows themselves. And silent as they were, they traveled with amazing speed in the tangled growth.

This was their home, and Bolan had learned from long, hard experience that you never fought a man on his own ground if you could help it. That was a sucker's game, and you didn't survive in a war by being a sucker. No, here he would go along and look for a way to choose his own ground. Unless they gave him no choice. Meanwhile he would watch and wait.

Hours passed in the changeless shadows of the dim rain forest. Bolan's mind was carried back to the other jungle where he had spent his youth, to the same endless march through the same fetid stink of decay, the neck-crawling fear of being a stranger in an unknown world.

More hours passed, and Marsha began to stumble. Even Olds. Bolan steadied them while the expressionless Indians watched and pushed on as the sun overhead began to slant toward evening.

Bolan used the sun to estimate their direction. If he was right, they had been moving steadily southwest, away from the river and toward the Brazilian-Colombian border—and closer to Maroa, where the crates of "mining equipment" had been before Ciudad Bolívar.

Closer, but still a long way. Much too far for anyone to walk, even the Indians. That meant they were being marched somewhere else, somewhere definite. Indians didn't push across country in a forced march on their own. These Indians were following someone's instructions.

Bolan heard the new river long before they came to it. Then, suddenly, the rain forest thinned, and they were in a village on the banks of a fast, deep river that flowed south.

It was the usual small Amazon/Orinoco settlement. There wasn't much cleared space along the river, where thatched huts stood in the shadows. However, there were two unusual features—a large tent was pitched beside the river, and a small motor launch bobbed against the bank next to it.

The man who stepped out of the tent was tall and lean, a swarthy fellow with black hair and a Roman nose. He wore a grayish brown tropical uniform with a heavy pistol hanging from a web belt, and his tight trousers were tucked into low black boots. White teeth smiled under a thin black mustache, and he spoke in what sounded like nasal Portuguese.

"Ah, visitors! Come and sit. Sit! I get so few visitors on my trips."

He motioned eagerly toward some camp chairs set out in front of his tent. The Indian warriors made no move to join or help him. Instead, they stood in a circle behind Bolan, Olds and Barr, discreetly closing around them. Women and children had come from the huts to look at the strangers, but showed little interest and soon returned to their work.

"So," the tall man said when they were seated. "Tell me everything—who you are, how you got here, what I can do to help you."

Olds translated the Portuguese for Bolan and Marsha.

"English!" the man exclaimed. "You are Americans?"

"I am," Bolan said. "They're British. What are you doing way out here, Mr.—"

"Captain Tostao of the Brazilian Interior Police and, alas, this is my territory to patrol. I don't get up so far that often. Maybe twice a year. The Yamano have instructions to bring any foreigners to me. Directly and unharmed. Now how did you get here?"

Marsha told the Brazilian police officer of their crash in the Cessna and the accidental death of the pilot. But she gave him their cover story of being on an assignment for an English magazine to photograph the upper reaches of the Rio Negro and said they had been flying to Içana on the Rio Negro in Brazil.

"You're very lucky the Yamano found you and brought you to me. I can take you down river in my launch."

"But aren't we still in Venezuela?" Marsha asked.

Captain Tostao shrugged. "The capitals and the mapmakers are far away. We go where we are needed. Sometimes a Venezuelan officer comes up the Orinoco. Sometimes a Colombian rides across the Ilanos to see who is alive. But since the river is the Negro here, I come up. In Brasilia, Bogotá, Caracas, they care little until someone discovers oil or metals."

"You said Yamanos?" Olds asked. "These Indians are Yamanos?"

"You know the Yamano?"

"A very warlike people. No wonder you said they were told to bring strangers to you unharmed."

"An instruction that took many years to impress upon them," Captain Tostao said. "I doubt there is a man in this village who hasn't killed at least one enemy, mostly quite a few more."

"And strangers with white skins are enemies by definition."

"Or so far outside their world they don't even count as enemies," the captain said. "You can never be sure which or when. They're changeable and unpredictable. All our work with them has barely scratched the surface."

As if his words had been instantly translated into reality, there was a loud commotion in the circle of the small, silent warriors. The squat leader turned sharply and faced an equally powerful younger man who stepped out of the circle. They spoke angrily to each other, making threatening gestures. Then the younger one said something, and the leader nodded and stepped aside. Striding over to Marsha, the young Indian grabbed her arm and pulled her out of her chair.

"Get your hands off me!" she cried.

Bolan jumped up and tossed the smaller man across the small clearing. The Indian whirled, his spear ready, aimed straight at Bolan. The big soldier froze. "What's he want, Tostao?"

"The woman, I think," the Brazilian said. His swarthy face was pale.

"Tell him to move off. The woman doesn't want him," Bolan said quietly.

The squat young warrior growled something furiously at Captain Tostao. The Brazilian was now very pale. "I can't. It is their code. You defended the woman, so she must belong to you. They get all their women here by fighting for them, which means he wants to fight you for Miss Barr."

Bolan stared at the small, powerful warrior with his spear and his bow. "You better tell him we don't do things that way."

"I can't do that. I can do nothing, American," the captain said. "You will have to fight him."

CHAPTER SIXTEEN

The Major flipped the intercom key. "Report."

A flat, neutral voice answered. "Captain Haggarty states the aerial survey showed the Cessna down in a river less than a hundred miles north of our base. Wing gone, no sign of life, but the aircraft isn't destroyed. No report at this hour from parapatrol."

The Major flipped off the switch and sat back. He had hoped the Cessna would have been totally destroyed and the bodies plainly visible. The small problem gnawed at him. On the surface it was nothing more than a minor irritation. All the experience of a lifetime told him it was nothing. Three routine agents on a routine backtrack that would come to a dead end in Maroa. He should forget it, dismiss it. Haggarty could handle it. But all the instincts of a lifetime wouldn't let him off so easily. Every alarm in his brain told him that this wasn't a routine matter.

He flipped the switch again. "I want any report from the parapatrol instantly. Wherever I am, break in. Clear?"

"Clear," the neutral voice said.

In the silent office the Major thought for a moment, shook his head grimly, then looked at his watch. The outer door opened and his staff sergeant came in.

"The reps are all in the briefing room."

The Major nodded. "Haggarty and Greenleaf?"

"The colonel's there. Captain Haggarty's in the field to the north."

"The field?"

"Helicopter. We've gotten some reports from the parapatrol on Indian tracks around the Cessna crash."

The Major frowned. "He didn't tell me that."

"Probably wanted to check it out first."

The Major swore. "Have him get to me as soon as he knows anything." He stood up. "Let's go."

The terrormaster strode angrily along the narrow corridors of his camouflaged headquarters to the large briefing room at the end. Damn! he thought. Why did these three agents bother him so much? Was it that they'd gotten this close? Or that the woman had escaped once? Or was it the shadowy, enigmatic American, Mack Bolan? He was a solitary maverick in some kind of war of his own, and no one but a fool worked alone on such a mission. Yet, apparently, this Bolan had survived a long time. Alone and deadly.

"The Major!"

He shook himself and realized he was standing inside the briefing room and being announced by his staff sergeant. Recovering quickly, he smiled at the fifty or so men at the long tables of the briefing room. "So glad you could all be here. I think I may have an item of great interest to everyone."

The fifty-odd faces didn't smile. They watched warily as the Major walked briskly to the front where the lectern stood on a platform before giant wall maps. He looked out over the colorful audience and smiled again. "I think you'll be quite pleased with what I am about to tell you."

There were faces of every age, skin color, eye shape and ethnic origin. Violent young faces; smooth, cunning, mature faces; crafty old faces. Uniforms of every color and shape and description. Turbans, fur caps, sun helmets, red headbands. Business suits and camouflage fatigues. Burnooses and berets, keffiyehs and sombreros. Men and women from almost every terrorist, guerilla and mercenary group in the world. Many of the organizations represented were deadly enemies, and everyone kept a wary eye on one another and a cold eye on the Major.

The Major went on smiling. "You are all here because you need, must have, weapons. You know my weapons are always good. You need cadre training, soldiers, plans, advisers, and I have all that. And now I'm about to offer an item for sale that will be of the greatest interest to your organizations. So great, believe me, none of you will be able to refuse it."

An old Afghan in a dirty turban said angrily, "We are fighters for justice! You speak to us like venal cutthroats!"

"Freedom fighters!" a swarthy Hispanic in U.S. fatigues shouted. "Not bandits who live by buying weapons."

"We build a better world," a scarred Filipino People's Army officer cried. "We do not deal in your tools of death."

"For the people!"

"Justice!"

"Peace!"

A Khmer Rouge leader stood up. "You think we came here to be huckstered like eager capitalist thieves only looking for an advantage over the competition? Is that what you think of us, Major?''

"Because you have never had any ideals beyond money," the Maoist Shining Path guerrilla said, "do not think others are not idealists."

Half of them were on their feet now, angry and threatening. There were shouts to leave. The Major held up his hands and nodded. He looked serious and solemn now. Slowly the hubbub calmed and the angry guerrillas and terrorists sat down again.

"Of course," the Major said. "Of course you are all idealists and freedom fighters." His voice was dry with an edge of sarcasm. "I never meant to imply you were looking out for yourselves. But, can we say, that in the interest of peace, freedom, justice and the abused people of the world, wouldn't you all like to have nuclear weapons?"

There was a rumble of anger again at the tone in the Major's voice—and then stunned silence.

"Nuclear?" the old Afghan majuhideen said.

"Atomic weapons?" the Khmer Rouge man said.

"For us?" the Shining Path soldier breathed.

The Major smiled once more as he looked around at all the faces staring up at him. "Tactical weapons of all kinds, which would be most useful to you. Possibly even a strategic bomb and a launch missile just for show. Keep the big powers in line, you might say."

The eyes of the assembled now glowed with fire— nuclear fire.

"What we could do to the big, arrogant capitalist powers!"

"Kick the Soviets out of our country!"

"Destroy all the rich men who strangle the world."

"Send the Marxists home to ruin their own countries."

"It will make the rich, arrogant powers on all sides helpless!"

"They would have everything to lose by a nuclear conflict with us, and nothing to gain!"

Laughter. "Who would drop a nuclear missile on Ethiopia? What is there to destroy?"

"There would be no advantage to them," a black guerrilla leader said, "but to us?"

"We have nothing to be destroyed. They have everything."

The death merchants surged forward and crowded around the raised platform in front of the Major.

"When, Major?"

"How can we get them?"

"Will it be soon?"

The Major smiled broadly this time. "Soon, my friends. Yes, soon. But I think we can start talking details even now—what you want, how many, the prices. Shall we get down to serious business?"

All around him the terrorists, guerrillas, mercenaries and death squad leaders nodded eagerly.

MACK BOLAN FACED the powerful Indian, who had dropped his spear and now had an arrow in his long bow aimed straight at the Executioner's heart. "The only weapon I've got is a combat knife."

"I can do nothing," Captain Tostao said. "If I tried to help, they would kill us all. That you have no weapon is his advantage."

"They won't give me weapons?"

"No," Captain Tostao said. "You're on your own. No rules, just life and death."

All the time Bolan talked to the Brazilian police officer he kept his eyes on the slight native. And the Indian never let his eyes leave Bolan, or his fingers stray from his bowstring. Instead, the Yamano watched and listened, as if he understood more English than anyone thought. But Bolan realized it was the tone of his and the captain's voices that the savage was listening to. He knew, without understanding the words, that Bolan was trying to avoid a fight.

The Indian knew exactly what he wanted and was ready to fight to the death to get it. But it was the woman he wanted, not the fight, and if Bolan backed down, that was okay with him. He didn't care how he got Marsha, only that he got her in the end. A man who wouldn't fight for what he wanted would never get what he wanted, but a man who put the fight above the goal was a fool.

"Tell him," Bolan said, talking to Tostao but staring at the Indian, "that the woman doesn't belong to me or him. She belongs to herself."

"He won't understand. I'm not sure I could even say that in their language. Women aren't people like men. The idea would have no meaning."

"Okay," Bolan said. "Tell him among my people that men and women are the same and that she doesn't want him to own her."

Captain Tostao spoke to the Yamano. The Indian smiled. The other men burst out laughing. Even the leader grinned. Across the small clearing some women turned to stare and snicker.

It was what Bolan had been waiting for.

He had to neutralize a weapon that killed at a distance, and at the same time get close enough to use his knife. Hunters with bows and arrows had to skirmish, take advantage of cover, sneak up on their target. The hardest target for a bow and arrow was something charging straight at it, fast. There would be time for one shot, a difficult one, and no more.

Bolan knew a samurai tactic for attacking a gunman when armed only with a sword: a sudden, fast, direct walk straight at the man. It made the gunman hesitate a split second, startled by the unexpected tactic and unsure of what the man with the sword planned to do. That momentary hesitation was all the swordsman needed, and Bolan was certain it would work better against a bow and arrow.

As the warriors laughed at the crazy notion that men and women were the same, that women could own anything, the Executioner moved. He drew his knife quickly as he walked toward the Indian. Surprised, the native stopped laughing, drew his arrow back . . . and hesitated.

Bolan raised his knife as if to throw. Alarmed, the warrior shot quickly, and at the same instant Bolan jumped to the left. The arrow grazed the soldier's right shoulder and flew past.

Then the Executioner was on top of the smaller man, grabbing at the bow and thrusting with his knife. He broke the bow in two and flung it away, but the fierce Indian recovered immediately, swept his long spear up from the dirt and lunged at Bolan. The soldier went in under the spear and slammed the warrior with a karate side kick, which sent the native sprawling.

As Bolan closed in with his knife, the Indian rolled and came up again with his spear. He thrust it at Bolan, and the soldier had to dive and roll to escape the lethal jab. The Yamano pressed his advantage, initiating a series of quick, violent spear thrusts, and Bolan had to backpedal rapidly.

They circled the small clearing. Bolan watched the Indian's eyes and saw white-hot rage emanating from them. The Yamano world was one where only the strong ruled and the best men would always die before they would give up. Death was the only decision to this battle.

Bolan saw this. He had come to respect, even admire, the wiry Indian as they struggled in the clearing dwarfed by the tropical rain forest. But he would have to kill him.

Bolan knew he could kill the warrior—he had the size and skill—but he wished there were another way to end it. However, there wasn't. The Yamano warrior wouldn't let it end any other way, and the fight went on.

Bolan drew first blood with a quick knife thrust that gashed the Indian's side. And second blood. The native had death in his eyes now. He knew he wouldn't win. He knew, yet didn't think for an instant of running, or escaping, or even stopping. He would die, and that was the only way for him. To survive because another warrior let him live was something alien to his existence.

The Indian doubled his fury, lunging, thrusting and parrying with even greater ferocity. Then, with a final shout, he penetrated Bolan's left arm with his spear. Bolan countered at the same moment and his knife found the Indian's heart.

The Yamano died instantly, the shout of triumph still on his lips as his eyes glazed over and he fell to the dirt in his own blood. Silence settled over the small village. The natives made no move to attack and avenge their fallen tribesman. Olds and Barr hurried to Bolan with the first-aid kit, and Marsha went to work on his wounded arm.

Captain Tostao walked up to the leader and spoke forcefully in the Yamano language. The leader nodded, said something to the other warriors, then turned back to the Brazilian policeman and spoke again.

The captain nodded to Bolan. "He says you have defended your woman. She is yours, and you are all free to leave. They will return your weapons, and I can take you downriver in the launch. Are you all right?"

"It's a clean wound, but I've given him a tetanus shot just in case," Marsha said.

"I'm going to have a stiff, sore left arm for a while," Bolan told the Brazilian. "But I can travel fine."

"Then I suggest we do that," Tostao said.

They all nodded. The Yamano warriors brought them their guns and the machete, and Captain Tostao gave orders for their gear to be put into the launch.

Turning to Bolan and his friends, he said, "Very well, you can get aboard. We—"

A sudden shower of arrows out of the shadows of the rain forest cut him short, though. They all dived for cover, with the Yamano warriors already firing back at unseen enemies.

CHAPTER SEVENTEEN

Captain Miles Haggarty gunned his Land Rover through the heavy terrain toward where the Major and Colonel Hugo Greenleaf bawled orders to Greenleaf's new recruits. The fledgling mercenaries were going through combat training with live ammo and buried charges.

Haggarty drove straight across the range, barely missing the exploding charges. The Major saw him and gave orders to cease fire. Haggarty screeched to a stop in front of the Major and Greenleaf and jumped out of his vehicle.

"Bolan, the woman and the MI6 agent survived the crash," Haggarty reported in disgust. "But I think the Yamano got them."

"You think?" the Major snarled.

"I'm certain. We found Yamano tracks all around the plane and followed the boot prints into the jungle." Haggarty shrugged. "Then we lost them. The Yamano are too damn good at covering their tracks."

The Major nodded at Greenleaf. "Take over. We'll talk about the results later."

He climbed into Haggarty's Land Rover, and the renegade Briton drove back toward the main base buildings. The Major wasn't in a good mood.

"Give it to me again. All of it."

Haggarty described how Bolan and his companions had picked up the trail of the Red Army weapons in Galveston and traced them back to Puerto Ordaz.

"Our guy there gave them a cock-and-bull story about the crates coming from Maroa and had their Cessna sabotaged. We figured that was it, but somehow they got the bloody plane down and walked away."

"Obviously one of them can fly a plane very well," the Major said dryly. "My guess would be the one named Bolan. He seems to be the key."

"Took more than that," Haggarty said as he drove along a narrow, rutted road hidden under the tall rain forest trees. "They had to get over the mountains without an engine, then find an open spot in the rain forest. Any opening's chancy enough, but they had to find one long and flat enough to land a plane. Talk about your bloody luck."

"I'd say they're having altogether too much luck, Captain."

"Well, it's over now. The Yamano have them, and that's all she wrote."

"Perhaps," the Major said. He scowled at the thick forest surrounding the secret road. "These people are becoming a nuisance. They're beginning to annoy me. It's time they were stopped permanently before they get any closer.

"Hell, Major, what damage could they do against our whole organization, anyway?"

"Probably little," the Major agreed. "This Bolan seems to be special, but one man isn't very disturbing in himself. As you say, what can he do? But if they aren't stopped, they'll begin to draw attention to the base, to our operation, and that we don't want. Alone they're nothing. It's who might come after them that concerns me."

"Not much sweat about that, Major," Haggarty said cheerfully as he reached the main base complex. "We've got people covering their trail and keeping a sharp eye on anyone looking for them."

"And them? When will you eliminate them?"

"I've got all the wickets covered. The situation's under control. I expect any minute to hear that the Yamano have skewered our troublesome friends. No matter what, though, they won't get near the base. And you can put that in the bank."

"I hope so, Captain. I hope so."

Haggarty brought the Land Rover to a bone-jarring halt in front of the Major's headquarters. He let the Major out and waved cheerily as he drove away. The Major stood for a time, staring thoughtfully after the Briton.

AFTER THE FIRST FLURRY of arrows from the dark of the rain forest, there was complete silence. One Yamano warrior lay dead with an arrow through his neck.

"It's a feud," the Brazilian police captain said, breathing hard as he crouched behind a hut. "We're caught in the middle, and it looks as if the attackers outnumber the villagers here pretty damn badly."

"Another tribe?" Bolan whispered next to the captain.

"Same tribe. Another village."

"This happens often?"

"No, it doesn't. There's usually lots of warning before a war starts between villages. Usually one or two warriors go out after a single enemy and ambush him. Not whole villages."

"How do they fight?" Bolan said urgently. "Are they any good?" The big soldier watched the forest. He saw Marsha and Olds behind the next hut, and single Yamano warriors spread all around the clearing, bows and spears ready and looking for a target. A lot of them hadn't even bothered to take cover.

"One-on-one they fight damn well," Captain Tostao said. "As an army, they don't have a chance. It's every man for himself. They run straight at the enemy and look for someone to bash."

It was typical of primitive fighters—the more primitive, the less efficient they were at fighting. All noise and violence and no real strategy or tactics.

"One-on-one they'll be sitting ducks, and so will we," Bolan said grimly. "Can we get them together and talk to them?"

Tostao shrugged. "I can try."

"Try fast," Bolan said.

The soldier watched the jungle for any sign of a renewed attack. There was nothing. They were out there, but their ideas of war were probably as primitive as the villagers. From what Captain Tostao had said, they were other Yamanos. This was Yamano territory, and no one else entered Yamano land.

As he waited for the Brazilian to persuade the Indians to meet him instead of blundering off into the jungle, looking for a head to bash, Bolan thought about the attack. There was something wrong with it. He had a strong hunch that it wasn't against the other Yamanos but against the strangers—them.

"We'll meet in the men's hut," Tostao panted as he slid back behind the hut. "It's the biggest one over there. Miss Barr and Olds are there now."

"Will the Yamano post sentries?"

"I doubt it."

"Then we better."

The Brazilian captain nodded as they both stood, zigzagged low across the small open space and dived behind the men's hut. No arrows were fired at them. What the hell were the damn attackers waiting for? Were they up to some trick? Were strangers advising them?

"I'll keep watch," Olds volunteered.

Marsha bent to go through the low entrance to the hut with Bolan and Captain Tostao. The Yamano warriors gaped at her—a woman in the men's hut! Then they saw the MAC-10 in her hands and watched her load and clip and cock the SMG. The older leader said something and they all stopped staring and squatted in the dimness. Even the most primitive people can learn new ways, recognize a different world with different rules and accept it when they have to. And when it could give them an edge on their enemies.

"We'll make this fast," Bolan said to Tostao. "Tell him I know how to beat the attackers, maybe capture them all."

The Brazilian policeman translated rapidly. The Yamano leader nodded, glancing at Bolan. Then all the Indians stared at the big soldier.

"Tell them I'm going to draw what we'll do in the dirt. Marsha, have you got your flashlight?"

"Here." She took the powerful light from a side pocket of her pack and turned it on.

The natives looked at the dirt floor of the hut. Bolan drew a crude diagram in the dirt floor with a stick as he talked and Tostao translated. "You'll split into two groups, in the center and on the right of the village. We'll be the third group on the left. Like the head and tusks of a wild pig."

Bolan waited while Tostao translated and the Yamano examined his crude drawing on the floor. It showed a straight line in the center and two curved lines right and left like the tusks of a pig or the horns of a bull.

"The head of the pig stands in the center, angry, breathing fire, waiting for an attack. The right tusk pretends to swing at the enemy in the jungle. But it stops short. Then the left tusk hooks massively at the enemy's exposed side and back. The enemy is driven into the head and the right tusk, wounded in the side and pinned against the head and right tusk."

Bolan watched them as Tostao finished his translation. They eyed the dirt for a time, then looked at Bolan again. The leader grinned, and the others nodded violently, their mouths open as if they could taste fresh meat. They seemed to think it would work, and they all looked at Bolan as if he had magic. They had never heard of the buffalo horns tactic of the Zulu king Chaka, but they understood it at once.

"Okay," Bolan said. "Let's go."

Outside in the sunlit clearing the village was quiet and deserted. Olds nodded toward the jungle. "I saw movement, but nothing's happened. They're waiting for something, Bolan."

"Tostao?" Bolan said.

"I think maybe they are waiting for our side to attack. That is the Yamano way."

"Would our side have been after them by now except for us?" Marsha asked the captain.

"Without a doubt."

"Then they must be getting edgy as hell," Bolan said. "Let's give them their attack."

The soldier gave last-minute instructions through Tostao, then led the Brazilian and his two British colleagues to the left, out of sight. They crawled and slipped from hut to hut until they reached the edge of the rain forest on the left.

Bolan made a hand signal to the Yamano leader on the far right of the village. Almost instantly the Yamano warriors in the center began to brandish their spears, draw their arrows back on their bowstrings, shout defiance and do a kind of war dance mocking the enemy in the forest.

The Executioner watched the vague shapes in the forest move toward the center. Then the attack began on the right. The Yamano warriors dashed into the forest with spears and bows ready, now that the shadows in the forest in front of them were gone.

"Now!" Bolan said. "Shoot to scare or wound. No killing unless we have to."

Guns drawn, Olds, Barr and Tostao followed Bolan into the dim jungle light. The soldier led them at a trot fifty yards into the forest, then swung sharply right to flank the attacking force. A single startled warrior appeared from behind a tree ahead.

"How do we tell them from ours?" Marsha cried.

"If they shoot, they're not ours!" Tostao said.

The single warrior raised his bow, and Bolan fired in the air, causing the native to shoot his bow wildly and run. The arrow missed everyone by six yards.

A group of warriors appeared ahead. They milled around in confusion, looked in the direction of the feint and pulled back. Bolan realized they had never seen an attack start and retreat without making any contact. Yamano warriors never ran without at least shooting an arrow. Then they heard Bolan and the others and whirled. "Fire over their heads!" Bolan cried.

The volley of semiautomatic and automatic fire sounded as loud as the thunder of artillery. But these were tough warriors. They stood their ground, raised bows and spears and howled defiance.

"They're going to attack!" Tostao cried.

The plucky tribesmen hurled their spears, and the four whites dived for cover.

"Damn!" Olds swore.

"Cecil?" Marsha cried.

"Winged me," the MI6 man said. "I'm all right. Carry on."

The warriors massed for a charge. They were as gutsy as any fighters Bolan had seen, and they wouldn't be stopped without losing blood. Demonstrations of power wouldn't stop them; they would have to feel the power.

"Fire to wound if you can!" Bolan commanded.

The heavy volley tore through the thick jungle growth, slashing vines and shattering trees. Six of the Indians fell, clutching at their arms, shoulders and legs.

The superior firepower was too much for the tribesmen. Even they knew that their arrows and spears were no match for the weapons of the intruders. They turned and ran, some limping due to wounds, some still trying to fight, hurling spears at their pursuers. Until they ran into the right tusk of the pig—the village Yamanos. They were now trapped between the two horns, outnumbered ahead and outgunned behind.

The attacking warriors stopped and looked wildly around them. When they saw the rest of the villagers from the center coming up, they knew they were finished. At that moment they dropped their last weapons, sat down on the jungle floor and waited passively as the village Yamano howled in savage triumph and rushed in to spear them.

"Tell them to stop!" Bolan yelled at Tostao.

The Brazilian barked orders in Yamano. Astonished, the warriors stopped. They looked with puzzlement at Bolan, knowing by instinct who was in command. Still, they had no understanding of why they were being told not to execute their defeated enemies.

"We have to talk to them," Bolan said to Tostao. "There's something about this attack I want to know."

HOURS HAD PASSED. The captured Yamano attackers sat in the men's hut of the village Yamanos. One villager crouched on each side of an enemy. Tostao and Olds were near the low door, watching. Marsha had put a sling on Old's wounded left arm and was now taking care of the wounded attackers, of whom only one had died. Bolan sat alone in the center of the hut, facing the captured Yamanos.

The defeated warriors and their village guards squatted naked and sweating in the fetid air of the hut. Wads of green tobacco were stuck between their lower teeth and lips, and long ropes of dark green slime dripped or hung from their nostrils, slimy strands so long that they drizzled down their chins and stuck to their pectorals.

To show friendliness, Captain Tostao had told the villagers to share their *ebene*, an hallucinogenic drug they blew up their noses, with the prisoners. Now they were all high on the drug, and one of the side effects was a runny nose.

"Ask them why they attacked," Bolan told the Brazilian policeman. "Tell them we think they came to attack the strangers, not the villagers. Ask them why they want the strangers to die."

Relaxed and released from fear by the *ebene*, an older warrior among the attackers began to jabber in a deep, angry voice so fast that Tostao was almost breathless in keeping up with the translation.

"Pale strangers destroy all people. Soon no more people anywhere. Land dead. People dead. See pale strangers with this village. This village betray people. This village let pale strangers live. This village bad. We kill."

The older man stopped, and Tostao spoke behind Bolan. "By people he means Yamano. The word means 'the people.' They are the only 'people.' No one else is really a person to them, so strangers are the same as animals and stones."

"How are the pale strangers killing the people?" Bolan asked.

Tostao translated. The old warrior waved his powerful arms. "Fish die in river. Pale men take people to work for them. Pale men take people women. Pale strangers kill people, send people away from village."

"What pale strangers?"

"Ones with many guns. Live in big village on river. Many days toward sun."

Bolan stood in the dim hut. "Tell them we want them to take us to where these strangers are."

CHAPTER EIGHTEEN

Bolan, Barr, Olds, Tostao and the defeated Yamanos, now eager friends, were ten miles southwest by nightfall. The Yamanos from the village where Tostao pitched his tent were glad to be rid of them all.

Tostao had tried to talk Bolan out of it. "It would be better if I took you downriver to Maroa and you flew out from there."

"Don't you want to know about white men killing Indians?"

"They didn't mean killing literally. They don't have a word for destroying things, only for killing people," the captain said. "It's too dangerous out there, American."

"You don't have to come."

"I can't let outsiders wander around."

"Suit yourself. I'm going to find out about these white men."

As night descended like a blanket over the rain forest, they pitched their camp beside a small tributary. Olds and Marsha set up the tent from the Cessna. Tostao had a Yamano pitch his travel tent. The rest of the Yamanos dropped where they had stopped and watched Bolan build a fire to cook their dinner of game and jungle greens hunted and gathered by the Indians.

After dinner Bolan took the first watch. Marsha sat up with him for a time, leaving Olds to crawl into the small tent to rest his wounded shoulder. Tostao came out of his tent and joined Bolan and Marsha at the fire. He lit a cigarette and offered one to the big soldier and the MI6 agent. They both shook their heads. The captain smoked and looked out into the black beyond the circle of firelight.

"You have maybe been in jungles before this, American?" the Brazilian asked.

"Maybe," Bolan said.

"I think, yes. You move here too easily, are not worried by the strange sounds, the smells."

Bolan said nothing. Marsha stared into the fire. The Brazilian seemed to search the forest with his eyes through the darkness around them.

"It is incredible this rain forest of ours. Dense, wet, endless, trackless. Snakes, jaguars, pumas, caimens, piranhas. Even dolphins that eat piranhas! Gold, diamonds, rubies, oil and a million other resources, and yet still almost untouched. The last untouched area on earth, and we have it. Empty and waiting."

"Waiting for what, Captain?" Marsha asked.

"Progress, Miss Barr. The future. A great future for Brazil, eh? We will open the whole basin. Drain it, make it ours. It will make us one of the great nations."

"Blacktop it?" Marsha said. "Build factories and condos? And what about the Indians? The Yamano?"

Tostao shrugged. "The Indians will join us, or they will cease to exist. They will become Brazilians and move ahead."

"That sounds a lot like genocide, Captain," Marsha said. "Move ahead to where? Exploitation, slave labor, welfare and starvation?"

"Progress means freedom for everyone, Tostao," Bolan added. "Not just for corporations and big governments. A lot of corporation big shots and politicians are just out to make a fat profit and help out their friends. They don't give a damn about the ordinary Joe or the Indians. They just want to grab everything they can for themselves. If you want to handle all this jungle right, then let the local guys and the Indians work it out."

The Brazilian shook his head and stood. "The future is much too important to be left to private citizens and amateurs."

"The future's a hell of a lot too important to be left to the politicians and the corporations," Bolan said. "And the future includes the trees, animals, everything. They have to figure into the equation, too."

Captain Tostao shrugged. "We disagree, American. Fortunately, in Brazil, we know how to deal with amateurs who try to stand in our way."

"I'll bet you do," Marsha said.

Tostao smiled. "We must discuss it more thoroughly sometime, Miss Barr. For now, it is time to sleep."

The Brazilian strode back to his tent and crawled in. Bolan nodded to Marsha. "You better hit the sack, too. You've got the last guard."

"You're right," she said, getting up. "Mack? Are we going to get out of this? Are we going to find the Major?"

"We'll find him," Bolan said. "And we'll get out of this."

They smiled at each other. She bent and kissed the soldier before she turned to walk to the tent and crawl in.

Alone, Bolan listened to the jungle night and watched the stars above the river. Guard was always a lonely time. He tried to think of how many times he'd pulled guard, in how many places. There were too many times to count, too many parts of the world to remember. So he let his mind go blank and sat in silence, alert yet almost asleep, until his duty ended and it was time to roust Olds.

Later, after Olds had relieved him, Bolan crawled into the tent beside the sleeping Marsha. He lay for a time under his thermal sheet and watched her. She was a beautiful woman, and he knew she was drawn to him as he was to her. But they had a job to do, and Steve Barr was out there somewhere, dead or alive. Until they knew which, Bolan would have to stop thinking of her as a woman. It was the only way.

MILES HAGGARTY RUBBED his tired eyes and yawned in the headquarters CQ office. Since joining the Major less than six months ago, he'd risen fast to be second in command and didn't have to pull CQ, but tonight was special. He looked at his watch. Past midnight. It shouldn't be too long now.

To pass the time, he leaned back in his chair and studied the giant wall map that showed where all the clients of the Major's worldwide organization operated. The blue pins were terrorist groups the Major supplied with weapons, ammo, information and sometimes experts for a particular attack. The red pins were mercenary units in the field, weapons and soldiers trained and supplied by the Major. The yellow pins were guerrilla forces who used the Major as a supplier, information source and recruiter of needed experts for special projects. And, finally, black pins showed the government armies and services who came to the Major for advice and help.

Haggarty shook his head with admiration. The Major had an operation anyone would envy. He worked with all sides in any conflict, and that included most of today's battles, big and small. It made no difference to the Major what anyone stood for, or fought for. There was no right and wrong, no good and evil. There was just profit for the Major. He didn't care who won or lost, who survived or died. Except himself.

The renegade Briton heard the footsteps on the polished floor of the corridor long before they reached the CQ office. The door opened and a short, burly Indian entered. Stark naked, he carried a metal ax and had a machete in a case slung across his back.

"How far?" Haggarty asked in Portuguese.

"Day, maybe two," the Indian said.

"All of them?"

"Woman, big American, skinny Englishman. Englishman is wounded by Yamano. Yamano with them. They go Yamano village on big river one day north."

"The village where we get workers?"

"Same village." The Indian grinned. "We get women, too. Make men very mad."

"I expect it does."

"In village tomorrow."

"Okay. Go back, report again tomorrow. Here."

Haggarty handed the Indian a small bag of white powder. The burly little man took it eagerly. Cocaine was far superior to the *ebene* his people snorted. He left in a hurry, and Haggarty soon followed him.

There was no light in the Major's office along the corridor. Haggarty went down and out into the night to his Land Rover. The shadowy figures of sentries moved everywhere, but no one stopped the captain. At the Major's private cottage there was a light in the front window. The Briton had expected there would be. Most of the time it seemed that the Major never slept at all.

"Come in," the Major called when Haggarty knocked.

The Briton stepped into the office of the Major's quarters.

"He showed up?"

Haggarty nodded. "They'll be a day away tomorrow. At that village we used to get workers and women."

"Those Yamano went for help?"

"Don't think so, Major. I think they spotted the three whites and attacked because they hate us."

"Which means they told them about us. About us using them for labor."

"I'd say so."

The Major leaned back in his desk chair and closed his eyes. His pale, heavy, Siberian face was thoughtful. He seemed to be almost asleep for a time. Haggarty waited. Then he opened his eyes and looked at the captain.

"It's this Bolan. He's the force that's brought them so far. No one's ever gotten this close. I have a strong feeling it's not the woman or the MI6 man. We've dealt with MI6 before. No, it's this Bolan, and it's time to get it over with." He stared at Haggarty. "Go out and get them. I want it ended, and I want this Bolan. I think he may be someone very special."

Haggarty nodded and left the office.

After the renegade English soldier had left the Major closed his eyes again in his silent office. He wanted this damn Bolan annoyance ended. Bolan sounded interesting, a man he could use, but he wanted it ended, even if they had to kill them all. He had enough problems with Dr. Claudius Lev and the other scientists. If this batch didn't come across soon, give him what he needed to develop the nuclear weapons, he'd kill them off and get a new batch.

BOLAN CAME AWAKE with every sense alert and his Beretta already in his big hand.

He held his breath.

The sounds of the night seemed normal: the whisper of the stream, the cries of monkeys, the rustle in the thick jungle floor. But something had awakened the soldier. His sixth sense told him something was wrong, and he'd learned a long time ago to trust all his senses first, his reason second.

Olds slept quietly beside him, and Marsha's sleeping bag was still empty. He slipped out from under the thin thermal sheet and listened again. Still he heard nothing.

Very carefully he snaked out of the tent, Beretta in hand. The night was still pitch-black, but a faint gray line of dawn seemed about to break over the narrow river. The fire had burned down to embers, and Marsha wasn't there.

Bolan stood up in the shadow of a tree, his hard eyes searching the darkness. There was no sign of Marsha or anything else, either—no blood, no struggle. He trotted silently across the clearing on the riverbank and counted the sleeping Yamanos. They were all there.

Then he heard a muffled sound from the left, and whirled. He heard it again, a muffled scream. Tostao's tent was pitched in the shadows beside the river on the left, and that was where the noise originated.

Bolan sprinted through the night to the tent and tore up the flap. Naked on the tent floor, Tostao struggled with a shape under him. Bolan got a glimpse of hiking boots, fatigue pants around the ankles of a pair of pale, slim legs, and a flash of dark bikini underpants. He saw the Brazilian's hand over a face with wild eyes.

Bolan reached into the tent and hurled the naked policeman aside. Marsha struggled up, panting, her hair wild and her eyes wilder. Her underpants were halfway down her legs and her bra had been torn off. Bolan looked at her large, soft breasts, tight with rage now, and at the curve of her full hips. She was a very beautiful woman, and Bolan felt her beauty. He also felt Tostao's hate.

"Merda!" the Brazilian spit, struggling to sit up. He glared at Marsha. "Vaca!"

Before he could say anything more, before Bolan could stop her, she was kneeling in front of the seated Brazilian. Her MAC-10 was under his chin, the barrel boring into his flesh. She clicked back the bolt. Her face was inches from his. She had her fatigue pants up now, but her naked breasts still swung in front of the Brazilian.

"Don't breathe," she said softly. "Don't even blink."

His eyes were wide with terror.

"Marsha?" Bolan said.

She didn't look at the big soldier, only into the eyes of the Brazilian policeman. "If you come near me again, I'll kill you. If you speak to me, I'll kill you. If you look at me, I'll kill you. Ever!"

Cunning came into his dark eyes, pushing out the terror. Cunning that said she would never do anything. "Is it such a crime to desire a beautiful woman?"

The MAC-10 dropped and the knife appeared in her hand as if by magic. She pressed the point into Tostao's neck until blood started to flow. "You think I won't kill you? I will. I don't care who you are or where we are. I'll watch you every minute. Bolan will watch you. Cecil will watch you. And to make you remember, I'll leave you a reminder.''

She slid the point of the razor-sharp knife inside Tostao's left nostril and slit the side of his nose for an inch. The blood poured down, and the Brazilian screamed, more from fear than pain. He tried to stand up, to find something to stop the bleeding.

''Let it bleed, so you'll remember,'' she said.

She watched the blood flow for a moment, staring into his eyes. Then she picked up her SMG, sheathed her knife and turned her back on him to find her bra and shirt.

Tostao had no more interest in her. He grabbed his shirt and pressed it to his nose, cursing and swearing at her, calling her a crazy bitch in Portuguese. When Marsha finished dressing, she crawled out of the tent. Bolan looked at the Brazilian. ''Try that again,'' he said, ''and if she doesn't kill you, I will.''

Tostao held the shirt tightly to his nose. He shrugged, then suddenly grinned. ''You can't blame a man for trying, eh, American? She's one great piece of woman.''

''You're lucky she didn't kill you,'' Bolan said. ''You won't be that lucky twice. Now get someone to bandage that nose, because we have to leave in two hours.''

Tostao laughed. ''Hey, American, one can never be sure with a woman. In Rio, tomorrow or next week, she could love me.''

''Get ready to travel,'' Bolan said, and left the tent.

Dawn was just breaking now over the river. Bolan went after Marsha, but he was thinking about the

Brazilian. He suddenly didn't trust the policeman, and not just because of Marsha and the attempted rape. There was something else.

CHAPTER NINETEEN

Throughout the morning Marsha slogged in the rain of the tropical rain forest with her MAC-10 slung around her neck and hanging in front. Her finger was on the trigger every time Tostao came near her.

"You want to talk about it?" Bolan asked as they plodded on in a steady downpour.

"No."

"I understand."

They followed the Yamano ahead.

"There's something wrong about him, Mack," she said. "And I don't mean the rape try."

"What do you think it is?"

"He's not worried enough. He should be worried by us or about us. He's the only official for thousands of miles. He should be worried about what we'll do here, or about what will happen to us. He could get in trouble over both."

That was how Bolan sized up the situation. But he let her talk.

"He came out of his tent last night as if he couldn't sleep," she said. "He sat with me, friendly. He talked about how lonely it was all the way out here, so far from Rio. I was tired, glad for some company, but I remember thinking he didn't act like a man who couldn't sleep. He was relaxed, unworried, you see? Very calm, his mind not worrying about us at all. His mind was on a woman, Mack, as if he had no problems.''

"As if he knows we won't be any problem," Bolan said.

"Yes! That's just what it's like." She paled in the downpour, and her hand whitened on the MAC-10 hanging from her neck. "He had a cigarette, then suddenly said he wanted to give me some material he had that might help us. He'd forgotten about it until then. He was so casual I never even thought of what I was doing. We got inside his tent and . . . it began."

She seemed to stumble, and Bolan caught her. For a moment she shivered against him, then pushed away and smiled up at the soldier. "I didn't thank you for finding me."

"I probably saved him, not you," Bolan said.

"No, you saved me. I'd only have killed him."

They marched in silence for a time in the steady torrent. Then Marsha went forward to talk to Olds about Tostao.

Bolan watched the Brazilian. He seemed unworried and relaxed. He hadn't done anything Bolan could pin down, but he was the only one who could speak to the Yamano. If he wanted to lead them in circles, get them lost, set up an ambush, it would be simple. And he didn't act worried about his attempt to rape Marsha, as if he was sure she would never tell anyone.

Bolan was still thinking about the Brazilian, wondering if they were being led on a wild-goose chase, when he heard a distant sound like faint thunder. It seemed to grow rapidly louder as they moved toward it. Bolan realized it was another river in this waterlogged land, this time with some kind of falls or rapids. The Yamano began to move faster, breaking into a ground-covering dog trot.

"What is it?" Marsha cried, jogging beside Bolan, her SMG bouncing as she moved.

"My guess is it's their home river," Bolan said. "We must be getting near the village."

"That means near to the white men," Olds said, coming back to them. "If it's the Major's people, we'd best be careful, eh?"

Bolan fell back to Tostao, who brought up the rear. "We must be close to their village," Bolan said. "Tell them to slow down and move quietly. We don't know who could be there."

"Nervous, American?" the Brazilian sneered.

"Careful, Captain. With strangers reported to be exploiting your Indians, I'd think you'd want to be careful, too."

Tostao laughed. "One or two Yamano more or less is no loss, American."

"Tell them what I said."

The captain smiled, shrugged as if it didn't really make a lot of difference how they acted and walked ahead to speak to the tribesmen. The Yamano calmed down as if they understood at once. They had all the instincts of real soldiers; Bolan wouldn't want to go up against them after they'd learned more about modern warfare.

A half hour later they came out of the forest on the banks of the large river below the rapids. A low moaning issued from the Yamano. Bolan and the others could only stare.

What had been a large village among the trees at the edge of the river was now a smoldering ruin. Every hut had been torched or hacked down, pots and weapons broken and smashed. Bodies lay bloody among the ruins, and floated in the backwaters of the river.

The Yamano rushed forward, howling and wailing as they searched among the corpses for their families. They beat their chests and screamed in rage at the empty river. Bolan, Barr and Olds walked among the corpses.

"Shot," Olds said.

"Automatic weapons from the look of the bodies," Bolan added.

"Mack," Marsha said, "you notice something?"

Bolan nodded. "No women. Some dead children, but all the rest are men."

"They must have taken the women," Olds said.

"Soldiers have their needs," Marsha said. "Especially mercenaries a long way from home."

Bolan said nothing. He knew there were men like that, a lot of them. Men who thought of women, especially foreign women, the same way the primitive Yamano did. The Yamano had love for their kids and their brothers and sisters, even their fellow warriors, but none for women. They had no concept of romantic love. Women were possessions, workers and sex objects, nothing more.

The soldier studied the scene. It looked as if the attack had come from the river, probably gunboats. With the rapids directly north of the village, the attackers had to have come from the south. He went to find the Yamano leader.

The older man was with his warriors, who were busy burying their dead. Olds and Tostao were helping them. The Brazilian seemed to be in shock; he was grim faced and sweating as he dug. Maybe Bolan and Marsha had been wrong about him, and he was no worse than any typical white male chauvinist who was the only power in a remote region. Whatever, Bolan knew he needed Tostao to talk to the Yamano leader.

"Where is the settlement of these white men who steal your women?"

Tostao translated, and the Yamano leader pointed downriver to the south and said something in his language. Tostao translated, "One day. Maybe less."

"Does he have canoes? Rafts?" Bolan asked.

The Yamano nodded.

"Show me," Bolan said.

They were hidden just north of the village in a backwater near the rapids. Ten crude dugout canoes. They wouldn't hold enough people with their supplies. Bolan studied them and decided they could be used in pairs with logs between to form rafts large enough to carry all of them. He told Tostao to explain to the Yamano what he wanted.

"They're not going to understand you," the Brazilian said. "It's not a concept they have."

"Then we'll have to show them," Bolan said.

After the dead had been buried, the Yamano warriors went into the forest to talk among themselves and decide what to do. Tostao announced their decision.

"They want to go with you to the white man's village. They know they can't fight these white men, but they want to be with you when you talk to them. They want to tell their story.''

"Good," Bolan said. "Tell them we'll show them how to build rafts to take us all there.''

The Yamano listened to the Brazilian policeman. They looked puzzled and confused, but they nodded when he told them they would go to the white man's village with the strangers.

It took the rest of the day and into the next morning to build the rafts. First Olds and Bolan took two canoes and, using hut posts that had survived the fire, built a single large raft that would hold at least six people. The Yamano watched in amazement. When Olds and Bolan demonstrated that the idea worked on the river, they were even more amazed at what they probably thought was magic. But they were a tough, practical people and, magic or not, they saw the idea work and were soon busy building the rest of the rafts under the guidance of Bolan and Olds.

They slept that night in the burned village and completed the rafts the next morning. By noon they were ready to start down river to where the white savages had their installation. Olds took the first raft, Marsha the second. They both had five Yamano warriors with them. The Yamano leader took the third raft with five of his men. Tostao took the fourth raft with two Yamano and most of the supplies. Bolan had the last with four Yamano.

Tostao smiled when he saw which raft he had. "You want to watch me, eh, American, so I will not chase the lady again?''

"That, too," Bolan said.

At exactly noon they pushed off and out into the river. Each of the whites steered their rafts with a long steering oar made from spears lashed together. The Yamano leader steered his raft, had understood quickly what he had to do, but they all floated slowly at first until he had learned the trick. The river current slowed as they moved away from the rapids, giving them all time to get the feel of their clumsy boats.

The Yamano had said there were no more rapids; Bolan hoped they were right. He wasn't even sure they could stop the clumsy rafts in time if the current caught them unaware.

"Watch for any speedup in the current," Bolan shouted to Olds in the lead raft. "And keep to the middle of the river!"

The MI6 man waved that he understood, and the rafts moved slowly with the current down the broad river.

The afternoon wore on slowly and nervously on the makeshift boats on the unknown river with an unknown enemy ahead in an unknown location. It sure as hell wasn't the best way to conduct a war. If the enemy *was* the Major, then he knew Bolan and the others were somewhere in the jungle, and that was an even worse way to conduct a war.

On the river, moving slowly with the current, they would be sitting ducks. Except that the river was wide enough to protect them from each jungle-covered bank as long as they stayed in the center.

Evening came, and they drifted on. Halfway to the killers, every mile increased the chances of running into an outpost. Bolan had no way of knowing how good a soldier the Major was. A good assassin and terrorist, sure, but assassins and terrorists were mostly lousy soldiers. With a little luck there wouldn't be any outposts and they could drift close and sneak up on wherever the Major had his headquarters. Provided these killers were the Major's men.

Eventually the river narrowed. An escarpment came down to the bank on the left, halving the river's width. Bolan stood up to call to Tostao and find out how long the narrows would last, but the Brazilian was gone.

Only the four Yamano rode on the raft ahead, one of them trying to steer the raft, which yawed back and forth; the current had already picked up as the river narrowed. Then Bolan saw the bobbing head in the river a hundred yards away—Tostao was swimming to the right bank.

"Steer!" Bolan ordered a Yamano, and dived in after the deserting policeman.

Swimming powerfully, the soldier gained rapidly. Unaware he was being chased, the Brazilian reached the bank. Bolan stopped swimming. Tostao glanced once downstream to where the rafts were nearing the narrows, then plunged on into the jungle.

Bolan slipped silently into the towering forest after the Brazilian. In the muted twilight he spotted Tostao trotting ahead. The Brazilian was running parallel to the river and the drifting rafts. Bolan followed, gaining slowly but not enough to be heard by the running policeman. He caught glimpses of the rafts through the trees as he ran. They had just reached the narrows. Then a white soldier appeared suddenly from behind a large tree ahead. He leveled his AK-74 at

Tostao. The Brazilian stopped and spoke quickly in English.

"Captain Tostao! The password is Bolan!"

The enemy soldier lowered his assault rifle. "Come on. They're waiting." The enemy turned and moved out to the south with Tostao behind him.

Bolan swore. He and Marsha had been right. The Brazilian had been working for these people all the time, sending messages probably and leading them into a trap. And the enemy soldier wasn't Brazilian, that was for sure. The rafts could be floating into an ambush!

But maybe there was still time.

The Executioner broke into a run, with the intention of heading off the enemy soldier and the Brazilian turncoat. He angled as silently as a ghost through the forest shadows toward the river, moving in long strides to intersect where the two would have to pass to join anyone at the river—*if* they were going to the river. It was a gamble he had to take to get close enough to use his knife.

He could see the narrowed river through the trees, the rafts still floating as close to the cliffs of the far shore as Olds and Marsha could steer them. And he heard the enemy soldier and Tostao close to his right in the dim jungle twilight.

Tostao passed first without seeing Bolan, then the unknown soldier. Bolan's arm went around the guy's throat, his knife up in under the ribs and into the man's heart. The scream strangled under the vise of Bolan's arm on his windpipe. Blood bubbled up through his lips as his eyes glazed, and Bolan let him slide silently to the ground.

The big soldier grabbed the AK-74 and looked straight into the terrified eyes of Tostao, ten yards ahead. The Brazilian raised his pistol with shaking hands.

Then, ahead of them, a savage fusillade from hundreds of guns exploded. Ambush! Tostao fired, then fired again, his trembling hands sending the bullets wild over Bolan's head.

There was no need to be silent now. Bolan leveled the AK-74 and cut the treacherous Brazilian to pieces with three bursts. The policeman bounced into the air backward, his blood and brains spattering the thick jungle vegetation.

Bolan ran past the gory mess without even looking at it; the Brazilian had died like the animal he had been. The Executioner had more important things on his mind now. If he could pull a diversion, he might still save his companions.

When he reached the riverbank, he saw the results of the ambush. The Yamano warriors were bloody and sprawled on their makeshift craft. The last two rafts, without Bolan or the Brazilian to command and steer, had drifted sideways and lay half-submerged in the river with no sign of life on them.

The middle raft, commanded by the Yamano leader, had made it to the far bank and was still being steered by the wounded leader with two of his men still moving. The first two rafts were fighting back. Bodies of Yamano warriors lay on the logs, but Marsha and Olds were returning fire. They had a chance to reach the point where the river widened again, which would increase their likelihood of escape.

Then Bolan saw the gunboats sweep upriver toward the rafts. There was nothing anyone could do against their machine guns. Bolan lay on the shore and watched Marsha and Olds stand and surrender. Both were pulled roughly aboard the gunboats, then the machine guns were turned on the rafts and the remaining Yamanos were slaughtered.

Helpless, Bolan watched until the gunboats were out of sight downstream. Then he stood and moved silently downstream until he caught up with the rear guard of the attacking force. They were all white, well equipped and moved with the disciplined precision of trained troops as they headed back south. Bolan fell into a light trot behind the enemy as night fell over the rain forest.

CHAPTER TWENTY

The Major stood at his window and looked down on his installation in the night. He admired his camouflaged barracks, parade grounds, warehouses and training courses as he waited for the report of Haggarty's operation. He had worked a lifetime since that first job in Siberia to accumulate the knowledge and investment to build it all, and he surveyed it with a quiet pride. Once he had the nuclear weapons, he would control every terrorist, mercenary and guerrilla in the world. They would all have to come to him, and then...

Greenleaf entered the office. "Haggarty's coming in."

The Major didn't turn. "He got them?"

"All the Yamano are dead. He's bringing two of them in. One got away."

The Major stared out the window at the night. "Bolan?"

"Yes."

He sighed. "He's either incredibly lucky or incredibly good. What do you think, Colonel?"

"I think a man makes his own luck," Greenleaf said.

The Major finally turned from the window. "Yes, so do I, Greenleaf. But let's forget Bolan for now. Out there he's totally alone in an unknown country. That good, I don't think anyone is.''

"Maybe," Greenleaf said.

The Major laughed. "Cheer up. We'll get him yet. And meanwhile we'll have a real full-scale Triumph, eh?"

"A triumph?"

"With a capital *T*, Colonel. An honored Roman custom. They were the greatest nation and people who ever occupied this earth of ours. A warrior people, who ruled or died and who brought the greatest benefits human beings have ever known."

"A victory parade?" Greenleaf said. "For who, Major? As I recall, a Triumph was to impress the populace."

"To impress our populace," the Major said. "The recruits, the trainees, the customers, eh? The Romans knew exactly what they were doing. How well do you know Roman history, Greenleaf?"

"Not very well, I'm afraid. They don't study it much in the British army the way they used to."

"Not in the Soviet army, either."

The Major left his window to sit and swivel restlessly in his desk chair. "The world's never really been the same since the Romans fell. There's a lesson there, Greenleaf. It wasn't the barbarians who brought them down. It was themsleves. They fell due to inner rot. Too much soft living, too many rights given to inferior peoples, too much resistance to the hard lessons of their early days. Their young men didn't want to fight anymore, didn't want to do their hard duty, so they hired hungrier people to fight for them and gave up their toughness and preparedness for the easy life at home. So when the barbarian attacks finally came, they had nothing left to fight back with and folded up like a house of cards, putting an end to the best nation of all time.''

He looked again at the night outside his window. ''In my own way, it's what I'm trying to do. The heart of Rome was its consuls—the citizen generals who fought its wars, led its conquests. The commanders of the Praetorian Guard later. The hard-nosed pros who preserved the nation, eh?'' He looked back at Greenleaf. ''They understood reality. They knew that their ruthless self-interest ended in building the best world for everyone. They made life better for all the people they conquered and took over. Wherever they went they ended by bringing greater peace, progress and safety than any of their subject peoples could have had on their own. And they did it through strength, power and readiness.''

''In the end,'' Greenleaf said, ''the winners will be those who are willing to fight the longest and hardest without letting sentiment get in the way.''

''Yes,'' the Major agreed. ''And we'd all do well to take the Romans as our example, beginning with the real Triumph tomorrow for Haggarty and his battalion.'' He smiled at the big mercenary. ''Now how about a beer to celebrate.''

''Pour.'' Greenleaf laughed.

THE ELITE COMPANY, with its spit and polish and state-of-the-art weapons, moved swiftly through the jungle. Bolan followed as closely as he could. They were a sharp unit, at least on parade, and had an alert, disciplined rear guard. He couldn't even get close enough to see what they were doing with Marsha and Olds.

Their perimeter flankers covered one another so well that Bolan couldn't take any of them out unobserved. Bolan knew he was seeing the results of the Major's mercenary training operation. The assassins and terrorists would be just as well trained. And if they got nuclear bombs... The big soldier wasn't easily scared, but that scared him.

Full darkness had settled over the jungle, and still the soldiers moved south. Bolan probed at the flanks, circled the rear guard, searched for any opening to slip inside their outer defenses, but he was stymied.

Two hours after nightfall they stopped and quickly set up camp. A mess unit had a hot dinner ready in half an hour. The Major overlooked nothing in his training, and Bolan had to lie on a small jungle ridge and watch the mercenaries eat.

They were set up well, but there was something relaxed about them, amateurish, as if they were well trained but had no real experience. He waited until the faint moon was down, then silently crawled up to the guard at the rear point.

The guy was half dozing. A single thrust of Bolan's knife and the man died without ever knowing there was anything to worry about. The big soldier took the dead man's AK-74, ammunition and four hand grenades. The other guards were too close together, and covered each other too well, awake or asleep; he wouldn't be able to move on them.

He found no food on the dead man, which was unfortunate. He was hungry, tired and alone, but he had ammo and firepower now, and he wouldn't be cold. Taking the thin thermal sheet from his field jacket pocket, he rolled up in it and tried to sleep with the hollow hunger rumbling in his stomach.

IT WAS AN HOUR before noon when the first blast of trumpets announced the entry of Haggarty's battalion into the camp. The platforms had been set up along the asphalt landing strip of the Major's vast installation. The Major and his staff, Greenleaf, and the other visiting mercenary commanders and guerrilla leaders stood on the platforms to watch Haggarty's battalion march past in its Triumph.

Ranked all around the platforms, on both sides of the strip, were the battalions of trainees, the other units of the Major's own elite troops, the locals from the town and silent Indian laborers. They all turned their heads in anticipation as the trumpets sounded outside the high gates. The beat of drums grew louder, and the solid tramp of five hundred booted feet marching in unison thundered through the green tropical rain forest all around.

Then the gates were flung open, and the vanguard in tailored gray fatigues marched in with their AK-74s at port arms. They gave a sharp eyes-right as they passed the Major and the visiting customers. Four of the tallest soldiers, wearing pale blue fatigues, followed, carrying the battalion colors and guidons, the ribbons of their battles hanging from the staffs. When they reached the reviewing stand, they dipped the colors to the horizontal, and the Major returned the salute. Behind them were the trumpeters and drummers sent out by the Major to bring them in with style. They blasted a long fanfare as they passed the platforms.

Then came the first company with their 5.56 mm British assault rifles slung muzzle down. They all marched briskly to the steady beat of the drums. In the middle, walking alone with their hands in cuffs and chained together by collars around their necks, came Marsha Barr and Cecil Olds. A single guard walked on either side of them.

Behind the captives, Haggarty and his platoon commanders rode in an open full-tracked personnel carrier, nodding at the ranks of their fellow mercenaries. The second company followed in gray fatigues. Finally the rear guard, armed with Walther sniping rifles, stepped past in perfect order, pride in the precision of their step.

Everyone raised a cheer, and the Major applauded. Then the last men in the rear guard seemed to suddenly rise in the air as if floating on a great cloud, a cloud of dust, blood, flesh and human parts that spread like a fog just inside the open gates, the result of two hand grenades.

"Haggarty!" the Major bawled.

The redheaded renegade came running to the rear of his column, shouting, "Go out and get him! Now!"

An AK-74 firing on full automatic greeted the men who charged the gate, cutting them down and sending the survivors clawing for the dirt. Screams rose from the civilians and moans from the shattered and dying men. On the platform the Major stared at the still-open gates, then he turned to Greenleaf. "Bolan," he said. "Go and help Haggarty. I'll pay you. Get him. Alive if you can. But get him."

BOLAN RELOADED the AK-74 as he ran through the rain forest in the noontime heat. He retrieved the second assault rifle, extra ammo and his last two grenades, all the while listening to the sounds of pursuit spilling out through the camp gates behind him.

There were two Land Rovers, the tracked personnel carrier and what sounded like a whole company of the Major's elite mercenaries. Bolan smiled—too much and too many to go after one man. He trotted deeper into the thick jungle. They were well trained, but they weren't experienced in real war, and neither was the Major.

NIGHT CAME AGAIN to the camouflaged training complex deep in the Amazon rain forest. Miles Haggarty slumped into a chair and faced the Major. "I called everything in except two patrols. We had too much out there. All we did was let him know where we were."

"Do they have contact?"

"Not when I left, but they will. They'll keep him on the run."

"Or he'll keep them," the Major said.

"One man is pretty damn hard to pin down in the jungle," Haggarty said. "But one man can't penetrate our defenses and get into the camp."

"He did."

"No," Haggarty said. "He shadowed the parade and took advantage of the Triumph and the fact that we didn't know he was out there. Quite simply, he hit and ran. That's a one-shot deal, Major. He can't do it again. We know he's there now, and the whole perimeter is closed."

The Major nodded. "It sounds good, but this Bolan seems to be very resourceful."

"As near as I can figure, backtracking our route, he's got two AK-74s, ammo for maybe another day and two grenades. That's not going to be much of a threat to us. And how long can he stay out there without any support? He doesn't even have food."

"How do we know he doesn't have support?"

Haggarty shrugged. "I suppose we don't. We don't know who he's working for, or even why he's down here."

"Maybe we better find out," the Major suggested.

The onetime assassin leaned toward his intercom, pressed a button and said, "Bring the woman and the MI6 man to my office. Yes, right now." He looked at Haggarty. "Maybe they can tell us who Bolan is working for, and what he's doing here."

Haggarty nodded. He got up and walked to the high window overlooking the whole base in the jungle night. He seemed to stare out into the jungle itself, as if wondering what the lone soldier was doing out in the vast darkness, what he was going to do next. The Major watched him thoughtfully again, but said nothing until there was a knock on the office door.

"Come in."

Haggarty turned back into the room and stood against the wall near the window. The door opened and guards brought in Marsha and Olds. They were still manacled, but the chains around their necks were gone now. Olds's arm was still bandaged, and there were new bandages on his neck and Marsha's leg from the fight on the rafts. The guards stood behind them as they faced the Major.

"I need to know why you backtracked on our weapons that were confiscated by the U.S. government. I need to know who you're working for," the Major said quietly.

"We're private citizens looking for this lady's husband," Olds said, his voice indignant. "We protest your vicious attack on us and the Yamano helping us! We protest this cold-blooded murder!"

"If that slimy Captain Tostao told you anything else," Marsha cried, "he's lying!"

The Major laughed. "I suppose this Mack Bolan is just helping you find the lady's husband?"

"Exactly," Marsha said. "You've been listening to the lies of that despicable Brazilian. Do you know—"

"Captain Tosao is dead," the Major said, shrugging. "I suppose he was pretty rotten, but it makes no difference now. Your friend Bolan killed him. Exactly how does that help you find this missing husband?"

"It doesn't," Olds said. "But if Bolan killed that swine, it was because he led us into your ambush."

The Major nodded. "That's probably right, and I guess he was trying to help you when he shot up our parade. The trouble is, don't you two think it's strange that such a well trained and expert killer should be working so hard to find someone's husband?''

Haggarty stepped away from the wall and stood closer to the two prisoners. "Not when the missing husband is an MI6 agent," the renegade British officer said. "Not when the wife's helper is also an MI6 agent, or when the loyal wife is retired from MI6.''

Olds glared at Haggarty, disgust all over his normally calm face. "How does it feel to be a traitor, Haggarty?''

"Rewarding," Haggarty said "How does it feel to serve a bankrupt government that hasn't got the guts to fight anyone but two-bit Argentinians?''

"What would a turncoat know about fighting anything, Mr. Haggarty?" Marsha said. "You certainly aren't down here to fight, are you? Money, isn't that your motive?''

"What I'm doing here isn't the question right now, Mrs. Barr. I'd say the question is what are you really doing here? Or, more accurately, what was your husband doing to turn up missing in this part of the world?''

"Was your husband investigating my actions, Mrs. Barr?" the Major asked.

Marsha said nothing.

"Because," the Major said, "if he was, he could have been one of the two agents we've had to execute over the past few years, and that would be too bad.''

Marsha went pale. Olds steadied her, and they stood defiantly in front of the Major and Haggarty.

"So he was investigating the Major," Haggarty said. "And so are you two."

Marsha pushed Olds away and turned on the scarred renegade. "He was serving his country, Haggarty. If he died, he died with honor and pride. Those are things a turncoat will never know."

Haggarty shrugged. "I simply joined a better organization with, believe it or not, better goals. The Major may be the best chance this stupid world has for real peace, Mrs. Barr. A peace through real strength, not through appeasing the Commies and their pawns. You might find we're not half-bad if you'd really look at us."

The Major smiled. "He's right, you know. We really aren't what we seem, and your Mack Bolan isn't going to help you."

"What makes you think that, Major?" Olds asked. "Bolan's an amazing chap."

"So I've noticed," the Major agreed. "Just who is he working for? I mean, he's obviously not MI6. CIA? Some other secret American agency? Himself?"

Marsha smiled. "You'll just have to catch him and ask him."

The Major shook his head. "Too much trouble. He's alone out there, and in the jungle, to be alone is to be as good as dead. He has no chance against man or nature. He can never penetrate this base alone, and without a source of supply he'll die out there."

"Maybe," Haggarty said, "you should tell him to give up. Join us, bring him in. I'm sure he's close enough to hear your voice on a loudspeaker."

Both Marsha and Olds remained silent.

"Then he'll die," the Major said. "Another skeleton on the jungle floor. In ten thousand years or so, a drop or two of oil for future engines, eh?"

CHAPTER TWENTY-ONE

The mercenary patrol passed below the low ridge where Mack Bolan lay hidden in a tiny brush-covered culvert. The soldier lay silent and invisible in the night, watching the patrol disappear along the jungle trail. Five minutes passed, and he heard soft, light steps moving through the jungle off the trail. Bolan flattened deeper into the culvert on the ridge and held his knife ready.

The second patrol came like the silent shadows of the jungle itself. It moved forward in a skirmish line extending deep into the trees on both sides of the trail. The men stepped as lightly as stalking jaguars, and their prey was Bolan.

It was a tactic used from the Romans to the Vietcong to trap patrols and guerrillas, and still worked against the untrained and inexperienced. But it wouldn't work against Bolan.

If a member of the second patrol came close enough to spot him, that soldier would be dead in an instant. But none did. They passed on both sides of his hiding place and were gone as silently as they had come.

Bolan waited another fifteen minutes. No one else came, so he slipped out of his hiding place and began to trot back toward the Major's jungle stronghold. He remained alert for any more patrols, but he didn't think there were any. His count said there were two twenty-man patrols out now and no more. They had all passed, and there should be nothing between him and the perimeter defenses.

Silently he ran through the forest, reaching the first perimeter outpost of the base without mishap. Now the problem was to get inside—and to get inside unseen. From his cover in the jungle he studied the main gate. A twenty-foot-high wire fence led away from the gate on both sides. The fence was topped with electrified barbed wire. That was no problem.

The problem was the two-man guard posts dug in and bunkered on both sides of the fence with an intricate field of fire that covered each other like a blanket. He slowly circled the entire base. The fence went all around, and so did the bunkered guard posts. Inside and outside, with two inside posts covering each outside post—even along the river where there were also camouflaged towers.

Bolan probed, looking for a weakness, but he found none. The posts were expertly placed, the mercenaries trained and efficient. Each post covered the others. With the fields of fire and vision overlapping, even if he could take out any single one without alarming the whole base, it would still not make a breach in the perimeter.

A bad performance of any single post wouldn't leave a hole in the defenses. An entire group of posts would have to be taken out before there was any hope of breaking through to the base itself. The Major really knew what he was doing. And soon he would have nuclear weapons if it turned out he *was* behind the thefts and kidnappings.

Worse, the mercenaries seemed to be well trained and dedicated, a lot more than most mercenaries Bolan had run into in his lonely war. It showed once again what the soldier had learned so many times—evil could be as efficient, organized and dedicated as good, lies as dedicated as the truth. A strong leader could inspire real men to the heights of dedication no matter how wrong and vicious the cause.

The Major's base was as impregnable as the best U.S. base in Nam. It would take a tough company to break through and make an effective diversion to give him an opening to get in and reach Marsha and Olds, to get in and find out what the Major was really up to. But he didn't have a company. He didn't even have a squad. All he had was himself. If the Yamano warriors hadn't . . .

The big soldier lay silent and watched the main gates with their guards and outposts, the high fence with its barbed wire fading into the distance. They were well trained and dedicated, maybe, but they had no real experience. His mind made up, he sprang to his feet and trotted back into the deep jungle, heading northeast, away from the camp.

MARSHA BARR AND CECIL OLDS had had a shower, breakfast and a good lunch. They wore clean clothes and had had their wounds newly treated and bandaged. Olds was clean-shaven and Marsha had washed her hair and blown it dry.

Clean, comfortable and well fed, they sat facing the Major in his office.

The Major smiled. "Better eh,"

"Much," Marsha said. "Why?"

The Major laughed.

"Blunt," Olds said, "but to the point. Why the kid gloves after the iron fist?"

"If chains and handcuffs don't work," the Major said, "try a full stomach and clean clothes."

"That won't work, either," Marsha said.

"Who knows?" the Major said. "You never know what can work until you try. The Romans ruled the known earth, and they didn't put a lot of faith in theories or absolutes. What worked, what was possible, what was best for them. You know the Romans?"

"Orgies and all that?" Olds said.

"Rather out for themselves, weren't they?" Marsha said.

"Of course they were." The Major stood and paced. "That's what the world's about—practical, logical, powerful and ruthless to their enemies. That's how they brought peace and order to the whole world, and that's how we'll do it." He turned and looked at them. "I need good people. All the people I can get. No man does big things alone. I have your countrymen Haggarty and Greenleaf. I'd like you to join me, too, but first I have to know everything you planned to do here, what MI6 knows about me, who this Bolan is and who he works for."

"You already asked us all that," Marsha said evenly.

"And I'll ask again and again," the Major said, "because I intend to know the answers one way or the other. Now, was your husband investigating my activities, Mrs. Barr? When was the last time you heard from him? Exactly what brought you down here?''

''I don't think this tactic is going to work any better than the handcuffs and chains,'' Marsha said.

The Major looked at Olds. ''What was Steve Barr's assignment from MI6?''

''You know, they never told me.''

''What was your assignment? How did the two of you find out about the Red Army in the Rockies?''

They said nothing.

''Who does Bolan work for?''

Silence.

''You understand that I can't let you leave here until I know why you were sent, what MI6 knows, who Bolan is and who sent him. I'll find out all of that. I always do. It's necessary that I find out, and when it's necessary there are ways no one can hold out against, believe me. It's not something I like, but I'm trying to save our civilization from the barbarians, the inferior people, the mongrels, and I'll do what I have to.''

They said nothing.

''No hurry. You're not going anywhere until I find out.'' The Major looked at them for a few minutes, then finally said, ''Let's talk about what happens after you tell me what you know. You need to think about life and death, about the wisdom of changing sides. Think about your self-interest. If you take good care of your own interests, the future will take care of itself.''

Marsha finally spoke. ''The future and our side are the same thing.''

"Loyalty? Remember what the Bible says. 'Put not your trust in princes.' Or in principles. Princes are never loyal to you in the end, and principles always fail you because they depend on other men. Other men rarely do anything when the chips are down, except save themselves."

They said nothing.

"For instance, if you're counting on Bolan to help you, I have a report that says he's gone already. He's nowhere out there. We have word that he was seen twenty miles north and moving fast away from here."

They said nothing.

"Even your Bolan knows when he's beaten, and you'd better think about that, too."

BOLAN SLEPT that night in the Yamano village that had been burned to the ground days ago, then continued northeast at dawn. During the second night he slept in the heart of the rain forest with only the chattering of monkeys to keep him company. By the third night he reached the Yamano village where they had met Captain Tostao. His motor launch was still moored in the river next to his tent.

Bolan found the leader and warriors in the men's hut. They were dripping with the green slime of *ebene* and greeted him warily, offering some of the drug and fingering their spears when the big soldier refused. Without Tostao he couldn't speak to them, so he squatted in the hut and tried to draw in the dirt the story of the failed expedition against the Major.

The natives squatted, too, their eyes wild with the hallucinogen, and stared suspiciously at Bolan. There was no way he could make them understand what he wanted. He kept trying, drawing the crude pictures, speaking broken English, but their faces remained confused.

Finally he gave up and left the hut to think about what else he could do. Every hour put Marsha and Olds in greater danger and gave the Major more time to develop his nuclear weapons. He knew Marsha and Olds would hold out as long as they could, but there were ways of questioning that no one could hold against forever.

He went into the dead Brazilian cop's tent. Maybe there were notes on the Yamano language he could use to get through to the Indians. He found no notes on the language, but plenty of evidence of Tostao's involvement with the Major, including a little black book with neatly entered payoffs. No wonder the Major could operate so easily. He was probably paying off every local official in all three countries. Deep down beneath the slimy belly of all the evil, from drug and porno kings to dealers in death and strutting dictators, were the bureaucrats and politicians on the take.

While he was looking at the black book, he heard something behind him. Beretta out and cocked, whirled around to see a young Yamano woman standing inside the tent. She said something to him, and the big soldier shook his head to show he didn't understand Yamano. She spoke again, and suddenly he realized she was speaking English!

"Where boss?" she repeated.

It was broken, barely understandable English, but it was English. She could help him get through to the warriors, tell them what he wanted to do. He realized that she must have been Tostao's woman; the Brazilian had taught her some English, not Portuguese, because he wouldn't have wanted her talking to his bosses or anyone who knew him.

"He go downriver," Bolan told her.

She didn't seem surprised. "When boss come back?"

"Soon," Bolan lied. She wasn't going to help him if she knew Tostao was dead. "You come. Boss send me get help."

"Help?"

"Need warriors."

Again she didn't seem surprised. She even smiled. "Boss be rich man."

Now Bolan wasn't surprised. The Brazilian must have used the Yamano warriors for his own purposes before, maybe to steal from other tribes. That would help him when he got her to tell the warriors his plan. "You come," he said. "Talk to warriors."

She followed him out of the tent and back to the men's hut. Bolan knew women weren't allowed into the hut, so he went in alone to find the village leader. The men were all lying around now, lost in the false dream world of drugs, but the leader wasn't there. Bolan went back out. "Where village chief?" he asked the woman.

"Chief?"

They had no concept of a chief.

"Old man lead boss."

She nodded, then led the soldier across the small clearing between huts to a hut larger and better than the others. Four women sat near it, working to prepare food, while a dozen children played in the dirt. It was the hut of the strongest killer in the village, the man with the most wives, spears, pots and children. She called out something in Yamano, and the leader of the village came out.

"Say I talk," Bolan told Tostao's woman.

The leader spoke and the woman translated. "What great warrior talk?"

"Tell him I have come from where many white men kill Yamano, steal women, burn villages."

The leader scowled. "Where this place?"

"Three days' journey."

"We go kill."

Bolan picked up a stick and drew a large circle with a smaller circle in the center. "Too many white men. Need many Yamano. Go to other villages, bring many warriors."

As he talked and the woman translated, he drew other small circles inside the big circle to indicate nearby villages. The leader stared at the ground, then at Bolan. His eyes grew wide and he shook his head violently. "Never do. Warriors kill."

"White man more danger."

The leader thought it over, then nodded. "Will try."

The Yamano headman went to the men's hut, and soon the rest of the warriors began to emerge, still half-stoned from the powerful hallucinogen. The older warrior explained everything to them. They argued, debated and resisted, but finally, with the smarter ones realizing that Bolan was right, they came around. They would go to other villages at the risk of their lives to convince the other warriors that the white men three days to the south were a great danger that had to be eliminated.

CHAPTER TWENTY-TWO

Captain Miles Haggarty stood before the Major. He was in dusty, sweat-stained fatigues. "No sign of him anywhere, Major. Looks to me like he's thrown it in and gone home. That report of him heading north seems to have been accurate. We haven't spotted any trace of anyone still out there."

The Major stood on the firing range, his old Springfield sniper rifle steadied by its sling as he pumped round after round into a three-hundred-yard target at five hundred yards.

"I don't trust this man, Haggarty. He's got nine lives. He's also smart and well trained. He'll be back."

"Then we'll stop him when he does come back."

"Just be sure you keep the guard up." The Major put two more slow shots into the tiny bull's-eye five hundred yards away. "Full security, patrols out, aerial surveillance, the works."

"For one man?"

"This one man seems to be special, and we don't know that he'll be back alone. He could bring an army this time."

Haggarty nodded but didn't leave. "How are we doing with the two prisoners?"

"Not good."

"The nice-guy treatment hasn't softened them up yet?"

"I don't think it's going to," the Major said, squeezing off two more bull's-eyes.

"I've seen it work a lot of times, Major," Haggarty said. "They get so comfortable that when we suddenly put the chains and pressure back on they can't handle it. You can take a lot if you're ready, but not if you're softened up."

"With these two I don't know." The Major shot six in rapid succession, and only one drifted out of the center. He swore. He was in a bad mood. The scientist Claudius Lev still hadn't cracked, and now it looked as if the two agents weren't going to, either, without the full treatment. The Major didn't like torture. It was a lot of trouble, and too many times the victim died before you got what you wanted. "I think you better try talking to them. Fellow countrymen, all that crap. But hammer it home that we won't wait much longer."

Haggarty nodded, climbed into his Land Rover and left the Major still shooting with the trainees at the range. He drove to the detention barracks where they were keeping the two MI6 agents. Striding in, he returned the salute of the guards on the door. But before he went to the detention room where they were holding the two prisoners, he knocked on an unmarked door at the far end of the barracks. The two mercenaries seated at the TV monitors, one blond, the other dark haired, jumped to attention, and Haggarty returned their salutes. Then he studied the monitors, which showed only empty rooms.

"No camera in the British agents' room?" the captain asked.

"No, sir. Major's orders," the blond monitor watcher said.

Haggarty nodded. It was part of the softening-up process. Take away all sense of being watched, all sources of resentment. As little as possible to remind them of their prisoner status, or their danger. Even the audio bugs were visible, built into the walls themselves, a lesson the Major had picked up in his days with the KGB.

"Heard anything?" Haggarty asked.

"They just talk about some guy named Steve," the dark-haired mercenary said. "About how they've been trying to find him."

"And a guy named Mack Bolan they figure'll bring help," the blond guy added.

"They don't say anything the Major wants to hear," said the dark-haired one.

"They don't say damn much about nothing," the blond groused.

"Standard," Haggarty said. "They're trained agents and they know anywhere they're locked up will be tapped. It's a reflex. The Major's decided to leave them strictly alone for at least a couple of more days to see if we can put them off their guard."

"Most of the time they don't talk at all," the blond mercenary said.

"I guess they do know they're bugged, eh, Captain?" said the other guy.

Haggarty nodded. "They know. You two take your break. I'll listen for a while."

The two mercenaries didn't need an invitation. They hurried off for the PX. Haggarty sat down at the computerized electronic surveillance unit. He listened for a time, but there was no sound from the barracks room where the two British agents were being kept. Then he got up and made sure the automatic door lock on the outer door was secure.

Stepping quickly back to the console, he went around behind it, took a screwdriver from his fatigue pocket, disconnected some wires and made some rapid reconnections. Finished, he returned to the front of the console and worked the computer keys. On the screen nothing showed; there was no alarm message to signal the reconnections he had made. Satisfied, he sat back and thought for a time. Then there was a knock on the door, and he opened it to let the two mercenaries back in.

"We brought you a Coke, Captain," the blond mercenary said.

"And a Snickers," added his dark-haired companion.

"Well, that's damn nice of you guys. Thanks." Haggarty took the Coke and candy bar and sat drinking and chatting with the two men for a while. "They sure don't talk much, do they? Are you sure their bugs are on?" he finally asked.

The blond mercenary ran a check and nodded. "Yep, computer says everything's go in that room."

"I guess you sleep a lot when you're a prisoner," Haggarty said.

"One thing they don't do," the dark-haired merc said. "A guy and a dame in a room and they don't do no screwing around. They got to be crazy, right?"

"They talk about this Steve guy like he was there with 'em, and we ain't heard no foolin' around," the other said.

"Maybe it's not so easy to get up interest when you're locked up," Haggarty suggested.

"Hell, wouldn't bother me none," the blond merc snorted.

"No way!" his dark-haired companion chimed in.

Haggarty laughed and left the room. Once outside he listened at the door, then turned and walked quickly along the corridors and up to the second floor. The room was at the far end. The captain glanced around, then used a key to open the door and shut it behind him.

Marsha Barr and Cecil Olds looked up as Haggarty came in. Olds was lying on a comfortable bunk, reading a week-old copy of the *Times* of London. Marsha sat in an armchair and watched the renegade Briton without expression.

"Well," Haggarty said, grinning, "How are my two favorite MI6 agents doing? Ready to tell us all about your assignment down here, and all that?"

Marsha sat immobile. "Do you have trouble sleeping at night, Captain?"

"None at all, old girl. Like a pink-arsed baby. The peace of a clear conscience."

"The mirror," Marsha said. "Do you have trouble looking into the mirror every morning?"

Haggarty sat down in the second armchair in the comfortable room that was more like a hotel than a prison. He looked from Marsha to Olds and back, then shook his head. "You know, this is getting us all nowhere. We've become bankrupt at home. They've all given up, really. Us, the States, Moscow. Nobody really fights for what they believe in anymore, for our whole civilization. The Major's right. We're all going to just lie down and die, give the world over to the wogs and Charlies and assorted Third World barbarians, who can't even take care of themselves. The Major's the last hope we have of keeping our way of life. That's why I joined up, and that's why he made me his second so fast. We've got the same goals, the same ideas, and we're the only chance Western civilization has.''

The wiry redhead, his long scar livid on his grim face, stood up restlessly and began to pace the room. ''I was tired of all the lying weak sisters who want to sell out to rabble not one-tenth as civilized as we are. I was sick of every two-bit radical, terrorist and dictator pushing England and the States around because we were supposed to feel so guilty for all we did in the past. Hell, what we did in the past was bring civilization to a bunch of shit-assed savages, give them more than they'd ever had or ever would have had on their own, and now we're supposed to all apologize for it.''

He turned suddenly and stared at Marsha and Olds. ''Well, I don't think we should apologize for anything. I think we're the best thing that ever happened to this world. Now I've signed up with the Major to make sure we stay the best thing, and so should you two. He needs you. He needs what you know and what you can do.''

''And what about the nuclear bombs?'' Olds asked. ''Or whatever he's doing with the fissionable material, the special alloys and the kidnapped nuclear scientists.'"

Haggarty waved his arms in a violent gesture. "Look, damn it, I'm trying to save you two. I'm trying to help. I've fixed it so the bugs are off. No one can hear us. The Major's only going to wait so long before he gets rid of you if you don't come across, or even if you do unless you join up. I did, and so can you two."

Marsha stared at the wiry redhead. She had been watching him from the moment he'd jumped up and begun to pace. Her eyes wide, she had watched every motion, seemed to listen to every nuance of his voice. Now she stood up. "Steve?"

Haggarty seemed to freeze in midmotion in the suddenly silent room.

"It's you, isn't it?" Marsha said. "You're Steve! The way you move, the way you gesture. Your voice. You're not Miles Haggarty. You're Steve Barr! You're my husband!"

Olds was up now. "By Christ, Marsha, it is!"

"Is this why MI6 wouldn't tell me what you were doing?" Marsha cried. "The hush-hush assignment? Working for an insane assassin who thinks he's going to save the world? Has MI6 gone as crazy as he is? Is Maggie Thatcher so paranoid she'd team up with a terrorist assassin just to stop the Communists?"

"No," Olds said. "They wouldn't even tell me what Steve's assignment was. His mission was too risky. Strictly need-to-know. It's deep cover, no contact. He's infiltrated the Major's organization by really working for him. That's it, isn't it, Steve?"

All this time Haggarty had stood silent in the room, as motionless as a statue. Even his eyes showed nothing as he listened to Marsha and Olds.

Now, when Olds spoke directly to him, he seemed to let out a long, slow breath and smiled at Marsha. Almost instantly his face belonged to a different man, and he walked to Marsha and took her in his arms. "I couldn't tell you," he said quietly. "We decided it was far too dangerous for you. I should have known better."

"Oh, Steve." She held on to him.

"I never thought for a moment you'd really try to follow me. But even if you did, I never imagined you would actually make it down here."

"I don't think we would have except for Mack Bolan. He's amazing, Steve. A strange, solitary man with an inner power you can't really pin down. It's as if he's fighting a personal war all alone. It seems as if he can do almost anything."

Steve Barr, in the face of Miles Haggarty, held her at arm's length for a moment. "Maybe he did too much. You're really in terrible danger, love. You and Cecil and probably Bolan, too, if he hasn't run off."

"Run off?"

"He hasn't been around for days. Our scouts report he was seen heading northeast, the way you guys came down three days ago." The undercover MI6 agent shook his head doubtfully. "You know, we don't really know anything about this Bolan."

"I know, Steve," Marsha said. "I've seen him in action. He's a man who sees a job that has to be done and no one else is doing it."

"So does the Major. Or that's what he pretends." He pulled her to him again, and they stood there for a time just holding each other.

Olds watched them. At first with a smile, and then, slowly, the smile faded and his face grew somber, almost grim. But he did nothing until Marsha took her head from Steve's shoulder and smiled up at him. Steve, in Haggarty's face, smiled down at her.

"What happened to the real Miles Haggarty, Steve?" Marsha asked.

"We've got him stashed in a safe place somewhere up in the Shetlands, I think. I didn't want to know the details in case I was caught. We found out he'd made contact with the Major and wanted to join him, but they'd never actually met. That's what gave us the idea. So we grabbed him and put him on ice, as the Americans say."

"And you took his place?"

"Yes."

Now Olds suddenly spoke up. "How did you get to be so important so quickly, Steve?"

Steve Barr glanced at Olds, and shrugged. Marsha looked up at him when he said nothing.

"By doing your job for the Major very well," Olds said. "Right, old man?"

Barr disengaged himself from his wife and turned to face Olds. "Something like that, Cecil."

"Doing the Major's job?" Marsha said, turning her head from Steve to Olds.

"Even if it meant going against everything you believe in? Going against England. Carrying out terrorist acts, bombings, guerrilla killings, the works," Olds said.

"Steve?" Marsha murmured, her voice wavering.

But Steve was looking at Olds. "What do you really want to know, Cecil?"

Olds stared back at the disguised MI6 man. "You said we were in great danger. Are you telling us you can't really help us, Steve?"

Barr looked at Marsha, then sat down again in the overstuffed armchair. He clasped his hands in front of him as he leaned forward. The knuckles of his hands were white. "If I try to get you out of here, let you escape, it could blow my cover." He looked up at them. "You understand?"

They said nothing.

"I've already taken a chance by cutting off the bugs in this room. No one can hear us, but if that trick is spotted my job's finished. I've done all I can to protect you two, hoped you'd lose the trail, give up. But you didn't. You joined up with this Bolan, and now you're in great danger."

He looked at Marsha. "If I help you to escape, I could blow the whole assignment, everything I've worked for all these months. We'd lose what chance we have of stopping the Major and his crazy plans. He'll get his nuclear weapons, sell them to every two-bit terrorist, guerrilla, mercenary and dictator. He'll blackmail the whole world. We can't let him do that. We can't!"

"There's no way you can help us without compromising the job, Steve?" Olds asked.

"I don't know. I'll do everything I can. Stall, anything. But I can't risk the assignment. I don't even know where he's doing the nuclear work yet. He hasn't let anyone know that except his personal aides. If even they know."

He was up again. "I've got to locate where he's doing the work, where he's holding the kidnapped scientists. I've got to find that fissionable material before he can turn it into weapons and sell it to every slimy little warlord in the world!"

Marsha spoke at last. "What do you want us to do, Steve?"

"Pretend to join him. You'll have to do a hell of an acting job. He's no fool. He's learned more about people, espionage and psychology in his years with the KGB and us than anyone I've ever run into." He paced the small room. "He'll question you, and test you, and maybe even make you kill for him. But it's the only way until I can find where the stuff is and get the word out so we can stop him."

"What if we can't convince him?" Marsha asked.

"You have to."

"Meaning that if we don't we're on our own," Olds said.

"We'll have to save ourselves," Marsha said. "Is that what you're telling us, Steve?"

"I'll try to help you," Barr said. "But I can't blow the mission, Marsha. It's too important."

They all looked at one another in the silence of the barracks room.

CHAPTER TWENTY-THREE

Mack Bolan guided the motor launch out into mid-river, drove it through figure eights and circled in tight turns. The boat handled well, responding quickly to its helm. Even against the current of the river it made speed. He would have to somehow get it overland to the big river.

The old surplus U.S. Army air-cooled .50-caliber machine gun mounted on the bow would add a lot to their firepower when they attacked the Major's base. He figured the mercenaries would be surprised; the Major wouldn't expect an attack by water. With any luck the Major wouldn't be expecting an attack from anywhere. Bolan knew he'd been watched on his trek north away from the base, and when they went back they'd travel at night. All the soldier needed was an opening to slip inside the base unseen. After that he'd take care of the rest.

As he brought the launch back to shore and tied it up, he heard the excited chattering of the children. They all ran across the clearing at the edge of the river toward the forest wall. It could mean only one thing—some warriors were returning from trying to recruit help from other villages.

Bolan walked to the center of the village. The returned warriors looked tired and jumpy. Some were wounded. The leader was with them. Bolan found

Tostao's woman and got her to make a rough translation of what had happened.

"Many enemies," the leader told Bolan through the woman. "Many fights."

"They didn't listen?"

"Not want, but talk. All warriors think bad white man steal women. We go back. They say will do. Will come village. Soon."

"All the villages you talked to?"

"All. Not like. Not trust. But come."

Bolan got the launch ready to roll. With Tostao's tools he made a cradle with wheels cut from logs. It was crude, and the jungle was thick, but it could be dragged and was worth it. The Major's base wasn't going to be easy to crack into. The big .50 would make a difference, and the launch would move the rafts downstream a lot faster.

As the big soldier worked, sweating in the heat and sun, the women helping, the warriors from the other villages came warily out of the rain forest one village at a time. It took two days for them all to arrive. In the end there were just under a hundred warriors.

They congregated in groups of ten to twenty, watching one another warily and making their camps as far apart as possible. It wasn't much of an army, and there was no way to be sure how well they would fight together or how long. But they were a force, something to give the Major pause, and better than nothing.

"Okay," Bolan told Tostao's woman. "Tell them we start at dusk."

She told them.

THERE WAS NO WARNING when the guards came for Marsha and Olds in the dead of night, only sudden flashlights and rough hands shaking them awake.

Half-asleep, they stumbled out of the comfortable beds and saw the squad of armed mercs shadowy behind the glare of the flashlights. The rifles jutting up over their backs seemed three times the size of ordinary rifles.

In a daze they were pushed out of the room half-naked, their clothes clutched in their arms. The squad of mercs fell in around them and half pushed, half dragged them along the barracks corridors, down the stairs and out into the jungle night.

"In!" an officer shouted.

They were in front of a low concrete building, squat and without windows like a blockhouse. There was nothing around it, no trees and no cover—a concrete cube out in the middle of nowhere with a heavy steel door and no light inside.

"In!"

The officer shoved them in through the black maw of the open doorway. Flashlights picked out a steep flight of descending steps. At the bottom a narrow corridor stretched lightless ahead. By the light of the flashlights, they were herded down the corridor, which was lined with steel doors.

"Stop!" the officer barked.

The mercs opened one of the massive doors, then hands pushed them into the blackness. Marsha fell to the floor.

Clang. The door closed, and then silence, not even the sounds of the departing mercs.

Marsha felt hands on her in the pitch-black and re-coiled.

"It's only me, Marsha," Olds assured her.

They stood together in the center of the cold, dank blackness.

"What's happening, Cecil?" Marsha asked.

"The switch treatment, I'd say," Olds said quietly. "Soften us up, then hit us. The kid gloves and the iron fist. You'd be surprised how often it works. It's so much harder to take pain after being comfortable, when you're not mentally ready. You feel vulnerable, confused. Just hang on."

She nodded in the absolute dark, shuddered, then whispered, "Why now, Cecil? I mean, do you think Steve knows they've done this?"

"No need to whisper. Just talk low. This place is all poured concrete and there's no electricity. It won't be bugged," Olds said, and shook his head. "He has to know, Marsha, but what can he do? It's a standard technique to break down someone you want to tell you things. It wouldn't be logical to oppose the Major if he decided this was the time to use the fist."

"An honest difference of opinion," Marsha said. "Why not? He said he'd do everything he could. And now this. It doesn't look to me like he's doing much to help us."

Olds tried to see her face in the darkness, but it was hopeless. "What are you thinking, Marsha?"

"What if Haggarty isn't Steve?" she said. "What if it's a ruse to get us to trust him and tell them what they want to know?"

Olds was silent for a time. Then he slowly sat down cross-legged on what he took to be a straw mattress. "He's your husband. You were sure when you saw him, talked to him."

"If Steve could impersonate Haggarty, why couldn't Haggarty impersonate Steve?"

"That would have to mean they've got Steve a prisoner and have watched him enough to imitate him. But why? They had no way of knowing we'd be the ones to reach here."

"No. You're probably right. It really is Steve," she said, then sat down, too. "But what if Steve really has joined the Major? If Haggarty could, why not Steve?"

Olds said nothing in the chill of the small, dark cell.

THEY HAD REACHED the burned village with the launch and the rafts had been built. Now Bolan and the Yamano waited for darkness. When it came, as suddenly as it always did in the rain forest, the warriors climbed aboard the rafts. Bolan took the helm of the launch. The Yamano leader and Tostao's woman were with him.

The big soldier had already taught the warriors how to steer the rafts well enough. Now he picked up the towline, tied it to the launch and moved out into the river. Soon he had the whole line of rafts moving downriver toward the Major's base.

Before dawn they passed through the narrow point where the other Yamano tribesmen had been ambushed and Marsha and Olds captured. At dawn they pulled into shore, camouflaged the rafts and launch and slept. Tomorrow they would reach the base and go into action. They all slept well. The Yamano warriors had no notion of fear of death, and Bolan had trained himself in the long years of his war never to worry about tomorrow. What would come, would come.

When the last light of day faded over the great rain forest, they were on their way downstream again. The book said you sent out scouts, and moved a vanguard ahead for point, but there was no way even to explain such civilized tactics to the Yamano warriors. They would have to fight the only way they knew how, and Bolan would have to find a way to make the best use of the results.

The second dawn found them under cover of the towering forest at the edge of the great river. So far they hadn't been spotted, but from now on every second was fraught with danger, even with, as Bolan hoped, the camp's guard down.

Mercenary, guerilla or regular, all armies were the same. When there was no immediate enemy breathing down their necks, they relaxed and lost the edge that made the difference. Bolan was counting on this, and the surprise of being hit from the river. With any luck, the inexperienced base defenders would overreact to the attack by the launch and give the Yamano a chance to break through the outer defenses. Then the mercs would panic, rush back to defend the center and give Bolan his chance to slip inside the camp.

That was the theory, anyway. The problem was to make it work with less than a hundred untrained warriors he couldn't talk to. But no one had ever said his war was going to be easy.

The Yamano didn't fight at night, so it was time. He got them all around him and, with the woman translating and the leader explaining, told them his plan. It was as simple as he could make it.

"I take a man for each raft. All other men go to the main gate inland. Get close to it. You hear machine gun firing on the river. You take ten pebbles from one hand and put them in the other. Then attack the camp."

They all thought, stared at Bolan, then each one slowly nodded. They understood what he was planning. Some grinned. There was going to be a great fight. The few with axes and machetes tested the edges. They would fight, and they would fight hard. Bolan hoped that would be good enough.

"Okay," he said to the leader through the woman, "we go at first sunlight."

The Yamano went first, into the towering shadows of the rain forest toward the main gate of the camp. Bolan detailed one man to steer each raft and piled enough brush on the rafts to make it look as if he had an army under cover. Then he waited. It should take them about half an hour. In the launch he would reach the river edge of the camp in ten minutes. He timed twenty minutes, then nodded to the Yamano leader and the woman.

"Let's go."

He had his Beretta, one of the captured AK-74s and two grenades. On the launch he checked out the .50-caliber and lined up the cans of link-belted ammo. The woman would lie on the deck and watch the feed, helping to reload, while the Yamano leader would steer.

"Cast off." Bolan gestured, and the woman untied the lines. The launch moved out into the current and picked up speed with the long line of rafts tied behind it. They moved ponderously downstream. With luck any outposts of the camp would think the procession was nothing more than a Brazilian police launch taking some natives on some kind of trading trip.

The first camouflaged guard tower of the camp came into sight. His watch told him he had three minutes to get into position. The distant guards in the tower leaned on the parapet and looked toward the procession. One had binoculars. Bolan joined the Yamano leader at the wheel and waved lazily at the almost-invisible tower.

The guards on the camouflaged platform went on staring at the launch and string of rafts, and then Bolan saw the place he wanted. Two hundred yards downstream the jungle thinned and a sloping bank came down to the water. The camp fence was no more than fifty yards in from the river.

Bolan saw the two guard posts that covered the stretch of fence, and no mercenaries were in sight. If the posts were manned, they were lying relaxed out of sight behind the sandbags in the morning sun. It was the logical place for the rafts to come ashore and make an attack, since it was out of range from the guard towers hidden in the rain forest on either side.

"Now," Bolan said quietly to the Yamano leader.

The warrior signaled to his tribesmen on each raft and turned the wheel to steer the launch in toward shore. Bolan watched as the rafts all moved toward land, then took the wheel. He suddenly gunned the engine full throttle, and the launch surged straight at the riverbank.

Ten yards out Bolan swung the launch hard to port. The boat turned, almost grazing the bank before heading back toward the center of the river. Bolan cut the line towing the rafts, and they whipped straight into the bank as the launch circled and came up behind them.

The whole maneuver took less than a minute. When it was over, the rafts had almost grounded on the bank, and Bolan was at the big machine gun on the launch. On the guard tower behind them one of the guards stood looking toward them as if puzzled. No one appeared over the sandbags of the two guard posts outside the fence directly in front of the rafts. The downstream tower didn't appear even to have noticed them yet.

Bolan grinned. No one expected an attack from the river, and no matter how many times the Major, Haggarty, Greenleaf or anyone else told the soldiers to be alert, they were relaxed and lazy. Armies never changed.

He opened fire. The heavy .50-caliber tracers flashed in a stream, riddling the platform of the upstream guard tower. Slammed by the massive bullets, one of the guards was lifted out and flung into the air, his flesh and bone raining down into the jungle. The second tried to swing his light machine gun to return fire, but his head exploded in a shower of blood as Bolan's slugs disintegrated his skull.

On the shore the Yamano warrior on each raft set up a shout and fired their arrows at the guard posts. Bolan swung the big .50 to fire over the rafts at the guard posts both inside and outside the fence.

Two heads raised, startled and shocked, above the sandbags. Bolan blasted both into red liquid gore that splashed all across the sandbags. Then mercenaries appeared behind the fence, and the Yamano shot two of them with arrows.

The guard posts opened up and three Yamano were riddled. Bolan could hear sirens screaming inside the camp. Sweating like a pig in the growing heat of the morning, he swung the machine gun right and left, trying to blast all sides. The Yamano woman changed belts as Bolan slammed open the receiver, slammed it shut and continued firing.

Squads of the Major's mercs were arriving now. Onshore the rafts were burning, the Yamano dying all across the open area. Bolan's .50 cut holes in the ranks of the Major's men, turning the riverbank into a slaughterhouse.

He had silenced the guard posts outside the fence. The soldiers lay scattered about in pools of blood across the sandbags. The upstream guard tower had toppled over, its legs cut from under it by the heavy machine gun. But more soldiers were massing behind the damaged fence, and the Yamano leader was down and dying on the launch.

Then Bolan heard distant firing; the Yamano were attacking the main gate. The last Indian on shore rushed the fence and hurled his feeble spear against it as a withering fire from the mercs chopped him into raw meat.

Bolan swung the launch into shore. It was already sinking, its hull holed by a hundred bullets. The Yamano woman had been shot to pieces. The big soldier slipped over the side into the river. Onshore the sirens wailed, recalling the squads of mercenaries to the main gate attack.

Bolan swam underwater until he saw the steep riverbank through the murky water. He surfaced under the jungle overhang on the edge of the bloody clearing where the rafts burned and the dead Yamano lay strewn in the red dirt. Mercenaries moved cautiously out through the blasted fence toward the burning rafts and the launch that lay half-submerged now where it had run into the bank.

There were only small groups of the Major's men. The rest had rushed back to face the new attack. Bolan slipped out of the river and through the shadows of the morning jungle toward the fence. Two mercenaries in the Major's gray fatigues suddenly faced him. The Beretta nailed the first one, but the second got off a shot. One shot. It missed. The Beretta made sure he didn't get another.

Bolan jumped over the still-moving bodies and reached the fence. He turned and ran along the steel mesh into the open space where his big .50 had blasted the holes. The dead and wounded mercs lay inside and outside the fence, but the only active soldiers were outside the fence down by the river.

The Executioner went through the torn fence and sprinted into the cover of the first buildings. Everyone was now at the main gate. The big soldier smiled grimly. They had overreacted as he had expected. It was one thing to be well trained, another to know what to do by instinct. Experience was the only teacher that made the right reaction automatic, stamped it deep into your bones. And Bolan had the experience.

He raced on through the deserted camp toward the main gate to take the defenders from the rear. They would overreact again, give the Yamano a chance to escape, and Bolan could melt back into the camp unseen.

Just then a squad came trotting across in front of him. They saw the big soldier, and he had to use one of his two grenades. He left the six men shattered and crawling on the bloody ground, their uniforms burning, their mouths screaming. They had wanted to make money from death and they had paid the price.

He reached the last building before the gates and stared out. Maybe three hundred gray-uniformed mercs were spread out on the ground, in the bunker posts, under cover, firing at the attacking Yamano. The powerful little warriors were all still outside the fence. They shot their arrows, hurled their spears, but none had come anywhere near the fence.

The road and cleared area in front of the gate was a sea of Indian bodies and blood. They didn't have a chance. They had no idea of modern warfare. All they had was incredible courage, bravery and ferocity, and not even twenty were still standing. It was too much for Bolan.

"Major!"

Standing behind the prone mercenaries, a lean, rangy man in razor-sharp gray fatigues turned slowly to look in the direction of the shout. He was well over six feet tall, muscular without being heavy, and his almost-white hair was without a helmet. He had a Colt .45 automatic at his hip and his combat boots were so polished that they reflected the sun. Beside him was the big, bluff Colonel Hugo Greenleaf in his camouflage fatigues.

Bolan stepped out with his last grenade in his big hand. "Call off your dogs, Major. I'm the guy you want. Let the Yamano go home."

Greenleaf said something to the Major. The tall white-haired commander shook his head. "Very well," he called, then turned and shouted orders.

The firing stopped, and the few surviving Yamano outside the fence saw Bolan. They understood instantly, hesitated for a long minute, then howled one last defiance and melted away into the rain forest.

The Major waited. Bolan tossed the grenade into the empty building beside him and raised his hands. The explosion was still echoing across the rain forest and the camp when the Major walked up to the big soldier.

"Mack Bolan, I presume?"

CHAPTER TWENTY-FOUR

The late-afternoon sun cast long shadows on the floor of the Major's office above his hidden base. Captain Miles Haggarty lounged in a chair. Colonel Hugo Greenleaf stood at the window.

"So we have them all now, eh?" the Major said. "All safely locked up. Now what do we do with them?"

"Bolan's never safely locked up anywhere from what I can tell," Greenleaf said. "I say we shoot them, and right now."

"Come on, old boy," Haggarty said easily. "No one is that good or dangerous. I think, given time, we can make them see our side. We can certainly use them. Two MI6 people with all they know about NATO, and this one-man army of a Yank. A real haul for us, right?"

"I say Bolan's too dangerous," Greenleaf insisted.

Haggarty grinned. "What do you say, Major?"

Their leader was silent for a time in the shaded office, then he looked at the two renegade Britons. "I say I very much like what I see about Bolan. Not the least of it being his daring. That was an almost insane attack on us, and yet the man damn near pulled it off. Do you realize that?" He stared at each of them in turn. "If he hadn't gotten softhearted, he'd have been inside the camp, unseen and unknown. No telling what damage he could have done. He's apparently fearless or, what's much better, totally able to overcome his fear and take giant risks.

"His willingness to take risks for what he feels he must do is absolutely amazing. And that's being alive, really being alive—the willingness to take any risk for what you feel must be done." The white-haired leader shook his head in both admiration and some doubt. "His only weakness appears to be softheartedness, and that could be corrected." He turned to Haggarty. "Tell me again all you know about him, Captain."

"There isn't a hell of a lot," Haggarty admitted. "And most of it is rumor, hearsay, guesses. I don't think I can add anything to what I've already told you. He seems to have come out of the Vietnam mess. Somewhere he picked up an anger that won't quit. The only thing anyone seems to be sure about is that he's a loner."

"How does he live?" the Major asked. "Who pays him?"

"Good question," Haggarty said. "As far as I know, no one's ever figured that out, either. He's a mystery, Major. No one has ever been sure what he's up to or how he gets paid or who he works for."

The Major's cold eyes seemed to glow in the shadowy room. There was almost awe in his voice. "Amazing in this day and age, when everyone knows everything, eh? When there are ten jackals to sell any piece of information to anyone. He's becoming more and more interesting. I think we have to have this Bolan with us, eh?"

Greenleaf came away from the window. "I don't know, Major. I'm not at all convinced that Bolan isn't a lot more of an American patriot than his record seems to show. Aside from mafiosi, profiteers and drug dealers, I've never heard of him attacking any Americans. From what little we know, he could be more of a one-man vigilante army against the enemies of the U.S. The one thing no one's ever accused him of is profiting from any of his kills. If he's a killer for hire, that would be pretty odd, wouldn't you say?"

The Major nodded. "Yes, I'd say that was odd. Haggarty?"

"Another of the mysteries about him," Haggarty agreed. "But the biggest problem might be getting him to join up with any organization."

"What would you say might induce him, Greenleaf?" the Major asked.

"If he's not a Yank patriot, money. He's got to be getting money somewhere, and if it's not from the States, then he has to be stealing it, and that means he's greedy under all the posing."

The Major looked at Haggarty. "Miles?"

"If he's what I think he is, then his biggest weakness is the softheartedness you saw, and personal loyalty. I'd say the best way to get him would be to make it a package—he joins up, or we kill the woman and Olds, too."

The Major studied Haggarty. "Okay, let's find out."

BOLAN SAT on the concrete floor of the narrow cell. There were no windows, a single steel door, a straw-filled mattress and a single blanket. It wasn't the worst prison he'd ever been in, but it would do.

The question was—how did he get out of it? There was always a way, a weakness, a flaw. The trick was to find it before they shot you.

He closed his eyes and imagined every inch of the cell. He'd explored it with his fingers already. The fingers were better in the dark. Sometimes the fingers were best even in the light—they sensed and remembered tiny flaws better than the eyes. Now he went over the cell inch by inch in his mind.

The memory in his fingers located nothing. The cell was poured, seamless concrete. There were no windows. No plumbing, therefore no pipes or drains. No electricity, so no wiring. The steel door was equally seamless, smooth and inset in the concrete so that there were no gaps around it. The cell was like a sealed box. The only good part was that there couldn't be any electronic bugs.

But the cell wasn't totally sealed—there was air. It had to come from somewhere.

Then, suddenly, he heard tapping. It was coming from the next cell. A slow, careful tapping. The pattern became clear—Morse code. Slowly he heard the name Marsha spelled out. He tapped back his own name. Marsha informed him that Olds was with her and that they were both okay.

At least they were still alive, and that meant the Major had a reason to keep them that way. It wasn't hard to figure. If the guy had some big plan to blackmail the world with nuclear weapons in the hands of terrorists, he could use all the inside know-how he could get. Two MI6 agents were a catch. But only if they would switch sides voluntarily.

Suddenly the tapping began again. This time it went on for a long time. Marsha, or Olds, was giving him a big message. He had nothing to write it on and had to commit it to memory the way he did with rendezvous data back in Nam. In the dark of the cell he closed his eyes again and concentrated.

Haggarty imposter. Is really Steve Barr. Undercover on our side. But cannot blow cover. Whatever he does, go along.

Bolan tapped back, You sure?

The answer that came back was yes. Bolan thought about it. Haggarty was doing a pretty damn good job of acting like the Major's right-hand man, even leaving Marsha in that wet rawhide garrote in the boathouse in British Columbia. Then, if he hadn't used such a slow method of death, Bolan and Olds would never have gotten to her in time. It was a hell of a risky maneuver if he had been trying to save her.

The soldier was about to tap out questions for more information, when the steel door suddenly swung open. Haggarty himself stood behind a flashlight. "Up and at 'em, Bolan. Major wants a chat."

Bolan peered at the renegade—or fake renegade.

"Don't be be difficult, old man. I can have you dragged out."

Bolan didn't move.

"We're taking the lady, up too. You wouldn't want us to manhandle her, would you?" Bolan got up slowly, and Haggarty smiled. "That's a good boy."

THE MAJOR WAS WORRIED. The stubborn Israeli scientist, Dr. Claudius Lev, still wouldn't cooperate, and finding a replacement of his caliber would set the program back months. And Lev knew it, too.

Then there were the three agents. How had they gotten onto him and managed to track him all the way down here? Bolan and the woman had located the Red Army unit in the Rockies. Somewhere there was a leak; he'd been sure of that for some time. Haggarty was convinced he'd removed any possible leaks in the chain up in New York, but the Major wasn't so sure. No, whatever had somehow led Bolan and the two Britons here was closer to home.

Alone, he waited for the three agents to be brought into the interrogation room. It was time to stop the games and get down to the nitty-gritty. He had the muscle. Now he would use it.

BOLAN, MARSHA AND OLDS sat strapped into the straight chairs facing the Major, Haggarty and Greenleaf. The room was small and soundproofed, with padded walls. There were wires on the chairs and steel rings and hooks set into the walls and ceiling.

"It's time," the Major said. "We have work to do and we can't play games with you any longer. While Bolan was loose, that was one thing. But now we have all three of you and we have to know."

Haggarty was cheerful. "It's quite simple, really. Are you in or are you out? There it is, right? In or out?"

Greenleaf shook his craggy head. "I say we take no chances, Major. We get rid of them now."

The Major walked slowly around the three strapped into the straight chairs. "I'm not really sure we could trust you even if you did agree to join us," the white-haired former assassin said. "The first thing you'll have to do if you want to join us and stay alive is to tell us everything you've learned about our operation and how you learned it, how you found us, all of it. Understand? Nothing left out."

"We found you through the Yamano," Bolan said. "You didn't treat them right, and they led us to you."

"What led you to the Yamano?" Greenleaf snapped.

Bolan shrugged. "The States is my territory. I've got my contacts and my intel sources."

"How did you get onto the Red Army unit?" the Major asked.

"You deal drugs, you've got no secrets," Bolan said. "Someone always needs a fix, and a strung-out junkie would sell his mother for a hit."

"How about a name, Mr. Bolan?" the Major prompted.

"Like I said, I've got my sources. I don't ask, and they don't tell me where they get their intel."

The Major nodded to Marsha and Olds. "And you two?"

"As Bolan said, old chap," Olds replied, shrugging, "you take payment for your arms in drugs, you have no secrets. MI6 also has its sources."

"But no names?"

"My dear chap, there were probably fifty names in the States alone who would have given us those Red Army terrorists and your arsenal for the price of an ounce of crack."

"Shit!" Greenleaf exploded. "Major, they're stalling and lying and they always will! I say get rid of them, and fast. I've seen too many first-class operations destroyed by taking unnecessary risks on unreliable people."

"All of them, Colonel? Even your fellow Englishmen?"

"Sorry and all that crap," Greenleaf said, "but my fellow Englishmen are the last people I'd trust to do anything against queen and country and all that, right, my dear?" He looked at Marsha.

"You once did a lot for queen and country yourself, didn't you, Hugo?" she shot back.

"I learned that queens and countries aren't grateful," Greenleaf said. "They have very short memories. Now I work for myself, as any sane man should."

"Bravo, Greenleaf," Haggarty said, clapping. "Sanity is a most admirable quality indeed. We work for ourselves, and I suggest that these three can be damn useful in helping us work for ourselves. Especially Bolan there. I don't know about you, Hugo, but I was bloody impressed by that crazy attack he damn near pulled off."

Bolan watched the disguised Steve Barr. The MI6 man could be playing a hellishly dangerous game, trying to use the Major's obvious admiration for Bolan to save all their asses. Or was he just trying to make them believe he was doing that? Who was he really fooling? The Major, or his wife and fellow MI6 man? Was he trying to save them or destroy them? He had them in his power, but they had him, too. They could take him with them.

Greenleaf seemed to be wondering about the disguised Haggarty, too. "Is that Mad Miles Haggarty talking? You sound like a schoolgirl, Haggarty. Where's the White Devil of the Congo?"

"And you sound more concerned about your macho reputation than about using your head, Greenleaf," Haggarty snapped.

"You know we don't need Bolan or anyone else," Greenleaf snarled.

"I didn't say we needed them. I said we could use them, and we fucking well can!"

Greenleaf stared at Haggarty. "What the fuck is it? Are you sweet on the woman? All we get with them is another possible risk! You want the woman? Okay, that I understand. Keep her in your room, but don't let her off a leash and get rid of the other two."

"You're a stupid asshole, Greenleaf! I'm talking long-range logistics, and you can't see past your dick."

"Christ! It *is* the woman!" He stared at Haggarty. "That stupid garrote trick in Canada. You talked the Major into that piece of idiocy, didn't you? Instead of just blowing her away, you come up with something that gave her the time to get rescued and on our tail again!''

Haggarty laughed. ''There it is, right? You've got the imagination of a bureaucrat. That was an experiment that could be damn useful in the future for interrogating prisoners. We have to have something between our ears besides an army manual. Sometimes an experiment goes wrong, but that doesn't mean it wasn't worth trying. With your thinking, Colonel, we'd still be fighting with stone axes!''

Greenleaf balled a big fist and strode toward the smaller man. ''Why you fucking—''

Haggarty leaped to meet the bigger man, fist up and legs set in the basic karate *shizen-tai* position. ''Asshole!''

''Stop!'' The Major's voice rang through the interrogation room. He shook his head, but there was a smile in his eyes. ''You two are getting too feisty for your own good. I like healthy competition, but let's remember we're all on the same side, eh? Whatever we decide to do with these three, I'll make the final decision. Understood?''

Haggarty and Greenleaf glared at each other, but both men nodded.

''Good,'' the Major said. ''Okay, Bolan, let's forget how you got here. Let's talk about what you planned to do. Just what *are* you doing down here? What are you after? Why did you come after me?''

''But we didn't,'' Bolan said mildly. ''We came down here to look for Marsha's husband, Steve Barr. That's all.''

"I see. And what made you think he would be in my camp?"

"We didn't," Bolan said. "We just knew he was somewhere in this area, knew he was working on the international arms trade. We traced those arms of yours to Venezuela and stumbled onto you after your people sabotaged our plane."

"That's bullshit and you know it," the Major said quietly. "But let it pass for now. I'd really like you on my side, especially you, Bolan. I can offer you a strong, tight organization that will make you a great deal of money. In a few years, maybe sooner, we'll be in position to do just about anything we want anywhere in the world. Power to do almost anything. How does that strike you?"

"That usually means power to rip off the little guy," Bolan said bluntly. "And I don't join, Major. I work alone to do what I have to do."

"That's a big mistake, Bolan. Efficiency and power lie in a strong organization. A single organization. In any decent operation of any kind, the bigger and more complete the organization the better. Take my business. There are far too many little warlords and bosses in the terror and arms business, and it's even worse in the narcotics trade. There are generals, bosses, king-pins, warlords from every two-bit country on earth."

The white-haired onetime assassin shook his head sadly. "Look at Lebanon. You have six governments and ten militias all fighting over the same pie. Look at the result. Their country is totally impotent now, and just about destroyed. No one has any real power. The Israelis and the Syrians can do anything they want.

What a stupid waste of men, time and money. No, Bolan, a one-man crusade is doomed to fail."

"If you say so," Bolan said.

"I do say. It's much better to have a central organization with control over everything. It's more efficient. It's safer. It has infinitely more power. In our field, when we've firmed up our position and eliminated the petty warlords, no one will ever be sure who a terrorist is working for, or who's paying the bills, or where the arms come from. Because we'll supply everything from ammo to personnel. We'll handle all terrorism and guerrilla action, supply everything, and if a mission fails, no one will know why and have to hire us to do it again!"

The Major laughed. "We will, in essence, corner the entire terrorism, guerrilla and mercenary market. No one will be able to fight a small war or pull off any guerrilla attacks without dealing with us. We'll work for no one but ourselves, have a market no matter which way the wind blows. No causes, Bolan, only profits."

"I thought you were out to save the world from itself, Major," Bolan needled.

The Major frowned. "I'll ask you one more time. Will you join us, Bolan?"

The interrogation room was as silent as an empty stadium. The Executioner looked straight at Haggarty. Now they would find out which side he was really on.

"I'm sorry," the Major said. "I take it your silence is your answer. Obviously we can't let you walk away. Any of you. I really hate to lose all this talent, but—"

"Talent's easy to find, Major," Greenleaf said. "Get rid of them."

"For once I agree with the colonel," Haggarty said, "but I have an idea how we can do both."

"Both?" the Major said.

"Get rid of them *and* use their talent. At least Bolan's talent and, eventually, the talents of all three. Haggarty smiled at the Major, then at Bolan, strapped in the chair.

CHAPTER TWENTY-FIVE

The giant triple TV screen dominated the tiered auditorium and the rows of seats packed with the mercenary trainees. On the platform below the giant screen, the Major sat on a high chair with a pointer in his hand.

On the center panel of the screen the trainees saw the blasted and cratered field with the frame houses, bunkers, concrete walls and narrow gullies. The left panel showed an empty interior of some kind of concrete structure. On the right the panel was taken up with Mack Bolan's sweating, dirt-stained face.

The Major laughed from his high seat on the platform. "You see how angry Bolan is. His adrenaline is pumped as high as it gets. Violence will do that to you. You will feel you are superman, can do anything. You'll *want* to do anything. You'll want to kill, destroy. Look at his eyes. If he had me in his hands now, he would tear me to pieces." The white-haired ex-assassin turned to his audience. "That adrenaline is what you need to do your job, to win, but it must be trained and controlled."

Suddenly the entire screen went blank.

The Major raised his pointer. "Bolan will take a break in the contest now while we remove the wounded. Our subject has obviously done very well. Four opponents disposed of. The best Roman gladiators disposed of no more than four opponents in a contest. We have shut Bolan inside the house to await his next opponent, perhaps his death. A soldier never knows when that death will come, but it could always be the next opponent, and that's why we must train and learn." He turned to the screen. "We will now run the replay so we can note the fine points of Mr. Bolan's work."

The screen lit up again, and Bolan seemed to fly out of the glassless window of the frame house. The hushed audience watched him check himself for wounds, then crawl in instant replay to the low ridge once more and peer over. The trainees watched the big soldier sight down his M-16, and then they were looking at a split screen with Bolan on the left and one of their own cadre on the right in the two-story house.

The Major froze the action. "Watch this carefully."

The screen moved again, and they saw Bolan count and squeeze off his shot, watched the mercenary instructor slump down, holding his shoulder and cursing in a stream of angry German.

"Look again," the Major said, running the sequence backward and then forward once more. "See Bolan counting? He's spotted Hans at the window twice. He knows ninety percent of the time an enemy at a window will look out every five seconds. So after he saw Hans the last time, he counted to five and fired! That's training and experience. Absolutely incredible seat-of-the-pants know-how."

The double screen started up after the shooting of the mercenary instructor, Hans, and the Major conducted the trainees through Bolan crawling with the cradled M-16 and the tripping of the first wire. "Bolan is so alert on a battlefield that he spotted the trip wire the instant he touched it. Not one in ten would be that quick. Bolan doesn't even have to think about it anymore. It's all part of his combat-trained brain."

On the screen the second mercenary tried to run around Bolan and take him from the rear. "Bolan's heard him. Walters just isn't good enough yet." They watched Bolan shoot the grenade in midair, saw the mercenary hit by his own grenade fragments, watched Bolan shoot the guy in the shoulder and dive back to the concrete wall.

"Why didn't he finish off Walters, sir?" a voice asked from the audience.

"Good question," the Major acknowledged. "Let's discuss that later, eh? Now watch how Bolan has spotted Lieutenant Nbomba and outfoxed him by doing the unexpected—moving straight to where Nbomba has come from! The man has excellent reflexes, and again he knows subconsciously what to listen for and what it means. He hears a faint click, and reacts instantly."

Bolan was up and charging straight through the cloud of dust and debris that covered him like a smoke screen. "Look at Lieutenant Nbomba standing up in the open waiting for Bolan to come at him from anywhere *except* through the explosion! Bolan does the unexpected and is on top of Nbomba before he can even get his weapon up. Our man is a sitting duck."

The Major's voice was scornful as they all saw Bolan shoot the mercenary officer's legs out from under him and run on. On the screen Bolan ate dirt when the fourth merc fired from inside the two-story house, kept the guy down with a quick shot from the M-16, then went for the house across the broken field.

"See how Bolan uses all the available cover? Perfect! He takes advantage of everything and anything. And when bold action is needed, that's what he does."

The hushed audience saw Bolan slam through the door of the two-story house, hit the floor and roll. They saw the merc in the house blast five frantic shots with his pistol, all at where Bolan had been but wasn't. They watched him knife the guy into a bloody heap and turn to stare up at the TV camera.

The replay ended.

"So," the Major said, "you've just seen one of the finest combat soldiers I've ever run into. Learn from what you've seen, and hope you never run into a Mack Bolan before you're ready." He looked around at them all. "All right, now we'll let Bolan loose again and pick up the contest where we left off."

The screen brightened, but on the left side only. The trainees saw the open fields, houses and bunkers of the combat training course, but the interior of the two-story house on the right was black.

"Technician?" the Major snapped.

"Sorry, sir, everything is working," a voice said over the loudspeaker. "I think the camera's out in the house."

"All the cameras in the house?"

"No, sir. Only the one in the ground-floor ceiling. I think that guy's shot it out."

The audience buzzed with a ripple of laughter.

"I see," the Major said. "Very well, let's see what he does when we open it up."

All the guerrilla and mercenary trainees in the packed auditorium leaned forward in their seats as the split screen showed two views of the combat course and the exterior of the two-story house.

IN THE DARKNESS of the empty house, Mack Bolan sat on the floor against a wall. His eyes were closed as he catnapped and took all the rest he could before it was time to move out. He had shot out the camera in the wall and checked the steel shutters that had come down over every exit. There was no way out until the Major and his game let him out, so he sat against the wall and emptied his mind. Until his sixth sense told him it was time.

He opened his eyes but he didn't move. The shot-out camera on the wall was moving like a blind eye searching for the light. Bolan smiled, then the steel shutters slid up and the game was on again.

"HE HAS, OF COURSE," the Major said in the auditorium, his pointer aimed at the screen, "become aware of the cameras and has shot out the one in the house in case I'm in radio contact with our gladiators and am helping them against him by reporting his movements! The man misses nothing, overlooks nothing. He's aware of every possible contingency."

The pointer jabbed at the image of a burly gray-uniformed mercenary sergeant on the screen. The sergeant was just outside the house, his AK-74 ready. "Sergeant Arroyo is going to take advantage of surprise and attack the instant we unseal the house. It isn't exactly fair play, but fair play has nothing to do with combat. Arroyo is one of our best men." As he spoke, the steel shutters went up on the screen, and the burly mercenary jumped into the house, already firing.

THE BURLY GUY in gray rocketed through the door, AK-74 blazing. The dark interior flickered like a movie screen, and the room rocked with the deafening thunder of the assault rifle. But there was nothing to shoot at except for an empty room.

The burly merc heard nothing when Bolan came out of the dark where he had been flattened beside the door, waiting. The Executioner shoved his commando knife in under the guy's rib cage. He let the guy drop, bleeding and groaning to the floor, without finishing him off. Picking up the AK-74, he ran up the stairs to the second floor, shot out the camera there and ran to a rear window. He slid out, hung for an instant, then dropped to the ground behind the house.

THE AUDIENCE HELD ITS collective breath and waited for the burly mercenary sergeant to come out of the house on the screen, but nothing happened.

"Second-floor camera!" the Major barked.

On the screen there was a momentary flash of something moving and then darkness. The audience gasped. Another voice cried, "He shot out that camera, too!"

"Where's Sergeant Arroyo?" another voice yelled.

The screen was now split between front and rear views of the two-story house.

"That's Bolan!" a third voice cried as the audience got into the action.

"But no Sergeant Arroyo!"

"Arroyo is probably dead," the Major said. "Bolan would have figured someone might try to pull what the sergeant did and would be ready just in case. He leaves as little as possible to chance. That's the key for all combat action, guerrilla operations or terrorist attacks. Remember it."

BOLAN SPRINTED around the house. He'd pretty well figured out how Haggarty had set up the combat contest. Each mercenary was sent out against him one at a time and from the opposite end of the course. The only edge they had was that they knew where the trip wires were. Did Haggarty figure he'd guess that?

Was Haggarty, or Steve Barr, playing the Major's game all the way, fooling Marsha and Olds? Or was he fooling the Major, stalling for time, keeping Marsha, Olds and Bolan alive as best he could, playing on the Major's weaknesses to try to save them all and destroy the operation?

At the front of the house he flattened. If he was right, they would now send his opponents from the smaller house at the far end where he had started. He knew there were TV cameras everywhere, and there was no way he could shoot them all out, even if he could spot them. His best bet was to try to keep under cover as much as possible.

Then, out of the corner of his eye, he saw a movement far to his left. This guy was staying down, crawling all the way. Bolan got down, too, and wriggled out to meet the merc.

THE MAJOR'S POINTER picked Bolan up as he came out from behind the two-story house on his belly. "Surprise, that's another key. He's seen Captain Takai crawling and he's going to meet him the same way. Takai hasn't seen him. Bolan maximizes any advantage, all the resources he has."

"We can't see him much, Major," a voice called out.

"And we won't. He now knows there are cameras everywhere and will stay hidden as much as possible. We aren't helping his opponents—he doesn't have to hide from us. But he doesn't know that, and he takes no chances. He never underestimates an enemy, never takes anything for granted, never becomes overconfident."

The tense trainees all stared at the screen as the two crawling men came closer and closer.

BOLAN LAY FLAT behind the concrete wall. He could hear the mercenary breathing on the other side. Which way would the man crawl? He put his commando dagger in his teeth and soundlessly palmed a grenade. Softly he rubbed it along the ground. It struck pebbles and gave off a dull, metallic click. He moved it lightly to the left, and again, as if it were dragging the dirt as he crawled to his left.

Carefully he placed the muzzle of the M-16 so that it barely stuck out beyond the wall on the left. Then he waited and listened. Dirt scraped on the other side of the wall, toward his left. He pushed the M-16 butt an inch farther. And again. The muzzle stuck out more and more from the wall. Silently he sat up with his back against the wall and his AK-74 in his hands. Once more he pushed the muzzle of the M-16 out.

The guy gave a banzai yell as he leaped around the wall and blasted away with his AK-74 at the ground where Bolan should have been crawling to come around the wall. The M-16 disintegrated into pieces, but the rifle wasn't the guy's target. The merc barely had time to look totally astonished before Bolan cut him down with a single burst in the arms with his own captured AK. In one motion the big soldier was up and on the bloody merc. He slammed his rifle butt into the guy's head and knocked him cold, then jumped back behind the wall to wait for the next opponent.

THERE WAS A RIPPLE of applause in the packed auditorium as Bolan cut down the sixth mercenary opponent.

"Yes, applaud," the Major said, his eyes making a sweeping glance over them all. "You're seeing a master soldier in action. You've seen skill, daring, a sixth sense, experience and great courage. But you've also seen one mistake. A fatal mistake in most cases." His hard eyes studied them all. "He refuses to kill his opponents. He had every one at his mercy, but finished off none of them."

There was a silence, and then a single voice spoke from somewhere among the trainees. "Maybe he won't kill without a good reason, sir. He knows this is only a contest."

The Major nodded. "Yes, but it goes much deeper than that. This is a contest to the death. Bolan is as aware of that as his opponents are. He's probably more aware because he's better and smarter. Yet he refused to kill men who would have killed him without thinking. It's a weakness in men like Mack Bolan. He's honest and honorable, a patriot, and that makes him soft. There is only one reason to kill an enemy."

The white-haired ex-assassin paused as if expecting an answer, but there was only silence as they all waited. "The only reason to kill is to stay alive yourself," he said slowly. "And a big part of doing that is to make sure the enemy knows you mean business. A few killings, and an enemy thinks twice before taking you on. As the contest goes on, our champions will get bolder, more daring, because they will know Bolan won't kill them!"

He stared at them all. "Bolan's skill and daring are magnificent. You can all learn by watching him. But also watch how much trouble he'll make for himself by not killing a fallen enemy. You've got to learn to kill a man who's down. That's your business."

There was a silence throughout the auditorium. The Major turned again to the screen, where Bolan was stalking a new opponent, who was advancing more boldly. Then suddenly, the side door of the auditorium opened and Miles Haggarty hurried in. His ruddy face was hard and grim. He reached the Major and whispered urgently in his ear. The Major stared at his second in command, then rushed off the stage.

"That's it!" Haggarty shouted. "Everyone back to the barracks and be ready to move out in ten minutes."

He picked up the platform telephone and spoke sharply into it. On the giant screen soldiers appeared all around the combat course, moving in to where Bolan and his new opponent slowly stood up and waited for them.

The contest was over.

CHAPTER TWENTY-SIX

It was the padded interrogation room that they took Mack Bolan to, not the concrete dungeon. Bolan sat alone on one of the chairs. No one strapped him in. No one guarded him in the room. No one questioned him.

All the way from the combat course to the headquarters building he had seen the mercenaries running around the base, units falling in with full combat gear, officers bawling orders. Something had happened. Something big.

Bolan paced the soundproofed room. Obviously someone was going to question him, so whatever was going on had to have some connection to him. But what? He was still thinking about it, when the door opened and Marsha was shoved inside.

Bolan picked her up and sat her on one of the chairs. She saw the straps and shuddered, as if she'd never seen them before.

"What are they going to do to us?"

Bolan held her shaking hand. "What makes you think they're going to do anything to us?"

"You haven't heard?"

"Heard what?"

"Cecil's escaped!"

Bolan stared at her.

"Escaped?"

"Yes! An hour or so ago. You didn't know?"

"I've been busy," Bolan said, and told her about the contest on the combat course. "They were watching me on closed-circuit television, using me as a training tool."

"My God! Did you . . . did you have to—"

"I didn't kill any of them. At least I tried not to."

She squeezed the big guy's hand. "I'm glad you didn't kill any of them. We came here to stop killing."

"Yeah," Bolan said. "Tell me about Olds. How did he escape?"

"After they took you away from here, they were taking us back to that dungeon, when Steve—I mean, Haggarty—told Cecil to pretend to be sick. Cecil put on a great act of someone with terrible stomach pains. Steve said it looked like dysentery to him, and that scared Greenleaf. Dysentery in a camp like this could put the whole base out of action. So Greenleaf ordered his men to take Cecil to the infirmary and get the doctor."

"This was all Haggarty's idea?"

"Yes. I told you he's Steve and that he's on our side."

"How do you know all of it? How do you know Olds escaped?"

"Steve came to the dungeon and told me. Then he had them bring me here."

"Okay, go on. How did Olds get away from the infirmary?"

"The infirmary is on the edge of the camp to keep infectious cases as far from the main population as possible. That's why Steve had Cecil pretend to be sick. Cecil somehow killed the doctor and two guards, slipped out a second-story window, dug under the fence and got away by dugout on the river.''

Bolan stared at her. "That's about as lucky as I've heard anyone get. How did he kill the doctor and guards by himself?''

"He got a gun from somewhere.''

"How did he get the gun? How did he dig under the fence? How did he find a canoe so easily?''

She shook her head. "I don't know, Mack.''

"I do," Bolan said. "Someone had to arrange all that, and the Major's going to figure it out pretty damn fast. And when he does . . .'' The big guy shook his head. "Someone's playing a hell of a dangerous game with all of our lives, Marsha.''

THE MAJOR RAGED at Miles Haggarty. "How? Tell me how someone under as heavy guard as that MI6 man was could escape and get out of a camp an army couldn't get into! How, Captain?''

Haggarty sat down in the Major's office, his hands clasped in his lap. "That's what I asked myself right off. So I did a bit of investigating while you got the troops on his tail.'' The wiry Briton lit a cigarette. "First thing I remembered was Olds going to the infirmary. We were taking him back from that interrogation before we put Bolan out in the area, when he suddenly doubled up as if someone had kicked him in the bloody belly. I examined him myself, talked to him, and it damn well sounded like dysentery to me.'' He drew on the cigarette and blew a stream of smoke into the office. "That's when I started thinking about Greenleaf. I mean, he decided awfully fast that we had to send Olds to the infirmary. He acted scared to death of dysentery on the base."

"I would have been, too," the Major snapped. "Dysentery on a crowded base could set us back a year or more."

"Yeah," Haggarty said, nodding, "that's what I figured at the time, too. But when Olds made his break, I started thinking a little harder. I mean, Olds had been pretty bloody isolated since he set foot on the base, right? His chances of spreading it began to seem a little thin, and at least Greenleaf could have held off until we talked to you, right?"

The Major said nothing, studying Haggarty.

"So I looked more carefully into just how Olds did bust out." Now he blew the smoke in a hard line between him and the silent Major. "There was no way he could have gotten hold of that gun on his own or by accident, Major. No way he knows just where to dig under the fence where the guard post happens to be unmanned just at that time. No way he knows just where to find a dugout and sail away."

The Major continued to study Haggarty. "What are you telling me?"

"I'm telling you I talked to people at the infirmary. I talked to supply, where the shovel he used came from. I talked to the guys at the empty guard post, and to the guys in the one guard tower still standing on that side."

"And?"

"They all saw some of Greenleaf's men around not too long before everything busted loose. It was one of the colonel's boys who got the shovel out of supply. Greenleaf's guys brought the orders that cleared the guard post. The tower guards saw some of Greenleaf's men around where Olds 'found' the dugout. And," he said, looking up at the Major, "I ran a weapons check. The only pistol I can find missing is a little SIG-Sauer P-230 7.65 mm kept by one of Greenleaf's barracks orderlies as an extra gun. He claims he doesn't know where it is or what happened to it. All three guys at the infirmary were killed by 7.65 mm bullets."

The Major walked slowly around his office, never taking his eyes off Miles Haggarty. "Where is Greenleaf?"

"Nowhere. I mean, he's out with his men after Olds. Or so he told everyone."

The Major walked on. "Find him."

"It's already being done. I want to talk to the prisoners, too."

"Do it."

Haggarty got up and left the office.

MARSHA BARR RESTED her head against Bolan's chest. The big guy held her close, trying to reassure her.

"If your husband arranged it all," Bolan said, "why? Why only Olds? Why not you, too?"

"I don't know, Mack."

They heard the door suddenly close. "I do," Bolan said.

Miles Haggarty stood alone just inside the closed door. He'd come so quietly into the soundproofed room that even Bolan's sharp hearing hadn't picked him up.

"I'm supposed to be interrogating you about the escape," the disguised MI6 agent told them.

"You're taking big risks, Steve," Marsha said. "Why now?"

"Time is getting away from us," Barr said. The voice coming from the ruddy face with the long scar was eerie. "From what the Major's let slip, he has most of the scientists working now. Some of the key ones who've been holding out. The others were already going along. I think he's just about ready to set up the reactor to produce his own bomb material, and I haven't been able to locate the nuclear installation or the scientists." He looked at Marsha. "And I couldn't stall the Major over you three much longer. I had to move, take the plunge."

"What plunge?" Bolan asked.

"Break Cecil out so he could try to locate the scientists and the nuclear lab. I know the general direction and the distance, but I've never been able to stay out alone long enough to find it."

"What makes you think Olds can find the place?" Bolan asked. "Especially with the Major's whole army out tracking him down."

"I couldn't stay out in the forest long enough because the Major would have become suspicious. Olds can take as long as it takes. And with any luck, our troops are all looking in the wrong direction."

"But what about you, Steve? How long can you stay unsuspected?" Marsha asked. "They've all got to realize Cecil couldn't have escaped by himself. It was all too neat, too smooth. It had to have been planned by someone else."

"The Major's already thought of that," Barr said. "And he knows who the planner is, the traitor."

"He knows? Marsha said. "But—"

"Greenleaf," Bolan said. "You framed Greenleaf."

"All the way and airtight," Barr said. "The Major will go for it even if deep down he's not that sure. First, because he trusted me on what he likes to think of as his infallible judgement. Second, because Hugo's too independent and the Major wants to take over his organization, anyway."

"Greenleaf will deny it, Steve," Marsha said. "And that leaves only you."

"He'll protest all the way," Barr agreed. "But I've set it up so that it all points to him, and the Major just won't admit to himself he could possibly be wrong about me."

"It's pretty damn tricky, Barr," Bolan said. "And cold-blooded. The Major will have to kill Greenleaf."

"I've got a job to do, Bolan," Barr said. "And so do you."

Marsha seemed to see her husband for the first time, and she blanched. "How do we know any of what you're telling us is true, Steve? How do we know you're not using us, too? How can we be sure Cecil *has* escaped?"

"I suppose you'll just have to trust me, Marsha," Barr said. "If you doubt me, all you have to do is reveal who I am and I'll be finished."

The three of them faced one another for a long minute of tension-filled silence.

"I think we can trust him," Bolan said at last. "He set up the garrote trick in British Columbia to give Olds time to rescue you if I hadn't. I figure the combat gladiator stuff was all his idea to stall the Major from getting rid of us. He's done everything he could, short of risking the mission."

"And that I won't risk," Barr said, looking at his wife. "Not even for us, love. The job's too important. I still have to locate and destroy the nuclear potential, if not the Major's whole operation."

"I understand, Steve," Marsha said, but her eyes said she didn't really.

Barr smiled at her and stepped closer to take her hand.

"What can we do?" Bolan asked the MI6 man.

But Barr never had a chance to answer. Feet pounded outside the door, which suddenly burst open. Barr just had time to drop Marsha's hand and step back before four mercenaries from Haggarty's company ran in.

"Captain! They've caught that Olds guy and arrested Colonel Greenleaf! The Major's going to court-martial both of them!"

"He's going to execute both of them!" another cried.

"I'll be right there," the bogus renegade said. "Stand by outside."

The soldiers nodded and closed the door behind them. Barr turned quickly back to Marsha and Bolan. "I'll try to talk him out of it. Meanwhile I convinced him to put you two back in the barracks room where we can listen to you. The dungeons were never wired, so be careful about what you say, and I'll get back as soon as I can."

"Be careful, Steve," Marsha said.

"Real careful," Bolan said. "It sounds as if the Major's flipped out this time."

"Yes," Barr said. "I've been worried about that. It's a kind of blood fever since he got the nuclear idea."

Then he was gone.

Three guards came in to take Bolan and Marsha back to the barracks room where Marsha and Olds had first been confined. The guards left in a hurry. Behind the locked door the two prisoners sat and waited.

Outside the barred window they could see armed soldiers everywhere. Time dragged slowly as they spoke only in signs, aware of the ears in the walls. Night came, and they slept.

IT WAS STILL DARK when the door was flung open and the squad of mercenaries armed to the teeth came in.

"Out! Now!"

Bolan and Marsha were marched along the silent corridors and out into the slowly graying dawn. With the mercs silent around them, they went across the dim camp to the large parade ground behind the headquarters building.

It looked as if every unit in the camp—trainees, volunteers and the Major's regulars—was in the ranks of soldiers formed into three sides of a square around the parade ground. One company, in the center of all the others, was unarmed. Bolan recognized the green leaf shoulder patch of Colonel Hugo Greenleaf's mercenaries. They stood sullen and silent among all the other armed units.

"Stand here," one of their guards ordered.

Bolan and Marsha stood at the open end of the three-sided square. They saw the two posts set into the dirt at the edge of the parade ground and they saw the Major standing alone and as erect as a statue at the exact center of the open-ended square.

The ranks of uniformed men were so silent that the distant cries of birds and monkeys in the tropical rain forest floated clear across the dawn. So did the footsteps of the fifteen men who marched from the nearest barrack. A twelve-man squad of armed mercenaries wearing the red wild-boar patch of Haggarty's company lockstepped into the area in two files. One man, who marched in front of the two files, was armed only with a side arm. And two men, unarmed and hatless, marched alone between the files.

"Mack!" Marsha cried.

One of the two unarmed men among the armed soldiers was Cecil Olds. The other was Colonel Hugo Greenleaf. The man in front with the side arm was Miles Haggarty.

"Yeah," Bolan said.

A low rumble emerged from the Greenleaf company of unarmed men as the squad appeared. Tall and massive among the armed squad, Hugo Greenleaf began to shout at the Major. "It's a lie! It's a frame! Someone's framing me and making a fool of you, Major. You've got a snake around you, you hear? A liar and a traitor! You're a fucking fool, you hear?"

The squad marched straight to the posts at the end of the parade ground. Two of the men had to hold Greenleaf, who struggled, raged and shouted more abuse at the Major.

Olds marched in silence. As he passed Marsha and Bolan, he smiled quietly and winked. He looked straight ahead as the mercenaries strapped him to a post. Greenleaf, meanwhile, continued to rant.

Finally Haggarty stepped out to face the Major. The ruddy redhead with the long scar on his face was pale, but he showed no emotion, and his voice was loud and steady as he read out the verdict of the court-martial. Cecil Olds was guilty of the murder of the camp doctor and at least four soldiers; Hugo Greenleaf was guilty of espionage, treason and murder. The sentences were death by firing squad.

The Major's voice rang clear. "The sentences will be carried out."

"Mack!" Marsha said. "Cecil!"

"I know," Bolan said.

"We've got to do something!"

"No," Bolan said, his voice flat, his eyes blank. "We can't do a damn thing and neither can Steve. We'd get us all killed and destroy the mission."

"But . . . Cecil?"

"He knows. He understands."

The firing squad took up position, and Haggarty raised his arm. "Ready."

Greenleaf's voice carried clear across the silent dawn. "It's a lie, you fucking fool!"

The Major stood like stone.

"Aim."

Olds glanced at Marsha and nodded once. Even Greenleaf was silent now.

The volley rang across the dawn and the rain forest, raising a cloud of shrieking birds that darkened the sky. The two men slumped forward. Haggarty drew his service pistol and walked stiffly and without expression to the two executed men. Stone-faced, he shot each once in the head in the ritual mercy of the coup de grace.

"Dismissed!" the Major barked, his voice carrying across the first rays of the morning sun.

CHAPTER TWENTY-SEVEN

In the hot barracks room the normal sounds of the hidden training base outside were subdued after the horror of the executions. On her bunk Marsha sobbed almost silently.

"He was such a quiet man, Mack. Not what most people would expect from an espionage agent."

"Did he have a family?" Bolan asked.

"I'm not sure. I think so, but he kept his private life apart from his work. Even when I was active in the service myself, I didn't know." She lay on her back and stared at the ceiling. "I think once he spoke of hoping his daughter would go to Cambridge, but I'm not sure. There may be a boy in the navy. I know he was nervous during the Falklands thing. I had the feeling then that a son was involved, but he never really said."

"Fighting for a decent life for everyone, for good people and what's right, has a hell of a lot of risks, Marsha," Bolan said. "We've all lost someone close to us in the fight, and a lot of good friends."

She dried her eyes and looked across the room to where Bolan stood at the window, watching the quiet camp below. "You, too? I mean, someone more than a friend?"

"Yes," Bolan said simply. "And a lot of good men I didn't even really know all that damn well." He turned and looked at her. "Men who did what they had to do. Just like your husband did this morning."

She shuddered, her voice almost a whisper. "Poor Steve. To have to...do that to..."

"Stop thinking about it," Bolan said sharply. "Olds was already dead. For Steve to have cracked then would have been to make his death nothing, useless. No, your husband did what he had to do. He's going to have to do a lot more, and maybe none of us are going to get out alive."

Bolan returned to his vigil at the window. Marsha lay silent for a time, then looked at the big soldier's back. "What are you watching for, Mack?"

"Your husband."

"Steve? Why?" She sat up. "You think the Major's going to do something to him, too!"

"No. I think Steve's going to have to come to us to do something. He still can't reveal himself. So the next move against the Major's big nuclear scheme is going to be up to one of us."

"What move?"

"That's what I'm waiting to find out. And I hope nothing's happened to your Steve. We'd have to start from scratch."

She stared at him, then began to cry again. She didn't get the chance to cry for long.

"There he is," Bolan said. "He's coming here."

The soldier left the window and lay on his bunk, closing his eyes. Marsha wiped her eyes, straightened her fatigues and smoothed her dark hair. The door opened.

"Keep the corridor secure," Haggarty said to someone. "I don't want anyone else coming in. Anyone. That clear?"

There was a muffled, "Yes, sir," and Steve Barr closed the door behind him. He just looked at them. Then he turned and stood with his face against the wall. Bolan said nothing. The disguised MI6 agent stood that way, his eyes looking at nothing but the blank wall, for a full minute. When he finally turned to look at them, there was nothing to show any emotion, only a deadness to his eyes and voice.

"Two men who have joined me against the Major are on listening duty. I've gotten maybe ten men ready to join me after...what happened. We have one more chance, and that's it."

"Then this time we do it," Bolan said.

"Steve..." Marsha began.

"No," he said. "The job. That's it. That's what we all came here for. That's what we have to do. Stop the Major. Nothing else."

"Easy, Barr," Bolan said. "Keep it cool and keep it calm if we're going to do what we have to do."

The MI6 man breathed hard, then nodded. "You're right of course. Okay." He came and sat on the bed beside his wife, took her hand and held it while he looked at Bolan. "You'll have to find the nuclear installation while Marsha and I cover."

Bolan nodded. "Yeah."

"Olds located where it is—a flat mesa northeast of here. There's no way in except on foot or by helicopter. It's not too far, but there's nothing there. Olds thought it had to be underground, but I'm not sure.

It's an area of ancient Indian cave dwellings that aren't used anymore. I've got some men ready to help now, as I said, and I've opened contact with the townspeople in Miradora who are fed up with the local big shots getting rich on payoffs to let the Major take over their town."

"Why not stop it, then?" Marsha asked.

"Because the Major's people outnumber them five to one, and he's got the area sealed off from the rest of the world. He pays off every local authority the way he did Tostao, and they pretend he doesn't exist. But I've got a lot of townspeople ready to fight when I give the signal."

"First we have to locate the nuclear stuff," Bolan said, "or he'll just move to another location. We've got to stop him cold here."

"Yes," Barr said.

"How do we do it, and when?"

"You tell me, Bolan. How do we find the actual location on a barren mesa?"

"Who *does* know where it is?"

"The Major and the staff and guards he has there."

"How does he get there?"

"Helicopter."

"Then the pilots know."

"He flies himself."

"Where do the staff and guards stay?"

"At the laboratory, as far as I can tell."

"Then there's only one way to find it," Bolan said. "The Major will have to show us himself."

Barr stared at him. "Of course. We have to get the Major to go there while you're watching. A two-man job."

"You here, me there. When, and how do you get me out?"

"As soon as possible. And getting you out will be easy now that I have help in town. The problem will be making sure the Major doesn't discover you're gone, and getting him to go there at the right time. But I think I can handle both of those." He turned to Marsha. "Love, my guys won't be on the listening post all the time. The next shift will be men still loyal to the Major. You're going to have to make them think Bolan is still in this room the whole time. They'll be listening. Any hint he's not here will send them running to the Major on the double."

"All right, Steve," Marsha said.

Bolan stood up. "Then let's get going."

AN HOUR LATER the camouflaged supply truck pulled up to the small side gate of the base. The two mercenaries in the cab wore the red wild-boar patch of Miles Haggarty's company. One leaned out and grinned at the gate guards and the men in the two armed guard posts inside the fence.

"Beer run," the soldier said, holding out his pass.

The gate guard looked at it carefully for both destination and signature. His partner checked the rear, where cases of empty bottles were stacked beside empty kegs. The second guard climbed up over the tailgate, looked around, then jumped down and nodded. The first guard waved the truck through.

The two soldiers waved at the solemn guards in the two outside guard posts before the truck disappeared along the road into the rain forest. Once out of sight of the gate and posts, the passenger merc tapped lightly on the rear of the cab. "You okay, Bolan?"

"The Executioner's faint voice was muffled. "I stink of stale beer in this keg, but that's all."

The two mercs laughed and drove on along the dirt road through the towering walls of green.

THE MAJOR SHOUTED orders at the surly troops sulking through the obstacle course. "I hated to have to do it, Miles," he said to Haggarty, "but spies and traitors have to be dealt with harshly. If you want to succeed, you must be ready to kill your enemies. I told that to the trainees when we watched Bolan in the arena, and a commander has to live by his own rules."

"They'll get over it, Major," Haggarty said.

"More of Bolan in the arena would do them good. They seemed to enjoy that. Have Bolan and the woman told you anything yet?"

"Not yet, but they will."

The Major turned to look at Haggarty. "You think going back to the soft treatment is a good idea?"

"After the executions, I'm sure of it. Everyone wants to live. Let them stew awhile, talk it over. Without Olds, the woman will be especially vulnerable and shaky."

"What's happening to them now?"

"I hope they're lying around worrying," Haggarty said. "I hope they're talking and we're listening."

The Major nodded thoughtfully as he watched Haggarty. "I hope you're right, Captain."

THE REMOTE LITTLE river town of Miradora had changed a lot since the Major and his base had come to the area. Dusty Avenida de los Angeles had fifteen cantinas on it now and five brothels, and the mayor had added a two-story prefabricated private office to the Quonset hut town hall for his own use.

On the river itself, with its own dock, was the new private warehouse where the supplies to be sold to the base were stored after coming upriver from Içana. The warehouse was owned by the mayor's brother. Prices quadrupled on the long trip from the sea upriver to Içana, then doubled again on the short trip from Içana to Miradora. The Major charged his clients and trainees double again. The clients asked for bigger contributions from their backers. Everyone was happy.

Except the ordinary people everywhere, even in Miradora. Their town had been stolen from them by a gang of thugs, and they wanted it back.

"The son-of-a-whore mayor and his brothers and sisters and fucking cousins kiss the ass of this crazy man with his toy soldiers and the rest of us eat dirt."

The speaker was a short, thick, peppery old man with a drooping white mustache and skin the color of saddle leather. He was waiting in the warehouse when Bolan crawled out of the beer keg. Since he was one of the few in Miradora who could speak English, Haggarty had recruited him to guide Bolan.

"Worked for *yanqui* oil drillers all over. Sure I take you to that mesa if it helps send this Major and his gang back where they came from."

The old man whistled as Bolan holstered his Beretta 93-R and slipped the commando knife into his boot. "The *rojo* with the scar says he will give us Miradora back so we can throw the mayor and all his family into the river. For that I will do anything. Come, *yanqui*."

"How much longer can we wait, Captain?" the Major asked.

"I know," Haggarty admitted. "I figured if we left them alone long enough the woman would break Bolan down for us, but he's a tough nut."

"We know that much already," the Major said dryly. "But that aside, we don't know any more than when they walked in here, do we?"

"We've just got to give it time, Major," Haggarty insisted. "You'll never get anything out of Bolan with threats or torture, believe me."

The Major tented his hands in his quiet office and studied Haggarty over the tips of his fingers. "I have believed you, Miles. Ever since you joined us. I believed you, and you've proven yourself right almost always. That's why I made you my second so quickly. I recognize talent, industry and imagination when I see it. You work hard, you have great skills and you're almost always right."

"Thank you," Haggarty said. "So give me—"

"Almost always right," the Major went on, ignoring Haggarty, "until recently. Recently you've been wrong quite a few times. Wrong and inefficient. Somehow whatever you suggest seems to go wrong, slow us down."

"No one's perfect, Major. I've been having a poor run, I suppose. But I'm sure this time. The only way to break Bolan is to wait."

But the Major wasn't listening; he seemed lost in his own thoughts. "Poor Hugo insisted he was framed, that someone else let Olds loose. I wonder if Hugo could have been right. I don't particularly care about Hugo. I wanted him out of the picture, anyway. I was ready to take over his contacts, clients and projects. But what if he was right?"

"I suppose it's possible," Haggarty acknowledged. "I never thought of Greenleaf as a turncoat or a fool, and it seemed as if he'd acted like both. Still, maybe he had a reason. I didn't mention it, but he said something odd while I was interrogating him after you had him arrested."

"And what was that, Miles?" The Major continued to stare at his second in command.

"That Olds had spotted something damn interesting out there on a mesa in the mountains. I suppose it was our secret nuclear lab, eh?"

The Major sat bolt upright. Haggarty went on as if he hadn't noticed the Major's alarm.

"Hugo said he marked it so he could find it again. Good thing he won't have the chance."

The Major froze. "Marked it?"

"Some sort of radio beacon, it sounded like. Hugo was good at that sort of thing. Standard merc procedure to locate supply drops and all that."

The Major was on his feet. "I'm going to give you one more day. If Bolan or the woman hasn't talked then, I'll take care of them myself."

The white-haired ex-assassin stalked out of his office.

MACK BOLAN FOLLOWED the old man up the first steep slope of the mesa as the jungle began to thin. The old guy climbed like a cat, zigzagging up the sheer sides at a steady pace even Bolan had to strain to keep up with.

The warrior saw the ancient Indian caves high above in the cliffs of the mesa. He studied them in the afternoon sun, but none of them seemed to be in use. "What's on top of the mesa?" he finally asked his old guide.

"*Nada*. Dirt and dust no good to anyone, not even our whore of a mayor."

They climbed on at the killing pace, sweat streaming down Bolan's body. The old man didn't seem to have any sweat in him, just gristle and leathery skin. His guide drove them up so fast that Bolan almost missed the warning outpost.

"Stop!"

Bolan got down on his belly and crawled to it.

It was a sophisticated type of electronic radar that scanned the slopes for anything that moved. The blip on a screen somewhere could be read by an experienced operator to tell exactly what kind of moving object it had picked up.

"What is it?" the old man asked, staring at the tiny unit that moved slowly right and left.

"A kind of radar," Bolan said. "It won't be the only one. My guess is they're set all around the whole mesa to pick up any intruder."

"Radar? What is radar? Come."

"Radar means they know we're here, old man."

The guide stopped. "They know?"

"They're watching us right now. On a screen."

The old man looked up at the distant summit of the mesa to find out who was watching him. If he couldn't see anyone, he didn't believe he was being watched.

"Believe it, old man," Bolan said. "Someone will be waiting for us somewhere up the slope, or they'll come down after us."

"Better they come down," the old man said.

"Much better," Bolan agreed.

They moved fifty yards farther, went to ground and waited. The slope and the rain forest were silent except for the birds and monkeys and the sudden movement of a small animal. Then the shadows seemed to move just above them. A two-man patrol of gray-clad mercenaries was working down the slope as silent and invisible as jungle animals.

Bolan glanced at the old man. The Brazilian, Venezuelan, or whatever he was, smiled. He produced a wicked-looking knife from somewhere in his loose clothes and held it like a man who knew how to use it.

The two mercs came on, alert and wary, but made the mistake of assuming the radar hadn't been spotted. They assumed their quarry was farther down the slope. A fatal mistake.

Bolan rose from the jungle duff as his man passed. He pulled the guy's head back and cut his throat with the commando dagger, then dropped the body on the ground and turned quickly to help the old man.

But he didn't need any help. His merc lay with both his throat and his belly cut wide open, spilling blood into the shadows of the forest.

"Come on," Bolan told him.

They moved on up toward where the jungle finally ended just below the crest of the mesa. The old man's pace hadn't slackened at all after his killing action. If anything, it had increased. Bolan wouldn't want to be in the shoes of the mayor of Miradora when the old man finally got to him.

The burst of automatic fire cut the old man in half, blowing him ten feet back down the slope. He died while he was still in the air, his dead legs still moving as if climbing upward. His eyes were empty, the death too sudden even to show surprise.

It hadn't been a two-man patrol; it had been a three-man one.

Bolan dived to the ground as the second burst of fire sprayed from above. He had made a mistake, assumed there were only two men, and the old man was dead.

The Executioner rolled, crawled and watched for the third burst. It came, tearing the jungle where Bolan had been. That was the third man's mistake.

Bolan zeroed in on where the burst had come from. He crawled forward, his eyes fixed on the spot, watching for any movement. There was none. The guy wasn't moving; he was waiting for Bolan to reveal himself. Another mistake.

Crawling silently, Bolan finally saw the gray merc among the shadows in the cover of a vine-covered tree trunk. The guy was looking the wrong way. Bolan stood up, Beretta in both hands. The mercenary heard him and tried to swing his assault rifle. But two shots blew him against the thick tree.

Bolan turned and moved up toward the summit again. There were no more mercenaries. He came out of the jungle just as he heard the approaching helicopter.

The warrior sprinted until the slope was too steep, then crawled, clawed and pulled himself up the last few yards to the crest.

Among the jumble of rocks at the edge of the mesa, he saw the chopper land in a swirl of dust that blew across the remote mesa. The helicopter touched down on what looked like a part of the mesa itself, but it wasn't. Bolan stared and saw the small building set down in a wide barranca at the edge of the mesa. He hadn't reached the summit, only the bottom side of the barranca, and the building was camouflaged to look like nothing more than a rocky outcrop from the barranca floor. The chopper had landed on the roof of the building.

The Major jumped out and sprinted to a large fake boulder on the building roof. It rose, and the Major disappeared inside. Then the boulder closed behind him. Bolan didn't hesitate. There was no way he could hide now. They would find the dead patrol and know something was wrong. The Major would certainly know what was wrong. There was no time for any plans, only action.

Bolan ran to the chopper, climbed in, started it up and took off for the base a few miles away. He hoped he could get back before the Major alerted them he was coming.

The final battle was on.

CHAPTER TWENTY-EIGHT

Mack Bolan brought the helicopter in low over the base and down toward the landing pad at the headquarters building. He flew with one hand, his Beretta in the other, and scanned the ground.

The mercenaries were still training below. The guards lounged in the posts, and officers strolled through the shadows under the trees and camouflage.

There was no alarm, no action, no emergency. Was it a trap? Or hadn't the Major realized the helicopter was gone yet?

He hovered over the landing pad. No one waited to attack or arrest him. The landing pad area was deserted. Then he saw the solitary figure stroll from the headquarters building toward the landing pad.

It was Steve Barr. The disguised MI6 man waved at him, as if he were waving to the Major. Bolan set the chopper down. Outside, Barr's face was expressionless. The Executioner shut off the engine and climbed out warily.

"Just walk with me," Barr said. "Don't act alarmed or look around or do anything."

Bolan walked beside the MI6 agent toward the headquarters building. He saw the Briton's men at the doors of the building. "The Major didn't call and alert the base?" he inquired.

"He called," Barr told him. "My men intercepted the call. You have to have some luck."

So that explained it. But the Major would be showing up anytime, and he would be mad as hell.

"We go for broke right now," Bolan said.

"We're ready," Barr said. "As ready as we're going to be."

Inside headquarters the disguised MI6 man hurried them into the communications center. His few men guarded it outside and monitored all communications inside. The Briton knew what he was doing.

"Mack!" Marsha hurried to him. "You're all right?"

"I'm alive," Bolan said. "'All right' might be going too far for us right now."

The big guy turned to the MI6 man. "You want to lay it out, what we have, what we don't have, what you figure we can do and how fast?"

"In about one minute flat," Barr said. "I've got twenty-five men of my unit who'll come with me. There might be some more, but we don't have time to find out. In town I've lined up most of the population not related to the mayor and his cronies. I've got a ton of plastic explosive, caps, wire and detonators. Maybe a hundred grenades, concussion and frag, and twenty shoulder-fired antitank missiles. Two night vision systems mounted on M-16s. Enough ammo for all our small arms. And that's it."

"And I know where the nuclear lab is," Bolan said. "Who does what?"

"There's only one way we have a chance," Barr said. "Take advantage of the Major's blood fever. He'll be plenty mad. If we can convince him we're all trying to escape north, he'll send the whole shooting match after us."

Marsha looked at the two men, first one, then the other. "You don't mean a chance to escape. You mean a chance to get the scientists and blow up the installation. That's all you're thinking about."

"Is there anything else to think about, love?" Barr asked.

"We can get away anytime," Bolan said.

"Of course," Marsha said. "So we're talking about one of us decoying the Major while the others go and take out the nuclear lab. Obviously I'm the most expendable in a fight, so I lead the Major away."

"Wrong," Bolan said.

"Wrong," Barr seconded. "Whoever plays the fox has to be so good the Major thinks it's all of us." He looked at Bolan. "Afraid that means you, old man."

Bolan nodded. Neither Marsha nor Steve had his combat experience, and they would need all of Barr's mercs to attack the Major's secret nuclear lab. Bolan didn't think there were more than a dozen guards at the nuclear building on the mesa. Barr, his mercs and the townspeople could handle that without him. The tough job would be fooling the Major.

"We'll all blow out of here in a big show and head north," Bolan said. "Everyone else veers off for the mesa while I lead the whole pack north."

"That's the ticket," Barr agreed.

"Then let's get the show on the road," Bolan said.

Barr's men smashed the communications equipment before they all slipped out of the headquarters building. At the motor pool the MI6 agent commandeered two trucks and a scout car from the duty officer.

"Destination, sir?" the merc officer asked.

"Miradora. Major wants a little show to remind them not to overcharge our guys too much."

The officer wrote it up in his report.

Bolan, Barr and Marsha climbed into the scout car and led the trucks to where the rest of Barr's mercs waited with all their matériel. They loaded the trucks and moved out. Just before they reached the side gate and the road to Miradora, they heard a helicopter coming in from the east.

"The Major, sir!" the field radio operator in the scout car exclaimed.

The raging voice on the radio came in thin and ragged, but it was the Major. "Come in, headquarters! Damn it, why don't you answer? Arrest Haggarty! Come in base HQ! Are you all asleep! Come in base HQ."

"It's from the chopper, sir," the radio operator said.

"He must have contacted a chopper in the air and diverted it to the nuclear lab," Bolan said.

"We better move!" Barr urged.

The Major's voice crackled on. "Come in, damn you all! Secure all gates! Arrest Haggarty! Come in . . ."

At the side gate ahead the guard commander came hurrying out of the guardhouse.

"He's contacted the guards on the gate radio!" Marsha cried.

The guard commander whirled as he heard them approaching. He bawled orders to the guards and guard posts, then tried to claw his pistol out of his holster.

"Drive through!" Barr yelled.

The guards hesitated, confused as the scout car and two trucks suddenly accelerated and roared toward them. The officer didn't hesitate. He got his pistol out and aimed it at the scout car.

"Down!" Bolan cried, unleathering his Beretta.

The merc shot wide of the oncoming scout car, but the Beretta bucked twice in Bolan's hands and blasted the merc officer into a bloody rag doll. Barr's guys raked the guard posts, and the startled guards sprawled for cover.

The scout car and trucks smashed through the gates and roared away down the dirt road between the walls of green. Behind them, the shocked guards recovered too late and sent a futile volley after the vanishing vehicles.

"Twenty minutes," Barr said, "and he has his advance after us."

"No problem," Bolan said. "The quicker he comes, the less he'll think it out. The trick is to make him confident that he's going to get us in the next half hour."

"Give him no time to think about us attacking his nuclear lab," Marsha said.

When they reached Miradora, Barr hurriedly met with the leaders of the opposition townspeople and told them what they had to do. The young ones would come with him and Marsha and his men to the lab on the mesa. The older people would set up the mayor and his cronies to tell the Major that all the escapees had headed north.

"I'll set the trail straight for that Yamano village they burned," Bolan said. "He knows I'm in with the Yamano and will figure we'd head for their territory, looking for help."

"It'll be night in half an hour and he'll have to chase you in the dark. So that's it," Barr said. "Except for one more thing. Wait right here."

The scar-faced redhead vanished into the house of one of the townspeople. Bolan looked at his watch. The Major would be after them just about now. Marsha stared back down the dirt road that ended at the town.

A sandy-haired, freckle-faced, clean-shaven man without sideburns or scars on his almost-boyish, innocent face came out of the house. "Okay," the newcomer said, "let's go."

"Steve!" Marsha exclaimed.

Bolan looked at the new man in Miles Haggarty's fatigues as the real Steve Barr walked to his wife and held her.

Barr shrugged at Bolan. "Wouldn't want you to think I really looked like Haggarty," he said. "In case we don't run into each other again, eh?"

"No," Bolan said. "Ready?"

"Let's do it," Barr said.

WITHOUT HAGGARTY or Greenleaf the Major took command of all his troops himself. Leaving the trainees and reps in the camp, they moved out along the single road into Miradora in the falling twilight. With any luck he'd have the bastards before dark.

The tall white-haired international terrorist rode alone with his driver in a command car between the second and third of his elite companies. He knew now that Captain Miles Haggarty was an imposter and had made a fool of him. He didn't give a damn about Greenleaf; he would have had to get rid of the unruly British mercenary sooner or later, anyway. But he was in a blind fury about Haggarty.

How could he have been so easily duped? Was he going soft? Had he become so arrogant that he was sure his judgment was perfect? So dazzled by his own great plans he had lost sight of everything he'd learned in all his years as an assassin, agent and terrorist? So overcome by a kind of blood fever he couldn't think straight?

Whatever, he'd been a damn fool, and now he had to do something about it. They had located the nuclear lab and the scientists. All right. But they wouldn't take what they knew out of the jungle. That knowledge would be buried in the trackless shadows of the rain forest with them.

It was dusk when he rode into Miradora. He waited in the command car until they brought the mayor to him. The stout, bearded man was nervous in the vaguely military mayor's uniform he had designed for himself.

"What has happened, Señor Major? Señor Haggarty comes, he takes food, water, breaks the radio in my office!"

"Where are they?"

The angry mayor mopped his sweating face in the glare of the vehicle headlights. "They tell me is special job for you, but they not fool the mayor, *sí*?"

"Where did they go, you fat fool!"

The mayor turned pale under his beard. "They... they go to end of road north."

Swearing, the Major ordered his troops forward. Flames suddenly jumped up ahead in the now-full black of a tropical night. It was the trucks. Then...but, no, they'd have used a timer to make him think they were still close.

Still, they were close enough. Maybe a half an hour ahead of him. The Major waved to the young lieutenant, who was the best man he had now.

"They're carrying food and water. Leave everything except the ammo in your guns and go after them. Don't kill Haggarty. I want him alive."

The young officer disappeared into the darkness, and the Major sat and looked at the flames of the burning vehicles. He'd get the rest of his force ready and move out after the lieutenant in twenty minutes. They wouldn't escape. Not if it took every man he had.

To THE EAST of Miradora Steve Barr urged his twenty-five men and the younger Miradorans on toward the hidden laboratory on the mesa.

"Steve!" Marsha cried out. She had seen the flames lighting the blackness far back on the northern edge of Miradora.

"Bolan must have set a timer on the trucks," Barr said. "Make the Major think he'd left only minutes earlier."

Marsha said nothing. She looked back, wondering if Bolan was safe, then shuddered for an instant when she thought about how close the Major and his men were. What if the Major wasn't fooled? If one of the Miradorans talked?

"Steve?"

"I know, love. All we can do is keep moving and hope we get the time to finish the job."

They marched on through the darkness, the Miradorans leading them like jungle cats.

MACK BOLAN SAW the flames to the south. He was high in a jungle tree almost two miles north. He smiled. They would all be so damn sure the fire had been set by a timer, all except the villager he'd paid to start the gasoline burning the moment the Major got near the trucks.

He checked his watch. The Major would send an advance guard to travel light and fast. As fresh as they were, they would cover the two miles through the night rain forest in about an hour.

The soldier slid down the tree and opened his heavy backpack to pull out ten small squares of plastic explosive, wire, caps and a detonator. Then he went to work.

TWO MILES TO THE SOUTH and twenty minutes later, the Major slung his mini-Uzi and marched out of the dusty river town of Miradora at the head of his main force. In his mind the image of the great Julius Caesar leading his legions across the Rubicon flashed like a movie on a screen.

The tropical rain forest closed in around him and his men, swallowing up the two full companies as if they were no more than a tiny squad. With an advance guard out front, there was no need to be cautious. They marched with powerful searchlights lighting the jungle. In an hour and a half they would catch up with the advance guard.

The gunfire exploded ahead exactly one hour after the column had left Miradora. Assault rifle fire. Then there was heavy answering fire from the Major's advance guard, and a series of rapid explosions like a shower of grenades.

"Forward!" the Major bawled.

The companies began to trot through the jungle, the bright lights showing the way.

MACK BOLAN LAY in the duff of the rain forest and sighted through the night vision system. The Major's advance guard came through the night fast and loose, confident of their superior power. Bolan squeezed off a single shot. The point scout sprawled backward, a third eye blossoming in the center of his head.

Next Bolan sprayed the three mercs of the connecting file with a single burst. The three went down as if axed, blood and flesh splattering the jungle. Bolan ran as fast as he could ten yards left, then fired a second burst that ripped and slashed the squad stumbling forward in a panic to find the elusive enemy. He raced twenty yards right, using the trees for cover, and hosed the confused mercs with another burst as they floundered in the dark, forgetting even to return fire as they fell over their wounded comrades.

"Down!" someone bawled in the darkness. "Down, you idiots! Fire! Fire!"

Bolan sprayed one last long volley that emptied his banana clip. He slung the M-16 and grabbed an AK-74, diving behind a thick tree trunk. The baffled and battered mercs fired a ragged volley. Then another. Bolan waited. The firing slowly stopped as the officers realized no one was firing back at them.

Bolan jumped up and ran straight ahead, away from the enemy. When he was thirty yards away, he began to make noise as he ran. The merc officers took the bait. "There they are! Get 'em!"

The mercs jumped up and ran eagerly after the enemies who had bloodied them. Bolan stopped and raked the night behind with the whole clip of the AK-

74. He heard the demoralized advance guard go down, then turned the handle of his small detonator.

The ten massive explosions went off, one after the other, right and left, some at the same time, until there was silence again. Then the screaming and moaning began all through the night. Men staggered around, arms and legs ripped off, eyes blinded, bodies bloody and riddled.

The ten plastic charges had exploded directly where the mercs had fallen to the ground. Bolan turned and headed north. It would be a while before they came after him this time.

CHAPTER TWENTY-NINE

On the jungle slope below the mesa, Marsha waited in the night with the villagers and the twenty-five red boar mercs of her husband's unit. They waited for the patrol to come out to check the single blip on the radar Steve Barr had made by advancing alone.

It was a three-man patrol again. First two men, then the third bringing up a distant rear. As the two reached where Marsha and the others waited, the red boar mercs swarmed around them. Pinned, stripped of their weapons, they stared in shock at their fellow mercenaries. Up the slope the third man unslung his AK-74 and aimed down the hill.

Steve Barr came out of the night behind him and knocked him cold with his rifle butt. "We can use all the help we can get," he said when he rejoined his men. "Maybe we can get them to join us."

The three mercenaries listened as Barr told them what they were doing and why. One of them was a corporal and had some experience.

"Nuclear weapons?" the corporal said.

"For terrorists?" another asked.

They agreed to join up with Barr and the others and thought they could get their fellow mercs inside the lab to go along.

"How many are there?" Barr asked.

"Twelve grunts, me and the lieutenant," the corporal said. "With two cooks, two orderlies, and Dr. Eugene Tellford. There's maybe fifteen scientists. None of them like being here except for Tellford. But none of them will fight."

"So there're fifteen plus the scientists inside now?"

"Twelve. We lost three guys yesterday. No one knows who got 'em, and they ain't sent replacements."

"Will any of them really stick with the Major?"

"The lieutenant, maybe, and Doc Tellford for sure. We figure the Doc's got a piece of the action."

"We can blast our way in," Barr said. "We've got the rockets, explosives and men."

They nodded.

"We'd rather not, though. We don't want to hurt any of the scientists or anyone else. Will you go back and talk to the others?"

The corporal mulled it over, then looked at the other two. They nodded. "You got a deal," the corporal said. "But you'll have to attack and make it look good. The guys won't go up alone against the lieutenant and Tellford."

Barr agreed, released the three mercs and watched them climb back up the slope to the hidden building in the barranca at the edge of the mesa.

THE MAJOR LOOKED at the carnage of bodies and human parts under the glare of his spotlights. The bloody-faced lieutenant, his head and arm heavily bandaged, had to be supported by the medics to make his report.

"They picked off our point and three connecting files, then opened fire. The men half panicked, forgot to return fire and ran into one another. It was terrible, sir. They need a lot more training."

"Or more experience," the Major snapped. "You get them calmed down?"

"Yes, sir. We went to ground, finally returned fire, and the enemy retreated. We heard them some thirty yards ahead and went after them. They opened up again. We reacted correctly this time, went down and returned fire."

Now his drained face went even whiter as he looked around at the shattered remains of his advance guard, at the dead and wounded being evacuated. "Then they hit us. I don't know if it was grenades, or if they have mortars, but they ripped us apart."

"Because they pinned you at exactly the spot they wanted," the Major said. "That's Bolan. He knows how to fight a war."

"Yes, sir," the lieutenant said.

"Go back and get yourself treated. We'll get them next time."

The dead and wounded were moved out to be carried back to Miradora and then the base hospital. The Major gave the order to move out after the fleeing renegades.

MACK BOLAN MOVED silently north out of the fake camp as the pursuit drew close again. The Major was swinging his point to the left to try to encircle and pin the fugitives against the river. Alone, Bolan could have been another thirty miles ahead. It would have been easy to escape the amateur soldiers pursuing him. But that wasn't his job.

His job was to keep the Major after him, lure the bloody international terrorist and his army farther and farther from the hidden nuclear installation on the mesa. To maintain contact and leave phony data like the "camp" he'd just set up to look as if at least thirty men had rested there.

If he could hold the Major until noon tomorrow, that would give Barr more than enough time. It was still two hours to midnight. There was a long night ahead.

ON THE FLAT ROOF of the hidden laboratory building, Steve, Marsha, the villagers and mercenaries waited. It was past 10:00 p.m., and there had been no signal from the three released mercs. Had they changed their allegiance again? Had they been caught? Had the others refused to join them and turned them in to the officer and Dr. Eugene Tellford?

"We can't wait any longer, Steve," Marsha said.

"No," Steve agreed. "No telling how long Mack can fool the Major."

He looked up and down the line. "Everyone ready? Count off if you are."

The numbers rolled down the line from both sides. Everyone was ready. Barr raised the anti-tank rocket launcher to his shoulder. "Here we go."

The rocket fired with no more sound than a pistol shot, no recoil, flash or back blast. Aimed at the fake boulder that closed the rooftop entrance to the building, the rocket slammed through the steel and blew the whole door wide open. The mercs and villagers ran across the flat roof toward the yawning black hole and the descending staircase.

ONCE MORE BOLAN waited with his M-16 and its night vision system. The Major's men advanced more carefully now, but still too fast. Their commander was driving them on to encircle and outflank the fugitives.

Five men led in a wedge this time, covering one another. But they were too close together, long and deep instead of wide. Bolan fired a burst, lobbed a grenade and ran to the right this time. The burst cut down three enemies, while the grenade got the other two.

They were in over their heads, amateurs who should have stayed home instead of getting into a dirty war they knew nothing about. Bolan fired a burst from the right, ran left and fired again. Then he zigzagged north once more, stopping to twist the handle of his detonator.

The jungle erupted in a series of shattering explosions, and once again groans, screams and shouts of rage tore through the night air. Confused, the survivors started shooting wildly.

"Cease fire!" the Major yelled. "Cease fire! You're shooting at each other!"

Bolan retreated north, leaving the frightened mercs behind once more.

THE MAJOR PACED up and down the sprawled ranks of the sullen troops. Midnight, and they hadn't gone ten miles yet! Worse, they'd suffered a hundred casualties at the hands of no more than thirty opponents! He was in a fury at such incompetence, but he was trying to hold it in. These were new troops; they weren't used to taking such punishment.

"They've been lucky so far, men. Very lucky. They have Bolan to lead them. But we can take them if we just keep up the pressure. They have to run out of ammo and grenades soon."

He had ordered a distribution of emergency rations, and gave them ten minutes to smoke afterward. But the time was almost up. His admiration for Bolan's fighting skills was beginning to change to a hatred that wouldn't be satisfied until the big soldier was dead.

"Major!" One of his few experienced subcommanders came hurrying up to him. "Look at this!"

The Major looked at the long strands of thin wire in the officer's hands. At two small metallic fragments. "What am I looking at, Lieutenant?"

"Blasting caps, Major, and wire. Those explosions weren't grenades. They were plastic explosive charges planted and wired and set off by a single detonator."

"One man?"

"That's what I think. And when I talked to survivors of both attacks, it sounded as if there wasn't all that much firing in front of them."

The Major stared at his lieutenant. "One man. He planted the plastic charges. Opened fire. Ran around firing while our men stumbled over their own feet. Lured them ahead and set off the charges at different distances so that they didn't explode at the same time."

The officer nodded.

"Bolan," the Major said. "But...where are the rest of them? Where...?"

He whirled around to his silent troops. "Everybody up! On your feet! On your feet! Officers, move them out! Back where we came from! On the double. Move them out, and then all officers to me! On the double now! Move it! Move it!"

All along the lines of sullen mercenaries, the noncoms and officers strode, ordering the men up. They turned what was left of the two companies back the way they had come, all except the hundred or more who would stay in the jungle forever.

STEVE BARR WAS the first one down the circular metal staircase into the long, lit corridor on the top floor of the secret nuclear laboratory. Marsha and his twenty-five mercenaries came next, followed by the villagers.

The corridor was empty.

"Find the stairs!" Barr ordered.

They spread out and located two flights of stairs down into the rest of the building.

"Marsha, take half. I'll take the other half. Keep alert, be ready. Go!"

They raced for the stairs at each end. The building was cool and silent except for the hum of air-conditioning. On the floor below, two of the mercenaries they'd captured outside ran along the corridor. One was the corporal.

"The lieutenant and Tellford are holding some of the guys, making them fight!"

"Where?"

"Bottom floor. The mess hall!"

"The others?"

"They're with us."

"The scientists?"

"Scared shitless in their quarters. Some of our guys are protecting them."

The laboratories were deserted as they checked all corridors and plunged on down to the bottom floor, which was lined with the solid doors of the scientists' quarters. Two mercs lay prone on the floor. Their AK-74s were trained on the open door of the dining hall.

"The lieutenant's got two guys in there with him and Tellford," the corporal told them.

"Tellford's got Dr. Lev, too!" one of the guys on the floor said.

"The kidnapped Israeli scientist?" Marsha asked.

"Yeah," the corporal said. "He's a hard-headed guy. Wouldn't help the Major one bit. They've been working him over pretty bad, but he's a rock."

It meant they couldn't use grenades or the anti-tank rocket launcher.

"I don't think our guys will fight for the lieutenant," the corporal said. "I laid it out for them, and I don't figure they want anything more to do with the Major."

"What about the cooks and the two orderlies?"

The corporal laughed. "They're hiding out in the kitchen, but they sure ain't married to the Major."

"So that leaves the lieutenant and and Dr. Tellford," Marsha said. "And they have Dr. Lev for a hostage."

The corporal nodded.

"Is there any way we can get into that dining hall without rushing it?" Barr asked the corporal.

"Back door and kitchen door, but I figure they got them covered, too."

"But you think there're only two of them who'll resist?" Marsha asked. "If we rush them from three directions, we should be able to take them."

"Sounds good," the corporal said.

Barr wasn't so certain. He wished they had Bolan with them, but they didn't have much choice. He could lead the attack on one door, Marsha the second door, the corporal the third.

"That's it, then," Barr said. "Who wants which door?"

"I'll take the kitchen," the corporal said. "I know how to get there."

"Right," Barr agreed. "Take two other men. Marsha, you take the door on this side, with two mercs. I'll take two up and around to the other side."

The corporal rounded up his two men.

The jump-off would be five minutes, to give Barr and the corporal time to get into position. With the rest of their men waiting in reserve, they were ready.

Marsha eyed her watch and listened in the corridor. There were no sounds from the dining hall. The big question was what would the two mercs in there do? They would soon find out.

"Time," Marsha said.

She sprinted down the corridor to the dining hall door. One merc stayed behind to cover. Marsha and the other one jumped in through the door and dived straight ahead for the shelter of a heavy table.

The thunder of an assault rifle shattered the enclosed space. Wood splintered above Marsha's head as slugs tore into the table. She heard her husband and the corporal charge through the other two doors. Cautiously she peered over the table. For an instant the action in the room seemed to freeze as in a movie.

The lieutenant was behind a barricade he had made from overturned tables. His rifle was aimed at Marsha's door. Two merc grunts stood behind him against the wall, rifles in their hands but pointed at the floor. A heavy, bearded man in a white laboratory coat huddled behind the tables, a Walther PPK in his hand. Looking furious beside him was a small old man in a rumpled business suit. Barr and his men crouched just inside the door. The corporal and his two mercs had slammed in from the kitchen, fanning out right and left.

Then the freeze frame broke into violent movement. The lieutenant swung his rifle toward the kitchen door, and the corporal and his men ducked. The two grunts behind the lieutenant dropped their pieces just as Tellford took a shot at Barr. Marsha raked the table with a burst, and everybody behind the table went down.

"Fire, you bastards!" the lieutenant bawled at the two reluctant merc grunts. "Pick up those weapons!"

There were sudden shots behind the barricade of tables, then silence. Steve, Marsha, the corporal and their men moved warily forward as the small old man in the business suit came up from behind the tables. He held one of the assault rifles the merc grunts had dropped.

"The stupid officer would have shot the young men," Dr. Claudius Lev said. "Tellford sold out his science. They forgot I fought in the Irgun. Or perhaps they didn't know."

Behind the table the two grunts were unhurt. Only the lieutenant and Dr. Eugene Tellford lay in pools of blood.

"Thank you, Doctor," Barr said. "Now let's free the others and destroy this place."

SOMETHING WAS WRONG.

Bolan listened in the jungle night. They were still coming, but it wasn't the same. Too slow and too few. Were they tired, or...?

Bolan turned and cat-footed quickly back toward the pursuing companies. As he moved closer he was more certain. They were walking. No more than a small platoon. He slid down into a steep little barranca and waited.

Two of them passed no more than a few feet from him. Their weapons were slung and they were walking slowly forward. Occasionally an officer fired into the air. The Major wasn't with them.

Bolan didn't have to guess what happened. His ruse had been discovered, the truth figured out. The Major and his army were on their way back to the hidden lab on the mesa.

He slipped out of the barranca and headed south again as fast as he could run.

CHAPTER THIRTY

The freed scientists were all gathered in the dining hall. Steve Barr faced them with Marsha beside him. "I know most of you aren't used to hard marches," Barr said. "I'd like to wait for daylight, but we can't. The Major's probably twenty-five miles away by now, maybe more, but just in case, I want to be out of here by 3:00 a.m. That's in half an hour."

"I'm sure we can all meet such a deadline," Dr. Claudius Lev said. "What's your plan, young man?"

"To get as far into the mountains and Venezuela as possible by daylight before we make contact with Venezuelan or British authorities."

"British?" Dr. Lev said.

"Yes, sir. We're British agents. We have contacts I think we can reach. I'm not at all sure of the local authorities if we could even find any this side of Ciudad Bolívar."

"That sounds realistic and practical," Dr. Lev sid. "We'll all be ready. But what happens to the nuclear matériel here, and the work my pliable colleagues have already done?"

"It will all be destroyed when we leave."

"Then we'll be ready even faster."

The scientists hurried along the corridors to gather whatever they had brought with them. The mercs finished planting the plastic explosives throughout the building. At five minutes before three they were ready to go. At four minutes before three the mercenary lookout came running and sliding down the stairs from the rooftop entrance.

"The Major! He's outside! With a couple of companies!"

BOLAN RAN ON THROUGH the dark jungle. The trail of the Major's troops had been easy to find and simple to follow. That made it a lot faster and easier for Bolan. They'd trampled down the undergrowth, giving him a clear path at full run, a path that cut across at an angle from Miradora and the hidden base straight toward the mesa and the nuclear laboratory.

The Major had figured it out, and Bolan wouldn't reach the mesa in time, not on foot.

He had estimated distance and checked time since he had started after the Major. If his mental calculations and dead reckoning were right, there would be a point where the trail of the Major's troops would pass closest to the base. When Bolan reached that point, he left the trail and turned in the night toward the base itself.

THE MAJOR STOOD at the edge of the mesa in the bright glare of his own lights. His voice boomed over the bullhorn aimed at the laboratory building in the narrow barranca. "Give it up, Haggarty, or whatever your name really is. It was a good try, but it didn't work. I've got you outnumbered a hundred to one. You haven't a chance."

The tall terrorist, his white hair shining in the glare of the lights, waited. No answer came from the building in the barranca.

"I don't want to kill those scientists you came to rescue," the Major called over the bullhorn. "I assume that's why you're here. But if I have to attack, it'll be them as well as you and those turncoats of mine. Now you wouldn't want that, would you, Captain?"

He waited again, calm and relaxed in front of his soldiers, spread around the building. "I'd really rather not destroy the building and all the work and have to start again. But I can get more scientists, more fissionable material, more alloys. It's all there for the taking. Still, it would be a waste of valuable time. I admit that. I can't offer to let you all go. That would be stupid. You would simply bring various forces down on me, but I can offer to let everything return to the way it was except for the woman and you. Only you two heroes eh? No one else gets hurt."

The Major looked at his watch. "I'll give you two minutes to send out the scientists and my renegade mercs. Then we're coming in. You can come out with them or not, as you wish. I'm now counting."

THE BASE WAS a ghost town in the night. Faint lights were on, but the gates were open and unmanned, the buildings empty. Bolan trotted silently across the open spaces under the tall trees and camouflage nets. No one challenged him.

The Major would have left some troops. The question was how many and where? The soldier moved on cautiously toward the headquarters building. The shadowy helicopters stood on their pads, lights showed in some windows of headquarters and a single guard walked slowly in front of the entrance.

The guy yawned and set his rifle down to light a cigarette. It was the last thing he ever did. Bolan's knife slid into his heart without a sound, his hand over the guy's mouth. He dragged the body into the bushes, wiped the knife and moved into the building among the late-night shadows.

There were no other guards, but he heard voices faintly from somewhere at the far end of the first corridor. That would be the CQ. But before that there was the door into the communications room, where they had smashed the equipment before escaping.

Bolan listened. Someone was talking softly inside. He opened the door and stepped in. The equipment had been repaired, enough of it anyway. A young merc sat at the console. Not much more than a boy, he talked lightly to some buddy on another radio. Then he heard Bolan and turned quickly.

"There's a dead guard outside. I don't think you want to die for the Major, do you son?"

THE CORPORAL HAD SHOWN Steve Barr the steel shutters installed by the Major to protect his laboratory in case of attack. "We figure we can't trust the Major with shit,'' he said. "We figure we got conned signing up down here. If we got to get killed, we figure we'd better do it trying to get rid of the Major and his terrorist bombs."

Barr smiled. "Thanks, Corporal. Maybe we can even hold out until Bolan gets some help, eh?"

"Maybe we can, sir. This place is a pretty tough nut to get into the way the Major set it up."

The young Miradoran villagers caught the spirit of defiance. "So we get blasted? Somebody got to stop this maniac and our fat pig of a mayor. Besides, we don't believe in the Major. We will fight, also."

"Give me a gun, young man," Dr. Lev said. "I think you know I can use one. The rest of these scientists will be useless. Better they stay safely down on the bottom floor."

The greatest danger came at the shattered rooftop entrance. There was no way to repair it in time. The corporal and Marsha took charge on the top floor with as much firepower as they could squeeze effectively into the corridor. Trying to boost morale, Barr visited every window where the thin ranks of the defenders were spread out.

The MI6 man was at a window facing the jungle slope, when the attackers burst over the edge and charged the building on the three exposed sides and the roof. "Take your time!" he said, running from merc to merc. "Make every shot count!"

The heaviest attacks came at the shattered top door, where the roof lights made running shadows, and at the third-floor double loading doors at the bottom of the barranca. The villagers and half the mercs not on the top floor were at the loading door and the windows around it, blazing away at the enemy mercs who charged through the outside loading lights.

"Semiautomatic," Barr urged his men. "Don't waste ammo until they're kicking at the doors. Slow and steady. That's right. Good shooting."

On the roof the Major's best company lay pinned down by a withering fire from the roof opening and grenades tossed by the corporal. But one man couldn't hold them long, and they surged forward, forcing the corporal and Marsha down into the top-floor corridor.

At the loading door the attack came from both sides as the Major's men tried to advance in the dead spots the window slits couldn't cover. The villagers and mercs cut them down in rows, piling the bodies on the floor of the lit barranca like cordwood. The Major's mercs took the punishment for five minutes, then vanished back into the night, leaving the barranca a sea of blood and moaning wounded.

"Good work!" Barr told his men. "They'll wait a while before they come again. Keep your eyes open. They'll come slow next time, crawling. Be alert."

On the top floor it had reversed. The attacking mercs could only come down the spiral stairs two at a time at most. The corporal and Marsha's men picked them off until the bodies lay piled six deep at the foot of the stairs. The blood ran in rivers over the polished floor, and the groans of the dead and dying echoed through the single corridor.

The attackers threw down grenades, slaughtering their own wounded but taking casualties among the defenders. Already six of the defending mercs were down. Marsha had been wounded in the left arm but fought on.

So far the corporal had had a charmed life. "Hang in there, guys," he cried. "Hang in!"

At the downstairs door the second attack was pressing hard through the dark of the barranca. They were much more cautious this time, crouching and crawling as they advanced. A rocket blew the loading doors in, and the attack flowed in a wave through the blasted doors.

The battered defenders retreated up the narrow corridor. Barr arrived with help, and a charge drove the Major's men out again. Once more the defenders closed the shattered doors.

On the top floor the corporal brought up the rocket launcher and swept the corridor clean of living attackers. On the roof the survivors ran back once more into the darkness of the night.

Throughout the building the defenders all lay at their posts, bloody, sweating and trying to breathe. Trying to breathe and not think. Could the Major make his untried mercenaries hit them again? If he could, their chances of survival were slim.

"JUST CONTACT the laboratory," Mack Bolan said quietly in the communications room of the Major's secret base.

The boy gulped, nodded and bent to the microphone. "Able Four, this is Able One, come in. Able Four, come in." He listened, then shook his head. "They're not receiving. I can't—"

"Keep trying," Bolan said.

The young mercenary recruit went on trying to raise the distant laboratory. He turned again to shake his head when the radio crackled.

"We don't have anything to say to you, Major," Barr's voice said. "Just—"

Bolan grabbed the mike. "Steve, this is Bolan. I'm at the base. The Major broke off, started back—"

"Hello, Mack," Steve's weary voice said. "You're a little late. He got here over an hour ago. We're under heavy attack."

"Tell me the situation."

"We've beaten off one attack. We've lost a third of our people, maybe thirty left all told. The Major's got at least a full company out there. I don't think his mercs are all that gung-ho. Maybe we can hold out one more time, but that will be it."

"I'm coming to join you," Bolan said.

"No!" Marsha's voice broke in. "Get away, Mack. Tell everyone about the Major. Bring in some muscle and get rid of him. We're finished, but don't let us die for nothing."

Barr's voice returned. "You couldn't get here in time, Mack. Even if we beat off another assault, that's it. We've got the place wired and can blow it in a minute. We can't let the Major take us or the scientists alive, or let the lab stand."

"Fifteen minutes, Barr!" Bolan said into the mike. "Hold on for fifteen minutes!"

"Mack, please," Marsha's distant voice begged. "You'll just die with us. It'll all be wasted."

"What can one man do, Bolan?" Barr questioned from the shattered laboratory.

"That depends on the man," Bolan said. "Hang on."

He brought his rifle butt down on the operator's skull, dragged him into a closet and locked it. Then he secured the communications room door and ran down the empty corridor and out into the night. At the armory he picked up four more rocket launchers and two boxes of grenades and lugged them out to the first helicopter. No one on the deserted base saw him take off and swing toward the nuclear laboratory.

The big soldier flew with one hand. He pulled grenades from the opened boxes and placed them on the floor of the chopper around him, then shouldered a rocket launcher and placed the others ready at hand. Peering ahead in the night, he watched the compass and the airspeed indicator.

Within minutes he saw the glare of the laboratory lights below. The attackers were advancing over the roof and up the slope toward the two doors. Some were falling, hit by fire from the building, but not enough even to slow them up or make them hit the dirt. They were at the doors as Bolan brought the chopper down. They seemed to hesitate for a moment as if they'd run into a wall. More bleeding and screaming bodies were blown away, but they didn't pull back.

Bolan swept down at an angle in the chopper. The heavy firing, yelling and screaming covered the sound of the helicopter swooping in.

He fired the rocket launcher into the mob stacked at the side loading door. The antipersonnel load swept the whole doorway clear in a single blast that left nothing but blood and bodies writhing in a heap like dying worms in a can.

The soldier pulled the helicopter up with one hand and hauled another rocket launcher onto his shoulder. The chopper slid up over the edge of the roof, and Bolan fired into the soldiers pouring down the stairs from the roof. The charge cleared the whole roof like the swing of a great scythe. The bodies twisted and moaned across the flat area, and some fell screaming over the edge.

Hauling the chopper up and around in a sharp turn, he zoomed down over the ranks still advancing toward the doors. He picked up grenades, pulled pins with his teeth and dropped them onto the massed mercenaries.

They'd seen him now, and were firing at him. The soldier went on swooping and banking while he dropped his grenades and bullets sang all around him, smashing through the fuselage. Then the attackers were streaming back from the doors, the defenders shooting some down as they ran.

Bolan raised his fist high and attacked the masses of retreating troops once more, his third rocket launcher on his shoulder. He had to hit them, and hit them again, before they reached the cover of the jungle. He didn't fool himself that he could stop them the next time. This time the surprise had been all on his side.

He swept in with the rocket launcher primed as bullets ripped and rocked the helicopter. Then he saw the Major. The white-haired, power-crazy ex-assassin stood behind his fleeing troops, trying to rally them. The onetime KGB agent was so intent, bawling so loudly, that he didn't realize the chopper was approaching until it was almost on top of him.

Then he heard it, turned and stared straight into Bolan's eyes. There was a moment of horror on the Major's flinty face as the Executioner fired the rocket launcher. Then the Major smiled. The rocket hit him dead center.

Bolan veered away, and a stream of bullets smashed into the engine. The chopper bucked and yawed as Bolan pulled it up until it was almost standing still, then everything quit and the aircraft settled into a lurch and crashed sideways into the slope.

The Executioner crawled out, Beretta in hand. All across the slope, and at the edge of the jungle, the decimated ranks of the weary and bloodstained mercenaries stood in silence and stared at the fallen helicopter.

Bolan rose to his knees. One of the subcommanders stared down at the shattered body of the Major. Then they all turned and began to run in the opposite direction. Without the Major there was nothing for them in the jungle or the base. They streamed away to vanish into the thick jungle below the mesa.

Bolan stood up, and Marsha and Steve Barr came out of the side double doors of the battered laboratory building.

"Thanks" Barr said.

"De nada," Bolan replied, holding his arm where blood streamed from a wound he hadn't even felt until now.

"I guess the right man can make a difference," Marsha said, smiling up at the big warrior.